Cold

Book 10 of the Jenny Watkins Mystery Series
1. Driven
2. Betrayed
3. Shattered
4. Exposed
5. Trapped
6. Vindicated
7. Possessed
8. Haunted
9. Targeted

To Mom: I hope I'm right.

WAIT!

This book comes with instructions

This book is paired with "House of Horrors" in the Hailey Newcomb Mystery Series. If you have a teen or tween in your life who likes to read, that person can read House of Horrors while you read Cold.

If you are at the end of chapter six in this book, for instance, and the tween/teen is at the end of chapter six in House of Horrors, you are at the same point in time. You get to see the same story unfold from two different points of view. I encourage you to discuss what's happening with the teen/tween to make it more fun!

Dedication

As always, I can't do this alone. I've had so many helpers with this book, and I must express my gratitude. First of all, to my amazing proofreaders…THANK YOU. Your input is invaluable to me. Here they are, in no particular order:

Amanda, Lucy and Cate Nevin
Dana and Eden Johnson
Karin and Anna Wallace
Scott and Grace Crespi
Jessica and Jami Loy
Trinitey Perkins-Rostine and Jessica Rostine
Jaime and Sydney Taylor
Jenni and Lily Margeson
Collen and Caroline Krezel
Jenn and Dylan Berardo
Monica, Brianna and Kiersten Filyaw
Rob and Tyler Toman
Tami and Mallory Chalker
Brianna, Abigail and Denise Wallace
Danielle Bon Tempo
Bill Demarest

Thanks also need to go out to my cover models:
Mallory Chalker
Mel Velante
Paul Ferreira
Rami Maleeb
Kayla James
And my beautiful "Steve," Brennen Ferreira

It always amazes me how complete strangers are willing to spend their afternoon doing a photo shoot with me for a book cover.

Lastly, thanks to my family: Scott, Hannah, Seneca, Evan and Julia. Without your love and support, none of this could happen.

Chapter 1

"May I speak with Jenny Larrabee, please?" Both the male voice and the phone number were unfamiliar.

Jenny's entire body instantly filled with apprehension. This was either a solicitor or something murder-related, and neither would have been good. "This is."

"Hi, Jenny. My name is Paul Schneider; I'm with the Hargrove Police department. How are you today?"

"I'm doing well." While that statement was currently true, Jenny wondered if her life was about to take a dramatic turn for the worse. She hoped this call was about her psychic ability and not informing her about a personal tragedy. Her nerves fluttered under her skin. "How are you?"

"Doing great. The reason I'm calling is because I just got a phone call from the folks at the Richmond PD in Virginia; they've got some unsolved murder cases there, and they're looking to get answers. They've heard about you and your ability to receive messages from the victims themselves, and they were wondering if you'd be able to go there and see what you can find out. In fact," he added, "they're extending that invitation to some other psychics as well. It seems they're willing to go the non-traditional route to see if they can get some of these cases in the books."

Jenny smiled knowingly; she'd been expecting a phone call like this one of these days, figuring that someone, somewhere, would want a little extra help with a case. "Sure, that can be arranged," she said. "When would they like me to go?"

"They didn't say," Officer Schneider replied. "They only called us because they didn't have your contact information. They'd like you to get in touch with them and make the arrangements, if you're willing." He recited the number to the Richmond Police Department.

With a brief expression of thanks, Jenny hung up with Officer Schneider and dialed the Richmond number, which was apparently a direct line. "Spicer," was all the man said upon answering.

"Um...hello," Jenny began, not sure whether this was Detective Spicer, Officer Spicer or simply Mr. Spicer. "My name is Jenny Larrabee; I received a phone call from the police department here in Hargrove, Tennessee, asking me if I'd be interested in coming to Richmond to help with some cold cases."

"Ah, yes, Mrs. Larrabee. Thank you for calling me back so quickly."

"No problem. I'm happy to help."

She heard him shifting around in the background. "We've got a few murder cases around here that have us completely stumped. We've exhausted all of our traditional means, and we're no better off than when we started. We're under the impression that these few cases are stranger killings, which are the hardest to solve, and that's why we're trying to enlist the help of some psychics."

"Do you think the cases are related?"

"I tend to doubt it," he replied. "The victims have little in common. That's why we're calling in as many psychics as we can; we figure we can assign each psychic a case and see how many of these we can solve."

"How many psychics are you talking about?"

"If you are willing to come, that would make four."

"Are Susan Leichart, Ingunn Epperly and Roddan Epperly on your guest list?"

After a short pause, he slowly said, "No...I don't know those names."

"Susan is my friend, and Roddan and Ingunn are my father and grandmother. They all have the same ability that I do."

"That's amazing," he replied. "Do you think you could get in touch with them?"

"Absolutely," Jenny said with certainty.

"Wow." The awe in Spicer's voice was obvious. "Anyway, we're hoping you could all come and stay for a few days; the only problem is that we don't have enough money in our budget to actually *pay* for your stay."

Jenny shook her head, although he couldn't see that through the phone. "Don't worry about that. I can cover that. In fact, I can cover that for everybody."

"What?"

Jenny explained her financial situation, letting him know that she'd been given a giant inheritance by her first client, with the instructions that she use that money to bring people answers. "This certainly qualifies," she concluded. "I can pay for the people's hotel stays, and even their airfare, if you can just get them to agree to come."

"That would be fabulous," Spicer replied, "although, one of our psychics is local and wouldn't need a hotel."

"Well, the offer stands for anyone who needs it." After a short pause, she smiled and admitted, "I'd love to meet some fellow psychics, and it would certainly be great to see my family and Susan again. They don't live close by." The thought of a reunion crossed her mind. "This should be fun, actually."

"I don't know if solving these murders is going to be *fun*."

"I'm sorry," Jenny said quickly, "I didn't mean that. Of course, the main purpose of the trip is to going to be business. I just thought the off-duty part might be interesting."

"I understand," he replied. "I just didn't want you to be under the impression that this trip was going to be entirely pleasurable. There will be aspects of it that are going to be very upsetting."

"I know," Jenny assured him. "Believe me, I've been down this road before; I'm aware that it can get quite ugly."

"Indeed," Spicer said softly. "Ugly might be an understatement."

With the trip arranged for the following week, the third week of June, Jenny started making some calls. Susan said she could find a way to make it happen; then the women spent a good deal of time catching up. Once that conversation was done, Jenny called her father, Roddan, even though it was somewhat early where he lived on the west coast.

"Hi, Pop, it's Jenny," she said when he picked up the phone.

"Hey, there, Jenny...is everything okay?"

She had to smirk. Being a parent herself now, she knew that worry was the standard reaction to an unexpected early-morning phone call. "Everything's fine. I just got an interesting call from the Richmond Police Department, that's all." She described the situation in detail, adding, "Would you be able to come out next week and add your two cents?"

The groan on the other end of the line made Jenny aware of his answer before he said it. "I'm not sure I have a full two cents to offer," he began. "Remember, my gift doesn't work like yours. I can tell what spirits are feeling, but as far as visions and pulls are concerned, I don't get those. I'm not sure how helpful I would be."

"You can still come," Jenny said pleasantly. "And don't sell yourself short; your input may make the difference in one of these cases."

Letting out a little laugh, he replied, "Thanks. You're very sweet. The problem is we're at our busy season here at work; this is the time of year that everyone wants to hike Mount Ranier. I'm not sure I'll be able to get that much time off with such short notice."

"I understand, and we'll definitely miss you. But, hey...if we do need your help, can we send you some pictures so you can see what the spirits are feeling?"

"Absolutely. You can always do that."

With a smile, she got off the phone with her father and dialed her grandmother, Amma, who readily agreed to meet Jenny in Richmond. After a return phone call to Spicer, Jenny handled the logistics and set up a hotel stay for all of the psychics, reserving one of the meeting rooms in the lobby to use as their headquarters.

With six-month-old Steve on her hip, she announced her plan to Zack and her mother, who both agreed to come along. As she started making a list of all the things she needed to pack for the trip, she couldn't help but smile. This was going to be quite an interesting stay in Virginia.

Chapter 2

Monday

"What room are you in?" Jenny asked Susan through the phone.

"Nine-twenty-one," Susan replied.

"Okay, I'll be there in a minute."

"Hurry," Susan remarked, "I can't wait to see that baby."

Jenny hung up the phone and called to Zack, "You ready?"

"Yeah," he replied, looking around the hotel room and patting his pockets. "I just need my phone...Ah, here it is." He walked over to the dresser and picked it up. "Is your mom coming with us?"

"She has a headache," Jenny explained. "She's just going to hang out in her room for a while." As the couple walked out the door and into the hallway, Jenny added, "I think it's from sitting in the backseat for so long. She gets carsick sometimes."

"Why didn't she sit in the front?" Zack asked.

"I told her to," Jenny replied, "but you know my mom. She wouldn't want to inconvenience one of us by making us sit in the backseat of our own car. Besides, the baby was in the back, and she had to sit with her little Steve."

Unable to find the stairs, the couple took the elevator down one flight to the ninth floor, where they found Susan standing in the hallway waiting for them. Seeing the baby, Susan let out a squeal and held out her arms. "There he is!" she exclaimed. "I've been dying to get my mitts on this guy for a long time."

Susan took the baby and gave Zack and Jenny hugs with her free arm. "It's great to see you," Susan said genuinely.

"You too," Jenny replied.

"Check it out," Zack noted. "Steve isn't crying."

Susan looked at the baby on her hip and stroked his cheek with her finger. "Of course he isn't crying. He knows he's with someone awesome."

Steve busied himself with trying to grab Susan's necklace.

"Lately he's been crying whenever strangers try to hold him," Zack explained.

"He's getting to be that age," Susan acknowledged as they walked back toward her room. "They get that whole 'separation anxiety' thing. Those are fun times," she added sarcastically. "You can't even leave the room for a second without them crying...Oh my Gosh, look at his shirt!"

Jenny had to smile; Steve had "Ladies' man" written in big letters across his belly. "Yeah, Zack picked it out."

With a smirk, Susan said, "I should have known."

They entered Susan's room and sat for a while, discussing their trips to Richmond as Susan gushed over the baby. A buzz on Jenny's phone caused her to glance at the screen; she was getting a call from her grandmother. "Hi, Amma," she said as she picked up, "are you on your way?"

"The GPS says fifteen minutes," Amma replied.

"Excellent. Did you have a good flight?"

"Eh," she said gruffly. "We didn't crash."

Jenny stifled a laugh, telling her grandmother she would meet her in the lobby when she arrived. After hanging up, Jenny held up a hand as she looked at Susan and said, "Before you judge me, I offered to pick her up at the airport, but she insisted on renting her own car."

"And you don't argue with her grandmother," Zack added.

"Headstrong, is she?" Susan asked, kissing Steve's oversized cheek.

"You could say that," Zack replied. "She's cool, though. She's in her seventies, but I don't think she's gotten that memo yet. She acts like she's thirty."

"That's awesome," Susan said. "I would like to be that way, but somehow I doubt I will. I already feel seventy, and I'm only in my forties."

"I feel a hundred sometimes," Jenny confessed.

"Quiet," Susan replied jokingly. "You're the youngest one in here."

"No, *he's* the youngest one in here." Jenny pointed at the baby. "And he's the reason I feel a hundred."

After a laughter-filled conversation with Susan, Jenny left and waited in the lobby for Amma to arrive. Within minutes, Amma walked through the double glass doors, carrying her suitcase even though it had wheels.

"Hi, Amma!" Jenny greeted her grandmother with a hug.

"Where's that handsome baby, eh?"

These days, Jenny felt like a mere extension of the baby, although she gladly accepted the role. Releasing the embrace, she explained, "He's upstairs with Zack and my friend Susan."

"I'll check in quickly, then," Amma said. "I have to see that great-grandbaby of mine."

After getting her key from the desk worker, Amma dropped off her suitcase in her room and then went with Jenny to where the others were. She walked in to find the baby looking content on Susan's shoulder, which was now covered with drool.

"There's my little man," Amma exclaimed. "Look at him—bald like his Grampa was."

Jenny couldn't help but smile. The man who had raised her, Frank Mongillo, was Italian, and all of his biological children in that family had been born with heads full of black hair. She had often wondered if the baldness that both she and Steve had shared was a trait of her real father—now she had her answer.

"Here," Susan said, standing up and walking toward Amma. "I've had my turn." She handed the baby over to Jenny's eager grandmother.

Once again, the baby didn't cry in the arms of this virtual stranger. Just as Jenny opened her mouth to say something about it, Amma commented, "He *does* have the gift." Turning to the baby, she bounced him in her arms and said, "Another little voice of the spirits, eh, little man?"

"That must be it," Jenny exclaimed, although no one knew what she was talking about. With a giggle, she explained what she was thinking. "He's not crying. He has been crying for everyone who has tried to hold him lately, but not for you two. It must be that he can sense you have the gift."

Susan smiled. "We must remind him of his mama."

The thought warmed Jenny's heart, although she turned to Susan and said, "Sorry about your shoulder."

"Are you kidding?" Susan replied. "I haven't had baby drool on me in so long; I love it."

Curling his lip and shaking his head, Zack announced, "I really don't understand women."

Jenny's mother was still getting over her headache while the others took the elevator to the lobby. "So, Jenny," Susan began, "do you know anything about these cases we're going to be working on?"

"Not a thing," Jenny confessed, "other than we're each going to be given our own case to focus on. They plan to present the details of the cases at this meeting."

The elevator doors slid open, and the group walked across the immaculate lobby toward the conference room. "Does Steve get his own case?" Susan asked.

With a laugh Jenny replied, "Not this time. Maybe next year."

"How many people are here?"

"I reserved a total of six rooms, although four of them are for us," Jenny said. "Apparently there's a girl here who is like twelve or thirteen; she's here with her mother. I hope this isn't too upsetting for her. There's also a husband and wife team, who live locally, and then one other person."

"Are any of them real?" Amma asked.

"I hope so," Jenny replied. "It would be a shame for the police to pin their hopes on a fraud."

Amma grunted in return. "Well, three of us are real. If we need to, we can double-up."

They entered the conference room, which featured a large screen and a podium in the front of the room. Three other people stood off to the left, having a casual conversation.

"I hope that's not them," Amma noted, gesturing toward the three people. "There's not a psychic in the bunch over there."

Jenny had gotten the same impression.

"Hello!" one of the group members called, waving over toward Jenny's bunch. "Are you the other psychics?"

"You should know that," Amma replied.

With a laugh, the man said, "Psychics don't know *everything*."

"Let it go, Amma," Jenny whispered through clenched teeth, using the hand that wasn't holding the baby to touch her arm.

"It's shameful, that's what it is," Amma grunted. Fortunately, she kept her tone soft so the others couldn't hear.

Jenny sighed and said, "You know as well as I do that the majority of people who claim they are psychics are frauds."

"Tell that to the families of these victims who are looking to find answers."

Jenny didn't bother to respond; Amma had a point. Due to a random assignment of cases, some of these victims would stand a chance of getting justice; the others would not.

"Why don't we go over here?" Zack proposed, gesturing toward the other side of the room. With a laugh just under the surface, he added, "That way, we can keep Amma out of trouble."

"Good idea," Jenny replied. The group made their way toward the right side of the room, away from the three frauds. While Jenny feared they may have appeared rude, she *knew* they would have appeared rude if they approached them with conversation. There was no way Amma would have been able to keep her mouth shut about their false claims.

"This is a nice hotel," Susan said once they settled in their spot. "Thank you for putting me up."

"No problem," Jenny replied. "It would have been better if we could have all gotten rooms near each other, but it was the best we could do with such a last-minute reservation."

Susan shook her head. "It's fine. We're only a few floors apart. At least we're all in the same building."

"I'm sorry." Jenny heard an unfamiliar female voice from behind her. She turned her head to see a woman who hadn't been in the room just a second ago. "But I have to say hello to this little man."

Turning further, Jenny smiled and said, "Go right ahead." She caught a glimpse of a middle-school girl with shoulder-length hair standing next to this woman, looking as if she'd rather be anywhere but there.

"Look at you," the woman squealed at Steve. "You are the cutest little thing."

"Mom." The girl's tone suggested she was completely and utterly embarrassed by her mother's behavior. Jenny bit her lip; she could remember being in both of those phases—the infantless woman who adored babies, and the middle schooler who was mortified by everything her mother did.

The woman ignored her daughter. "You're cutting some toofers, aren't you?" The woman reached out, and the baby wrapped his drool-covered hand around her pointer finger, giving her one of his charming, slobbery smiles.

"Mom!" The girl was apparently even more mortified.

The woman flashed a playfully-unhappy look at her daughter. "You're no fun. The baby likes me." Returning her attention to Steve, she added, "Yeah, that's right. You like me, huh, sweetie?"

Apparently, he did like this woman, as evidenced by his big smile and kicking feet. "Just be warned," Jenny began, "in a minute he's going to try to eat your finger."

"He's teething?" the woman asked.

"Big time." Feeling the familiar sensation of being in the presence of another psychic, Jenny turned to the uncomfortable young girl and said, "You must be Hailey."

"Yes." The girl's reply was simple, reminding Jenny of those awkward years when conversations with adults were painful. She would never want to go back to that phase, ever.

Trying her best to make Hailey feel comfortable, Jenny shifted the baby onto her other hip and said, "I'm Jenny Larrabee." She extended her hand, which the girl reluctantly shook. Jenny noticed the familiar sensation of coming into contact with another person with the gift. Speaking softly, Jenny added, "It's nice to see another real psychic here."

"The rest are fakes," Amma noted bluntly…and loudly.

"Amma," Jenny said, slapping her forehead. "Not so loud."

"What?" Amma replied. "It's true."

Closing her eyes for a moment, Jenny sighed and declared, "That's my grandmother; you can call her Amma."

"Everybody does," Amma agreed.

Touching his shoulder, Jenny added, "This is my husband, Zack, and over here is my friend, Susan. My mother is with us, too, but she's still in her hotel room, sleeping off a headache."

"Hi," was all she said, the poor girl.

"I'm Hailey's mother, Leslie Newcomb," the woman announced, her finger still firmly in Steve's grasp. Shaking her head, she asked, "How do you know that Hailey is a real psychic…and the others aren't?"

"Psychics have the ability to sense when they are in the presence of other psychics," Jenny explained. "I can tell Hailey has the gift."

"That's amazing," Leslie replied. "She's never been around another psychic before, so we didn't know that."

"Do you want your finger back?" Zack asked Leslie, somewhat randomly. "You may have to take it back by force. I don't think Steve's going to give it up voluntarily."

"No, he can have it for a while," Hailey's mother replied. "I am enjoying this. Look at those tiny little fingers." She placed her free hand on her heart. "Oh my Gosh, I love other people's babies."

Jenny laughed heartily. "I completely get that. Do you want to hold him?"

Her mother gasped yet again. "Do you think he'll let me?"

"There's only one way to find out."

Leslie managed to get her finger free and placed her hands under Steve's arms, lovingly bringing him over to her and situating him close to her. Almost immediately, Steve began to fuss, reaching over for Jenny. "Okay," Leslie said with a smirk, "I guess we have our answer."

"Sorry," Jenny replied, taking the baby back. "He's all about mom these days."

"No need to apologize," Leslie said. "I get it. I've had two myself, and they were the same way at that age."

"I'd like to try something," Jenny announced, wanting to test her theory. Turning to Hailey, she asked, "Would you be willing to hold him for a second?"

"Me?" Hailey seemed shocked by the request.

"Do you mind?" Jenny asked her.

Hailey's answer was reluctant. "I guess not." Awkwardly taking the baby, Hailey held him, and, as Jenny suspected, he was perfectly content.

"Would you look at that?" Leslie said with astonishment. Addressing Hailey, she added, "I guess you have the knack."

"She has the *gift*," Jenny explained. "Steve, the baby, doesn't really know my grandmother or Susan, but he didn't cry when they held him. If anyone else tries? Forget it. I think he can recognize the feeling of having a psychic hold him."

"You mean the *baby* can tell who is a psychic?" Leslie asked. "Does that mean he has the gift, too?"

"It runs in my family," Jenny explained.

"Can I have everybody's attention please?" A male voice permeated the room, causing the crowd to turn toward the podium. A man in a suit spoke into the microphone, and a slide that read "Cold Cases" appeared on the screen. "If you would please have a seat, I'd like to get started."

Jenny reached over and took the baby back. "Thanks for holding him," she whispered to Hailey, who didn't reply.

The group, which now included Leslie and Hailey, all took a seat at one of the round tables. "Thank you," the man added, "and thank you for coming out today; I'm hoping you'll be able to give us the answers we haven't been able to get on our own…"

Chapter 3

"I'm Detective Darnell Spicer," the man behind the podium continued. "I have spoken with many of you on the phone, but I realize I haven't provided many details about what you will be doing during your time in Richmond. Therefore, I'd like to begin by giving you a better idea of why you are here.

"Up on the screen, I will present six cold cases that have been hand-selected by our department. These cases have left us stumped, yes, but so have many others over the years. These particular murders have stuck with us, however, due to the innocent nature of the victims. We have many cases where drug deals go bad, or rival gangs do drive-bys, and those do often go unsolved. However, these six individuals had done nothing to put themselves in danger. They were productive members of society, going about their daily lives, when they became the victims of foul play. We would like be able to provide their families with answers and make sure the perpetrators get the punishment they deserve.

"Each of you will be given a case to focus on, except for you two." The detective used two fingers to point at a man and a woman at the other table. "I know you are a team, so you will be given one to work on together." Returning his attention to the whole group, he added, "First, I will present a brief overview of every case so you can see what it is we are dealing with."

The presenter clicked the instrument in his hand, causing the slide to change. The picture of a man appeared; his smile was wide, and he looked as if he had been friendly during his lifetime. "This is Luis Alvarez, Hispanic male," Detective Spicer announced. "He was forty-four at the time of his death six years ago. He was married with two teenage daughters. He worked for the power company as a linesman, and in his spare time he volunteered as the coach for his daughters' soccer teams. He also donated his time to the local boys and girls clubs, teaching those kids soccer skills and organizing scrimmage games among the lower-income children of this city."

Jenny couldn't help but shake her head; this man deserved a person-of-the-year award, not to end up on a slideshow of cold cases.

"One night," Detective Spicer went on, "after some storms had left people without electricity, Luis worked into the early hours of the morning restoring power. He was last seen by his coworkers at about four a.m. getting into his car to head home. He never made it. Two days later, he was found shot to death in the trunk of his own car, which was thirty miles away, abandoned in a parking lot. Robbery didn't appear to be a motive; his wallet still had cash and credit cards in it when they found it in his pocket."

The image on the screen changed again, this time featuring a girl who appeared to be in high school. She, too, looked like she had been happy when the picture was taken. "This is Ebony Carter, age seventeen, African-American. She was a junior at Grove Hills High School in the city's east end. She was an honor student, hoping to eventually go to medical school. She was actively involved in her church and volunteered at the local soup kitchen, serving meals to the homeless.

"Her mother worked, so Ebony would routinely come home from school to an empty apartment. One day, five years ago, her mother got home around five o'clock to find that Ebony wasn't there. She called friends and family, asking if anyone had seen Ebony, but nobody had. She was last seen getting off the school bus, but her backpack wasn't at the apartment, leading officials to believe she never made it home."

"Give that case to someone over here," Amma said loudly.

Jenny's eyes quickly darted to her grandmother, fearful of what Amma was about to say next.

When Detective Spicer didn't respond, Amma continued, "Make sure one of us gets it." She tapped the table with her finger.

Realizing that it was going to be nearly impossible to keep Amma quiet about the frauds, Jenny just sighed and put her head down. Zack, however, giggled under his breath.

The detective glanced down at the podium, stating, "I have that case down as being assigned to Jenny Larrabee."

"Good," Amma said. "That's fine."

Jenny listened a little more intently, knowing this was her case. With a look of confusion, Detective Spicer continued, "Ebony's body was found by some hunters a few weeks later in a remote wooded area about an hour west of here. It appears she died from a single gunshot wound to the head."

Those words hurt Jenny's soul. There she was, with her beautiful little baby boy on her lap, hearing about another mother whose equally-beautiful daughter was abducted and senselessly murdered. Jenny heard herself grunt involuntarily, giving Steve a kiss on the head simply because she still could.

Detective Spicer went on to describe four more cases, each as upsetting as the first two. Jenny found herself periodically glancing over at Hailey, making sure the child was okay. It was disturbing enough for Jenny to hear these details; she couldn't imagine hearing it when she was still in middle school.

Strangely, Hailey seemed to be taking it better than Jenny was.

"I have files for each person, and I will pass those out to you," Detective Spicer added. "You will receive photographs of your assigned victim, both while they were alive and once their bodies were discovered." He turned to Hailey's mother. "Mom, you may want to look at those first and use your judgment about whether your daughter should see them."

Leslie nodded with understanding.

"You will have photographs of the crime scenes, or at least the places where the remains were found. In some instances, the actual murder site is still unknown. You will be given the victims' home addresses, as well as the locations of their work or school and other places they used to frequent. We are also presenting you with one of the victim's belongings, just in case that will help bring you some insight. I have to admit, I don't fully understand how psychic ability works, but we will do whatever we can to help you. We literally have nowhere else to turn with these cases, so any information you can give us will be valuable."

With that, Amma grunted, causing fear to radiate under Jenny's skin. She silently prayed that Amma would behave herself and not make a comment about the fictitious information coming from the other table. Thankfully, Amma stopped with a grunt.

Detective Spicer wrapped up by saying, "Without further ado, let's go ahead and get these files passed out. The families have waited long enough for justice; I don't want to make them wait any longer."

As the detective gathered up some folders and envelopes to distribute, Jenny scooped up Steve and handed him over to Zack. The baby didn't seem too pleased with that decision, immediately reaching for his mommy with both hands. While Jenny found that flattering, she wished the baby would be more content with his father. That would have made Jenny's life a whole lot easier…not just at the moment, but always.

Before long, a folder and a large envelope were placed in front of Jenny. She puffed out a quick breath before she opened them, already knowing she had been assigned the Ebony Carter case. She couldn't imagine anything more horrifying than coming home from work on an ordinary day, only to find that the teenager who was supposed to be on the couch wasn't there.

She wasn't anywhere.

Jenny imagined her mother fearing the worst but rationalizing the best. Ebony was at a friend's house but forgot to call. Ebony had plans to stay after school but didn't mention it. Something innocent and simple had to be behind this. It couldn't be that she was missing.

She most surely wasn't going to turn up dead. That stuff only happened in movies.

Jenny wanted to vomit.

She opened the folder, quickly rummaging through the photographs and written statements, getting a feel for what she had been given. Glancing into the envelope, she saw a few pieces of jewelry resting in the bottom. The sight of those saddened her. Had they been gifts? Did Ebony go out to the store and pick them out herself? Jenny closed the envelope, tucking both the belongings and those thoughts away for later. She could feel a good cry coming on, and she didn't want to have that here.

She didn't have too long to feel sad; before she knew it, Amma was getting up out of her seat and heading toward the other table. "Oh, dear," Jenny muttered under her breath. More loudly, she called, "Amma, what are you doing?"

Amma didn't reply. Instead, she picked up a picture from the husband-and-wife team's case and studied it. Turning to Detective Spicer, she announced, "When I'm done with my case, I can work on this one. I can definitely get something from this victim."

"Do you want to trade?" the detective asked innocently. That poor, unsuspecting man had no idea what she was getting at.

"No," Amma replied nonchalantly, "I just want this one to get solved." She picked up a photograph from the other case, announcing, "This one, too."

"Seriously," Zack began softly, leaning in toward Jenny, "Amma needs a babysitter."

"You're not kidding," Jenny whispered back.

Putting the picture back on the table, she once again said to Detective Spicer, "I'll work on those when I'm done with my own." Without another word, she headed back to her table.

"Amma," Jenny said once she had been seated, "I can't believe you just did that."

Amma looked surprised. "What?"

"You essentially called them out as frauds."

"So?"

Jenny wanted to say a million things, but this was her grandmother—a grown woman who had the right to act under her own free will. Jenny just wished her 'free will' directed her to conduct herself a little more tactfully. As a result, Jenny just rested her forehead in her hand.

"What are we here for, eh?" Amma asked, gesturing to the other table with her thumb. "To make those people over there feel welcome? Or to get answers for these families?" She waved a picture from her folder in the air. "I want to get these people some justice. Period."

Jenny let out a sigh. Amma was right. If Jenny sat politely and adhered to the rules of society, those two families would never get their answers. Sadly, Jenny was still at a point in her life where she would have allowed that to happen. As uncouth as Amma could have seemed sometimes, she definitely had the right idea, and her heart was full of nothing but good intentions.

Jenny decided she could probably learn a thing or two from Amma.

Zack spoke loudly, clearly trying to change the subject. "So," he said to Jenny, "are you getting anything?"

Jenny shook her head. "No, and I probably won't here. There's too much interference. We've got six victims all trying to tell their stories in one place. It won't work...at least, not for me. I'll need to go back to the room and try when it's quiet."

At that moment, as if on cue, the baby started to fuss. "Quiet?" Zack asked. "Yeah, good luck with that."

Chapter 4

Tuesday.

"Hi, may I speak with Rhonda please?" Jenny asked.

"This is."

"Hi, Rhonda, my name is Jenny Larrabee." Jenny softened her tone. "I am calling to let you know that I have been assigned to work on your daughter, Ebony's, case."

A long, slow sigh indicated this was an emotional moment for Rhonda. "I hope you have better luck than the people who have tried before you." There was no animosity in her voice. "But I'm glad to know they're looking into it again."

"Well, they're trying a different angle this time. I'm a psychic, and they're hoping I can get some information that they haven't been able to get before."

Jenny was met with silence.

"I've been able to solve many murders in the past. I'm hoping I can add Ebony's to my list."

"I am, too," Rhonda whispered softly, but the doubt in her voice was obvious.

"I'd like to meet with you, if I could. I want to get a better feel for Ebony's routines and where she may have been on the day in question."

"She should have been walking home from the school bus," Rhonda said plainly. "Her bus driver saw her get off, and her instructions were to always go straight home unless she had express permission to do something else, and, on this day, she didn't."

"Okay," Jenny replied, "that's actually helpful. I can walk along the route she would have been taking home, and hopefully something will come to me."

"I hate that route," Rhonda said solemnly.

"You don't have to come with me," Jenny replied compassionately. Rhonda's hatred of that stretch of road was certainly justified. "If you want, I can walk it before I meet with you; that way, I can let you know what I find out."

She released another sigh. "That would be great. I don't live near there anymore, though; I had to move once Ebony was..." She didn't finish the sentence. Her tone became even sadder when she whispered, "She was my only child, you know."

Jenny hung her head. Although, with this heartbreak came new motivation. "I have the location of where her bus dropped her off, and I have your old address..."

"She used to cut through an alleyway on her way home," Rhonda told her. "It was between..."

"Wait! Don't tell me," Jenny said quickly. "Sorry to interrupt, but I want Ebony to show me the way. If I go to the bus stop, she should be able to lead me along the path she took home."

"She can show you that?" Rhonda asked. Although her voice remained solemn, it reflected a bit of optimism.

"They usually can," Jenny replied. "I hope she won't prove to be an exception."

Jenny couldn't find a parking space anywhere near where the bus would have dropped Ebony off, so she parallel parked a couple of blocks away. She felt like she'd stepped into an oven as she and Zack got out of the car.

"It's hotter than three Hells out here," Zack said, "and it's barely ten in the morning."

"It sure is," Jenny said, fanning her face with her hand. Although she wasn't familiar with Richmond, she couldn't help but feel like they weren't in the best section of the city. The run-down houses looked like they hadn't seen care in a long time. In their short walk, Jenny and Zack passed a liquor store and a laundromat; both were remarkably busy for mid-morning on a Thursday, indicating the residents around here didn't exactly work nine-to-five.

Although plenty of people were milling about, Jenny didn't take comfort in the crowds or the fact that it was daylight. According to her calculations, Ebony had been accosted in the middle of the afternoon, probably under conditions similar to these.

She was glad she was carrying her gun in her purse.

After walking for a few minutes, she found herself looking at street names hanging from wires at an intersection. "Here it is," Jenny announced. "This is where the bus would have dropped her off." She looked around, getting a little nervous because she wasn't feeling anything. She hadn't gotten any messages from Ebony at all, actually, and she was beginning to wonder if Ebony's spirit had already crossed over. If that were the case, Jenny would have been of no help at all.

Closing her eyes, Jenny let out a shallow exhale; she did *not* want to have to look Rhonda in the eye and tell her there was nothing she could do to solve Ebony's murder.

And then she felt it.

"This way," Jenny said, raising her arm to point down Elkins Avenue. She said nothing more as she headed in that direction, unwilling to compromise the contact.

Holding the strap of her gun-concealing purse with both hands, she relaxed the rest of her body, allowing herself to follow Ebony's lead. After a block and a half, she felt the urge to turn right down a narrow, paved path between two buildings. Jenny's instincts would have told her not to go down that alleyway; it didn't look like a safe shortcut. However, she was following the lead of an invincible seventeen year old girl who traveled that route every day, so she didn't have a choice.

Taking the turn, she quickly found herself in a sort of no-man's-land—an area of gravel, broken pavement and weeds that served as a parking lot between the backs of the surrounding buildings. Continuing her walk, Jenny could see a brick façade appear between two old houses, on the opposite side of the next street. Based on the feeling of familiarity it invoked, she knew this to be Ebony's apartment building.

Without warning, splitting pain shot through the back of Jenny's head. Everything went black.

Unsure whether this was Ebony's experience or her own, Jenny placed her hands on the back of her head, noticing that nothing felt unusual. She stood up straighter as the pain went away, looking around to find bright sunshine and Zack with a concerned expression on his face.

"I guess we know where the attack happened," Zack said.

Jenny released a good deal of anxiety with a deep sigh. "We sure do. The problem is that I have no idea who did it. She clearly got hit from behind, and she didn't see it coming."

"Did it kill her?" Zack asked.

Thinking about the vision one more time, she concluded, "That's not the impression that I'm getting. I think I would have felt some sort of release if it did—the feeling of her soul leaving her body. I didn't get that."

"So, the person who hit her over the head—you think he took her?"

The implications of this experience were hitting Jenny all at once. Choking down her disgust, she looked at her husband and replied, "That's exactly what I think."

Chapter 5

"I don't want to tell her this," Jenny admitted as she and Zack approached Rhonda's home. "The only thing worse than knowing your daughter had been killed would be to know she suffered beforehand." Jenny shuddered involuntarily.

"Unfortunately, you don't get to make up the truth," Zack said.

"Oh, but wouldn't it be nice if I could?" Jenny knocked on the door to the apartment, where Rhonda said she would be home to greet them. As promised, Rhonda opened the door, dressed in a way that suggested she'd left work to come to this meeting.

"You must be Jenny," Rhonda said with an expressionless face.

"Yes, ma'am." Jenny was used to the idea that people weren't delighted to see her. She served as a reminder that a loved one had been lost—in this case, a child. This was the most unbearable loss of all, as far as Jenny was concerned. Nonetheless, Jenny remained cheerful and added, "And this is my husband, Zack."

"Nice to meet you both," Rhonda replied mechanically, opening the door wider. "Please, come in."

"Thank you for agreeing to meet with us," Jenny said after they'd been situated in the living room. "I know you had to take time off of work for this."

"It's just a long lunch," Rhonda replied. "An early long lunch. I'll stay later tonight to make up for it."

"What do you do?" Jenny asked as everybody took a seat.

"I work in a dental office; I do record keeping."

"Well, thank you again," Jenny added. "I will try to be short so that I don't keep you."

Rhonda held up her hand and shook her head. "This is far more important."

With a slight smile, Jenny nodded, silently acknowledging that she understood. Although, she couldn't help but notice that Rhonda didn't appear to be that much older than she and Zack; either Rhonda looked amazing for her age, or she had been very young when Ebony was born.

"Were you able to find anything out this morning?" Rhonda asked.

Jenny sighed as she leaned forward, resting her elbows on her knees and interlacing her fingers. "Somewhat. I figured out the path she used to take home. She went down an alleyway between a brick house and a light blue one, cutting through a vacant lot before she crossed the street to your apartment."

"That's right," Rhonda said solemnly.

"I get the feeling that the assault took place in that vacant lot. Somebody snuck up behind her and hit her on the head, knocking her out."

A long, tense silence filled the room, broken only when Rhonda remarked, "That's not what killed her."

Jenny's voice was little more than a whisper. "I know it's not."

"She clearly wasn't shot there," Rhonda added as she kept her distant eyes focused on nothing. "Somebody would have heard it if she was."

Although Rhonda wasn't looking at her, Jenny nodded. "I believe the person who knocked her out took her elsewhere."

"Do you know where?"

"Not yet," Jenny admitted, "but we've just started."

"I have a question," Zack asked in a tone much louder than the women had been using. Both ladies turned to face him. "Why was she alone? I mean, if you lived in an apartment building, I would assume there would be other kids getting off the bus and walking with her."

"She was in the gifted program," Rhonda explained. "She went to a magnet school, so it wasn't the same bus that the other kids took. There was only one other boy who got off at her stop, and he went the opposite direction."

"She was a very bright young lady, wasn't she?" Jenny asked compassionately. "I hear she was looking to become a doctor."

"She was," Rhonda agreed quietly. "She wanted to help people, and she was smart enough to do it. She had a bright future in front of her."

Jenny remained silent, getting the feeling that Rhonda had more to say. She was right.

"I was very young when I had Ebony...barely sixteen." Rhonda shook her head. "The Good Lord blessed me with intelligence, too, but it didn't stop me from making bad decisions. Having a high IQ doesn't necessarily mean a high self-esteem, and I allowed myself to get into a pretty bad position at a young age. I had to drop out of high school to raise the baby. I did *not* want that for my little girl, so from day one I stressed the importance of getting a good education. I wanted her to experience all the things I couldn't—I take that back. I wanted her to experience all the things that I *could have* if I'd made better choices.

"Ebony had her head on straight," Rhonda continued. "She had goals, and she knew exactly what she needed to do to achieve them. I have no doubt she would have gone on to college and medical school, and I'm positive she would have done it on scholarship. She was already applying for some and she wasn't even a senior yet."

Rhonda shook her head again. "I often ask God, *why Ebony?* I mean, I wouldn't wish this on anyone's daughter, but why Ebony? She was such a good kid. She had so much potential. I do feel bad for myself that she was taken, but I also feel bad for the world. Do you know how much good she would have done if she had been allowed to grow up? Do you know what this world was robbed of when that—*person*—killed my daughter?"

Jenny could hardly stand hearing these words. The thought of losing Steve in less than twenty years was unimaginable—even more so if he was murdered. She felt as if she couldn't breathe, and she was just listening to the story. Living it must have been hell.

Rhonda paused for a moment, gathering herself. "I try not to hold on to any anger. I keep the words of Martin Luther King in my mind: *let no man pull you low enough to hate him.* But that's hard to live by some days. I realize that keeping hate and anger inside only hurts me—it doesn't affect the person responsible for this—so I just throw my hands up to God and pray that He will make this right. God's judgment is based in truth. God knows what happened, even if I never do find out. I have faith that justice will be served where it matters the most; God will make sure of that."

"You're a better person than I am," Zack said.

Rhonda smiled slightly and replied, "No, I'm not. I'm just trying to live by Ebony's example. She had very strong faith and an affinity for Dr. King, so I believe this is the way she would have wanted me to handle the situation."

Jenny cleared her throat, announcing, "Well, I'd like to try to get some justice for her here on earth, if I could. That's why I'm here."

"I would like that, too," Rhonda said. "I do realize that if the killer is still out there, he could do this again to someone else's little girl. I wouldn't wish this on anybody."

Jenny nodded, trying to stay positive and focused. "Let's see what we can do. I'm sure you've answered all of this already, but I am hoping that the answers can trigger something in me that the other investigators couldn't get. Did Ebony have any enemies?"

Rhonda laughed at the idea. "Enemies? No."

"Was there any gang activity around at the time? Maybe she was part of some kind of initiation?"

"Gang activity was everywhere around us. I couldn't afford to live in an area where it wasn't. But the police have already investigated that angle. Do you know how difficult it would be to figure out which gang did it—or which member?"

"With traditional means, yes," Jenny began, "I agree, that would be nearly impossible to solve. But I have insight. Ebony may know who did this to her now, even if she didn't know at the time who attacked her in the vacant lot. She might be able to lead me to him if I get close enough."

Rhonda shook her head, her eyebrows furrowed. "I don't want you poking around in any gang activity. The only thing worse than losing Ebony would be to have somebody get killed trying to find justice for her."

"She's got a point," Zack said, putting his arm around Jenny's shoulder.

Jenny agreed in her own mind, but said nothing. "Is there anyone else—anywhere you can steer me—that can help me find her killer?"

"That's the problem," Rhonda replied with disgust. "I have no idea at all who may have done this. I think it was random, and she was just in the wrong place at the wrong time."

"Those are the hardest cases to solve," Jenny muttered.

Rhonda looked Jenny in the eye, staring intently and nodding. "So I've been told."

Chapter 6

"I want to go back to the hotel, feed Steve, grab some lunch and regroup," Jenny announced as they climbed back into the car, which was even hotter than it had been outside. Turning the key, blasting the air conditioning and rolling down the windows, she typed the hotel's address into the GPS.

"I'd like to take a shower," Zack replied. "I'm sweating like I've just run a marathon."

The GPS predicted a short drive to the hotel. "I guess later on we can go to the area where Ebony's body was found?" Jenny said, ignoring Zack's statement. "That might be our best bet for finding her killer." They pulled out of the parking spot and headed down the road.

"Do they know if it was a dumpsite or if she was killed there?"

"If memory serves," Jenny began, "which it may not, I don't think they were able to tell. Too much time had gone by, and too much evidence had been destroyed." She followed the directions that her phone spat out, taking a left on a one-way street. "They didn't find her body until a few weeks later." She shook her head, the reality of the tragedy even more pronounced now that she'd met Rhonda. "Could you imagine what those weeks were like for her mother?"

"No," Zack said flatly, "I honestly can't."

Jenny gripped the steering wheel tighter and said, "I just want to go to the hotel and hold Steve...and maybe never let him go."

Before long, the couple had parked the car and was headed into the lobby of the hotel. The cold air felt amazing as it wrapped around Jenny's skin once she walked through the doors. It must have been thirty degrees cooler inside than outside.

"Hey," Zack said with a point, "we know those people."

Jenny looked up in time to see Leslie and Hailey, the mother and daughter from the night before, waiting for the elevator. "Hello," Jenny called as they approached, "how are you ladies this morning?" With a giggle, she added, "Or maybe it's afternoon by now. I don't even know."

Leslie shrugged. "It's somewhere around there. We're doing well; how are you?"

Jenny managed a smile and said, "Okay. We just had a tough interview with a grieving mother, but I guess that's the reason we're here."

With a ding, the elevator doors slid open and the group stepped on. "What floor?" Leslie asked.

"Ten," Zack replied.

"Oh, really? Us, too." After a short moment of silence, Leslie began, "We just had an interesting vision in a parking lot. Well, *she* did," she added, placing her hand on Hailey's shoulder. The young girl only smiled.

A bit of dread came over Jenny; she hated the thought of a middle school girl having to deal with the ugliness that she had seen. "Was it violent?" Jenny asked, wincing.

"No, not violent," Leslie replied, "just disturbing. It seems our victim was ambushed in the parking lot of a convenience store. He was taken away in his own car at gunpoint. I'm thinking it was a carjacking that must have gone wrong."

"That's terrible," Jenny remarked, deciding to keep the details of her case secret. This school-aged girl didn't need to know what happened to another student who was just walking home from the bus.

"We want to go back to the parking lot tonight, when it's dark and less busy," Leslie continued as the doors slid open. They all walked out and lingered in the area where the elevators were housed. "I want an officer to come with us, though," Leslie added. "It's clearly a dangerous place, especially at night."

"You could bring Jenny with you," Zack announced, putting his arm around her. "She's a pistol-packin' mama."

Smacking her forehead, Jenny said, "Can you say that a little louder, please? The people on the third floor didn't hear you."

"Are you really carrying a gun?" Leslie asked in a whisper.

Unsure of what Leslie thought of that, Jenny held up her hand and quickly said, "I only bring it to sketchy places. When I'm at home, or here, I keep it locked up and I hold on to the key. I have a baby, so I'm not taking any chances of him getting his hands on it."

"No, I understand," Leslie replied. "I actually thought about it when we were in the parking lot today. We might be safer if I had a gun."

"Mom," Hailey said, mortified, "you want to carry a gun?"

"I do if it means protecting you," Leslie replied.

The middle schooler didn't seem any less embarrassed.

"Do you want us to come with you tonight?" Zack asked. "The offer before was actually serious, even though I used the phrase *pistol packin' mama*."

Leslie seemed ready to dismiss the offer when Jenny asked, "Which case was yours?"

"Luis Alvarez," Hailey said.

"Luis Alvarez," Jenny repeated. "Was that the father who volunteered as a soccer coach?"

"Yes, that's him," Leslie confirmed.

Addressing the mother, Jenny said, "Can I talk to you alone for a second?"

Looking both confused and apprehensive, Leslie agreed, and the two women stepped around the corner down one of the halls toward the guest rooms.

"I would actually like to come with you to the parking lot," Jenny explained. "Luis seems like he was a great guy, and he was the father of two girls. I'm not sure he'd want to expose Hailey to certain images, but they may be essential to the case. I worked with a psychic child in the past, and that's what happened—the spirit spared him from the most disturbing visions and gave them to me. Do you mind if I come along so I can get the scary ones?"

Leslie's eyes were wide. "No, not at all. Thank you for thinking of her that way."

"No problem," Jenny replied. "I've seen some things that I wouldn't wish on any child."

Looking worried, Leslie asked, "Do you think it was a mistake to bring her here?"

"No." She shook her head. "Not when you consider the victim she's been given. I'm pretty sure Luis wouldn't do anything to upset her."

Leslie let out a breath and lowered her shoulders, hanging her head.

"It'll be okay, Mom," Jenny said, rubbing Leslie's back. "It just takes some getting used to." The women started walking toward Zack and Hailey. "Do you want to get some lunch downstairs?" Jenny asked. "We'll be down there shortly. We'd love it if you could join us."

"That would be great," Leslie replied. "I'd like to talk to you a little bit about how this whole psychic thing works. We're pretty new at this."

"Do you want to meet in the lobby in half an hour?" Jenny posed.

"That's perfect."

Jenny looked up at Zack. "We'll be going with them to the parking lot tonight." Turning to Leslie, she added, "What time were you thinking of going?"

Leslie turned to Hailey. "I don't know, hon. What do you think?"

Hailey shrugged, saying, "I want to go when it's most likely going to be empty—just like it was when Luis went there."

"That was at, like, four in the morning," Leslie said.

"That's okay with me," Jenny replied, "if that's the best time to go. I have a baby; I'm used to getting up in the middle of the night."

Leslie looked concerned. "Are you sure that will be safe?"

Zack lifted a thumb in Jenny's direction. "She's been going to target practice every Tuesday afternoon for months."

Letting out a laugh, Leslie said, "Well, then…four a.m. it is."

Chapter 7

The hotel restaurant was nearly empty, so Leslie and Hailey were easy to spot. They were sitting next to each other at a table big enough for six and had thoughtfully gotten a high chair to put at the end.

"Hello," Jenny said cheerfully as she approached. "Look how sweet you are, getting a high chair for Steve."

"I figured we'd need it," Leslie replied.

Jenny gestured to her mom. "This is my mother, Isabelle. Mom, this is Hailey and Leslie."

"Are you both psychic?" Isabelle asked with a smile.

"No, just my daughter," Leslie said.

After configuring Steve into his seat, Jenny sat at the end of the table, with her mother and Zack sitting on the same side. "This is actually perfect," Jenny noted. "I called Amma, and she said she'd hopefully be joining us. She said to go ahead and order in case she can't make it. Susan can't come because she's hot on the trail of her suspect."

"Oh, yeah?" Leslie asked. "She's making good progress?"

"Well," Jenny replied with a laugh, "I don't know about making good progress, but she's far away at the moment. Her victim lived an hour from here, so Susan is there visiting with her family. She said she already grabbed something to eat on the way."

The waitress came by and took drink orders, during which time Jenny could sense poor Hailey's discomfort. No middle school student wanted to sit with a bunch of adult strangers at lunch. "So," Jenny began in her best teacher tone, "have you used the pool yet, Hailey?"

Nodding awkwardly, Hailey said, "We went yesterday before the meeting."

"That's cool," Jenny replied. "Are you planning to go again?"

Hailey looked at her mother. "I don't know."

"I'm not sure," Leslie said, the tone of her voice suggesting they wouldn't be. "Someone is paying for us to stay here. I'm sure the person who picked up the tab is doing it because they want us to solve the case, not use the pool."

An inner tug-of-war began within Jenny, resulting in the comment, "I'm sure the person who paid for the rooms wouldn't mind if Hailey took a break and went swimming."

"I don't know," Leslie said. "I would feel guilty."

Closing her eyes, Jenny announced, "I paid for the room." Opening her eyes back up again, she could see the astonishment on both Hailey and Leslie's faces.

"*You* paid for the room?" Leslie asked.

Holding up her hand, Jenny explained, "Not really." She let out a sigh and added, "My first client was Elanor Whitby; she was the founder of Choices magazine, so she was obviously quite wealthy. I was able to solve a mystery for her right before she died, and she left me the majority of her estate. I was shocked, to say the least...but with the money came some instructions: I was to use the inheritance to help people in the same way I'd helped her. So while, yes, I put the rooms on my credit card, the money is actually coming from Elanor—and I can assure you she wouldn't mind if Hailey took some time to be a kid while she was here."

Leslie appeared humbled. "Well, thank you...on both counts." The waitress reappeared with drinks and left with their lunch orders.

Jenny leaned forward on her elbows, interlacing her fingers. "So," she began, addressing Leslie, "you said you had some questions about how this whole psychic thing works because you're *new at this*. Does that mean Hailey just started showing signs of having this ability?"

"It started over winter break," Leslie replied, her face showing displeasure. "We live in a house that backs up to a lake, and Hailey got new ice skates for Christmas. She decided to give them a try, and she ended up falling through the ice."

Jenny's mouth fell open; her ancestor had also fallen through ice, and it was what led to the ability in her own family.

Even though there was obviously a happy ending, Leslie still appeared to have a difficult time recounting the story. "Thank God, thank God, thank God our neighbor was outside when it happened. He's an EMT, and he'd actually had some training on ice rescues, so he was able to get her out and resuscitate her." Shaking her head with her eyes closed, Leslie remarked, "I am just so grateful he was outside at that moment."

"There's something I haven't told you about that, actually," Hailey announced sheepishly.

Leslie looked at her daughter with dismay. "What is it?"

Clearing her throat uncomfortably, Hailey admitted, "It wasn't a coincidence that Mr. Glass was outside. Mrs. Glass made sure he went out there."

"You mean Diane?"

Hailey nodded. "Mr. Glass told me that he felt sad about Mrs. Glass all of a sudden, and he had this really strong urge to go outside and get some fresh air. That was right before I fell through the ice. And when I was under the water, the only thing I remember was hearing Mrs. Glass's voice telling me not to worry because help was on the way."

With her mouth agape, Leslie sat motionless.

Hailey continued, "I think Mrs. Glass knew the ice was too thin to skate on and that I'd be in trouble." Looking down, she added, "I think she did something to make Mr. Glass to remember her at that moment and need the fresh air."

Jenny smiled, softly saying, "I'm assuming Mrs. Glass was his wife?"

Hailey nodded slightly. "She died of cancer a few years ago."

Jenny let her eyes shift over to Leslie, who appeared to be on the verge of tears. She reached out her hand and placed it on top of Leslie's, telling Hailey, "When you heard Mrs. Glass's voice, you must have been on your way to cross over, but she told you not to. I guess she had faith that her husband would be able to save you if you just held on a little longer."

Leslie gave Jenny's hand a squeeze, saying, "By 'cross over,' you mean..." She left it at that.

With a nod, Jenny whispered, "Yes. But even if she had crossed, I assure you, she'd be in a beautiful place. I know you would miss her terribly, but there is something amazing on the other side. If the worst did happen, you could take comfort in knowing that Hailey would be okay, right where she was."

"I'd much rather have her here," Leslie replied.

"Of course," Jenny said cheerfully, letting go of Leslie's hand. "But I wanted to let you know that, just in case it's true of anyone else you love and miss."

Motion caused Jenny to look toward the entrance of the restaurant. Amma was headed in their direction, her gait just as quick and powerful as ever. "I finally made it," Amma announced as she sat in the empty chair next to Leslie. "Sorry I'm late, but I had a criminal to apprehend."

"*Apprehend*?" Zack asked with dismay. "You caught yours?"

Amma looked as if she didn't understand the question. "Yeah."

"So soon?" Zack asked.

"Yeah," Amma said again. "Did you order food already?"

After an uncharacteristic moment of speechlessness, Zack replied, "Yes, we ordered...But you seriously solved your case this fast?"

"It wasn't hard," Amma replied. "The spirit was angry. She was killed by hit man and it was made to look random, but he had been hired by her husband." She let out a hearty laugh. "Too bad her husband was stupid enough to pay the hit man in front of a surveillance camera. She knew that, too, and apparently had been desperate to tell somebody that since she was killed last year. Oh...excuse me." She raised her hand to flag down the waitress. "Can I please have a steak and cheese sub and a glass of milk?"

A tangible silence filled the table until Zack asked, "You said you apprehended him...by that you meant the police, right? Not you, personally?"

"The police are about to get him," she replied, "but I had a message to deliver to him, first."

Jenny closed her eyes, afraid to hear the rest.

Zack asked, "You went up to a man who has hired hitmen in the past and said something to him?"

"Yeah," Amma said, acting as if nothing was strange about that. "I went to his job and found him. His wife had me say, 'You haven't heard the last from Katie.' Her name was Kate, to everyone else. He was the only one to call her Katie. Boy, you should have seen the look on his face when I said that. He was spooked to the core. I mean, imagine if some random old lady walked up to you and delivered a message like that. It would be scary if you were guilty."

"Don't you think that was a little dangerous?" Isabelle asked.

"Nah," Amma replied with a dismissive wave of her hand. "I have a Taser in my bag. If he got nasty, I would have let him have it."

"You have a *Taser*?" Jenny asked, shocked.

"You have a gun," Amma replied factually.

"How do you know I have a...?" Jenny began, stopping herself to instead ask, "How did you get a Taser on a plane?"

"I didn't," Amma replied. "I bought it here. You can have it when I'm done since I can't bring it back with me. Although, you don't need it if you have the real McCoy, now, do you?" Turning to Leslie, she asked, "Did you drive here or fly?"

"We drove," Leslie replied.

"Do you want it, then?"

Shrugging one shoulder, Leslie said, "That might not be a bad idea."

"Mom!" Hailey's embarrassment surfaced again. Jenny wouldn't go back to being that age if her life depended on it.

"Good gracious, child, relax," Leslie told her.

Amma patted Leslie's hand. "I'll give it to you before I go." Leaning forward to get a better view of Hailey, she added, "It wouldn't hurt you to learn how to use it, either."

Before this got controversial, Jenny loudly said, "Anyway, Leslie, you were saying that Hailey fell through the ice. I imagine her psychic ability started after that."

"That's right. She started having visions before she even left the hospital."

"That makes sense," Jenny replied. "A near-death experience can cause someone to get the ability. It means she was on her way to the other side—she opened that door, so to speak—and it doesn't close when the person comes back to life."

Leslie responded with a long sigh.

"It happened in my family," Jenny told her. "My great, great..." Turning to Amma, she asked, "How many 'greats' do I need to say?"

"You?" Amma replied. "Four."

Jenny continued, "My great-great-great-great grandmother had a near death experience, and, ever since then, some of her descendants have been born with the ability."

"You mean Hailey could have kids with it?" Leslie asked with surprise, placing her hand on Hailey's shoulder.

Jenny nodded. "Yup."

"Or grandkids," Amma added. "Sometimes it skips a generation."

Leslie put her other hand on her forehead, clearly trying to absorb the fact that her life had changed more than she originally thought.

"Are you ready for this, Mom?" Jenny asked Leslie, unable to mask her grin.

With a sigh, Leslie replied, "I'm not even ready for this afternoon. We're going to meet with Luis's family, and I know that's not going to be easy."

"Yeah, we did that this morning," Jenny said. "It never is easy. But look at it this way—your afternoon is going to be more productive than mine."

"Why? What do you have planned?"

"Not much," Jenny remarked flatly. "Just a visit to the dumpsite that, hopefully, will yield something. But maybe it won't. That's the problem. At this point in my case, we have absolutely nothing to go on."

Chapter 8

"If this doesn't give us any clues," Jenny remarked from behind the wheel, "I don't know what we're going to do. It's possible she never regained consciousness and has no idea who did this to her."

The car worked its way down the rural road, surrounded by farmland. "She might have had no idea who did it to her while she was alive," Zack began, "but do you think she could have figured it out after she died?"

Jenny shrugged. "Your guess is as good as mine."

"According to this, you need to take a right up here," Zack told her with a point. Jenny did as she was told, and the road quickly disappeared into the woods. Zack kept his eye on the odometer, announcing, "In one-point-three miles, you will need to pull over and park."

"This isn't exactly the widest road I've ever been on," she replied. "Do you think the car will be safe if I park it here?"

"It's not wide, but it's kind of straight. Other cars should be able to see it from far away—that is, if there are any other cars. This doesn't seem to be a high traffic area."

After watching the correct number of miles tick by, Jenny stopped the car along the side of the road, putting on the hazard lights. With a quick, nervous glance in both directions, she got out of the car, hoping she wouldn't come back to find a mangled piece of wreckage.

Her worries were soon replaced by a pull that directed her toward the trees. "I've got something," she told Zack mechanically. Without another word, she headed into the woods with Zack trailing a few steps behind her.

Bugs swarmed her head as sweat dripped down her face. Her legs itched from mosquito bites and small plants brushing up against her calves. She was aware of this but chose to ignore it, realizing Ebony's ordeal had been far worse. Considering what the young honor student had gone through, Jenny didn't dare complain about being uncomfortable from bug bites and scratches.

The tug from within Jenny grew stronger until it eventually stopped, leading her to the conclusion that she had reached her destination. Allowing herself to come back into the present, Jenny pointed to the earth and said, "This is the spot. This is where her body was found." A scary thought occurred to her as she asked Zack, "Who found her again?"

"Hunters," Zack replied.

Looking around nervously, she asked, "Should we be wearing orange? Are we in danger of being shot?"

"It isn't season, unless you're hunting for predators," he told her. "I think we're good."

"Predators?"

"Coyotes and stuff."

Standing perfectly still, Jenny surveyed her surroundings with just her eyes. "You mean there are coyotes out here?"

"Probably not," he replied, "but it would be legal to shoot them if we saw some. Do you have your gun with you, Annie Oakley?"

"No, I do *not* have my gun with me."

He shrugged nonchalantly. "You don't have a license to hunt anyway."

"I think you are missing my point."

"Relax," he said with a smile, "I don't think people are very high on a coyote's list of desired foods. Besides, the odds of seeing a coyote around here are pretty slim. Snakes, on the other hand..."

"I swear to God," Jenny declared, "you are not funny."

With a new desire to be quick, she took three steps forward, standing in the exact spot that was calling her. Closing her eyes and lifting her face to the sky, she allowed herself to absorb the message that was being sent. Once it disappeared, she turned to Zack and announced, "She wasn't killed here. It was just a dumpsite."

"No fear?" Zack asked. He apparently knew the routine well.

"No fear," she reiterated. "Not from her, anyway. I only got peace from her. I, on the other hand, am a different story." She looked around her feet for snakes.

"So, I guess there's nothing to be learned here?" Zack posed.

Swatting bugs away from her face, Jenny replied, "Unfortunately, no." She sighed impatiently and added, "Let's get out of here. This place is miserable."

It was not lost on Jenny that this 'miserable place' was where a beautiful young woman was tossed aside like trash. Eagerly heading back out of the woods, she made a vow that she wouldn't give up. The clues may not have been coming easily, but she would find a way to make it work.

That is, if she didn't die from a venomous snake bite first.

"I'm kind of at a loss," Jenny admitted as they drove back toward the city. She reached down under the steering wheel to scratch her itchy leg. "I'm not sure where to go or what to do from here."

"Have you ever been to Richmond before?" Zack asked.

"Only driving through on the highway." She wasn't sure what he was getting at.

"Well, maybe we ought to tour the city," he suggested. "There's a lot of history here. And while we're driving around, something might come to you."

"I guess that's as good of a plan as any." She switched hands, scratching the mosquito bites on her other leg. "I want to go back to the hotel and shower first, though—and douse myself with hydrocortisone." She glanced at the clock. "And feed the baby."

"Yeah," Zack added, "that sounds good. I could actually use a little something to eat, myself."

"You eat as often as Steve does," Jenny said, "and that's disturbing."

"Well, it takes a lot of calories to keep up this manly physique," he replied, puffing his chest out.

Jenny responded only with a shake of her head, wondering if Steve was going to grow up to be a giant goofball like his father. Deep down inside, she hoped he did.

Once she had a shower and felt like a human being again, Jenny played with Steve in the hotel room while Zack looked up the best sights to see in Richmond. "There's lots of Civil War stuff around here," he noted.

"I'm not entirely sure that Civil War sites are the best places for me to go, all things considered," Jenny replied. "I can imagine there's a lot of 'spiritual unrest' associated with them."

"We can go to Hollywood Cemetery," he added. "James Monroe and John Tyler are buried there. You could see if the ex-presidents have anything exciting to say."

"Is there anything less death oriented?"

"There's a place called Maymont. It looks like it's got some nice gardens, a nature center and a petting zoo."

"Ooh, a nature center and a petting zoo. Maybe Steve would like that."

"Well, if we're going to bring the baby, now's probably a good time to go, don't you think? He just ate and napped, so he should be good for a while."

"Sounds good," Jenny agreed. "Is Maymont far from here?"

"It says less than ten minutes."

"That's perfect." Before long, the couple was headed out with the baby, negotiating the streets of downtown Richmond. Their trip brought them through an older section of the city, where skyscrapers turned into hundred-year-old row houses with quaint porches and small yards. Keeping one ear on the GPS and both eyes on the heavy traffic along the one-way streets, Jenny gripped the wheel tightly, trying to make sure they arrived at Maymont in one piece. Passing through an intersection, Jenny felt an overwhelming urge to head down the cross street even though the GPS has told her to go straight. "Uh oh," she said. "It looks like our plans might get canceled."

"You got something?" Zack asked.

"Back there, I did," she replied, gesturing over her shoulder with her thumb. "Somehow, I'm going to have to try to get back there again."

"It's the city. Just keep turning right; eventually, you'll make a square."

After passing a one-way cross street that headed in the wrong direction, Jenny turned right at the following intersection. After three more turns, she was back in the place she'd felt the original pull. Taking that right, she went only a short distance before the buzz inside her grew frantic. Even Steve started to make sounds, indicating he was bothered by it, too. As she drove along, the feeling inside her stopped abruptly, letting her know she had passed it. "Dammit," she said, "I have to make another circle."

After driving around one more time, she found a parking space along the side of the road, shortly before the buzzing reached its maximum. "Do you want to wait in here with the air conditioning running?" Jenny asked. "I don't think I'll be that long."

"Yeah, Steve and I will stay behind. Holler if you need me. Or shoot."

Jenny playfully rolled her eyes and got out of the car, immediately struck by both the heat and the intensity of the emotion coming from that area.

Something huge and quite upsetting had happened nearby.

Walking a few houses down, Jenny felt the pull leading her to a large, stone house that stood close to the sidewalk. It was an older building with pointed windows, giving it an almost churchlike appearance. The bars on the windows, however, had the opposite effect, making it look more like a place of imprisonment than a place of worship.

A shudder worked its way up Jenny's spine as she looked at this immense structure. She couldn't help but feel like she was staring into the gateway to Hell.

Voices swirled around her head with dizzying speed. She closed her eyes, trying to maintain her balance even though she felt like she was spinning at a million miles an hour. So much was trying to be said at this moment, but she couldn't hear any of it. It was as if she was trying to make out a single voice from a large, chattering crowd.

"Wow," she said to herself in a whisper, amazed by the intensity surrounding this house. Reaching into her purse, she pulled out her phone and dialed a familiar number. After a few rings she heard a male voice.

"Hello, Jenny."

"Hi, Kyle. How are you doing?"

"Oh, surviving," he replied. "Trying to stay cool in the Georgia heat."

"Good luck with that," she said, although it was difficult to make small talk at the moment.

Kyle responded with only a grunt.

"Listen, I'm in Richmond, Virginia right now, and I've got some terrible vibes coming from a house here. And I do mean terrible. Can you find out a little bit about it for me?"

"Sure. What's the address?"

Jenny looked at the building for the house number, then glanced at the corner for a street name. "It looks like eight-twenty-two South Bayhill Avenue."

After a pause, he replied, "Got it."

"Specifically, I'm wondering who lived here five years ago. I'm assuming the pull I just got is related to a case I'm working on, but, then again, it might not be. There seems to be a lot going on with this building…maybe more than just my case."

"Okay. I can just get the complete ownership history on the house and give you the whole thing. That way, if it turns out to be something unrelated to your case, you can still have the information on who lived there at the time frame you want to focus on."

"Thanks," she replied with a shaky exhale. "You're the best."

"You actually sound a little frazzled this time," Kyle remarked.

"I am frazzled," she said nervously, glancing up at the house. "Something tells me that this is going to be a bad one."

Chapter 9

"We should probably have the baby sleep in my mother's room tonight," Jenny told Zack on their way home from Maymont. "If we're getting up at three-thirty in the morning to go to a parking lot, we certainly don't need to wake Steve in the process."

"Ooh," Zack replied, "I like that idea."

Based on his excitement, Jenny determined she wouldn't be going straight to sleep that night. She mentally prepared herself for the sex she'd be having later.

Her phone rang, so she pressed the button on her steering wheel to answer it. "Hello?"

"Hi, Jenny, it's Kyle."

"Hey. That was quick. Did you have any luck finding out who owns the home?"

"Well, yes and no. It's a rental unit with eight apartments, and I was able to figure out the landlord's name, but the individual tenants are a mystery. That's atypical; usually the renters are just as easy to determine as the landlord."

Jenny thought about that for a moment. "How can people live there without a record of it? Don't they need to get mail?"

"I mean, there could be a couple of different explanations for it. The tenants could be illegals, or there could be something fishy about the way the landlord does business."

"There's clearly something fishy about that place," Jenny muttered with disgust. "Is it possible that he had no renters and he kept the apartments empty?"

"It's possible. You'll have to talk to the guy...or I could, if you'd rather. He might be the one responsible for all of the bad stuff going on there, so I don't necessarily want you meeting with him in person."

Jenny smiled; Kyle was like her third father. "I'll let the police handle it; how about that?"

"That sounds good to me."

"Can you text me the landlord's information? I'm driving right now, so I can't write anything down. Although, I'll be back at the hotel in, like, two minutes."

"Sure, I can do that. At the rate I type, though, you'll be back in your room before you get the message."

She was in the parking lot when her phone chirped. Glancing at the screen, she told Zack, "It looks like the landlord's name is Andrei Petrovich."

"Ah, a nice Irish boy," Zack replied.

Jenny made a face and then shook her head rapidly. "It seems reasonable that someone named Andrei Petrovich could have some connections with some illegal immigrants and oh, dear God." She stopped in her tracks.

"What's the matter?"

Remembering that Ebony was dead, Jenny determined that her momentary thought didn't apply to her, but there may have been some other girls who were very much alive and were in trouble. "Do you think we might be dealing with human trafficking?"

"Does that really happen here?"

"I don't know, but I don't want to eliminate that as a possibility." Jenny resumed her walk toward the hotel, carrying a fussing Steve in his car seat. She shook her head again, this time with disgust, desperately hoping she was wrong about her theory. After sucking in a breath, she calmly stated, "I guess I shouldn't jump to conclusions. Just because the guy has a foreign name, that doesn't mean he's involved in shady, foreign business dealings."

"Well, he has a foreign name and an apartment building with no registered tenants and a bunch of pissed off spirits hanging around there. And let's not forget you were most likely led there by an abducted teenage girl."

"Oh, God." Jenny hung her head as they entered the hotel lobby. While she felt relief with the cooler air, Steve continued to squiggle and whine, and her mind was still in a horrible place. "If this ends up being a human trafficking case, you're going to have to hold on to my gun for me. I swear, if I discover Andrei whatever-his-name-is is selling young girls, I would save the taxpayers the cost of a trial and shoot the son of a bitch myself."

Wednesday

The three-thirty alarm was painful. With half-closed eyes, Jenny reached over and silenced the phone that was playing some cheerful little jingle. Hearing Zack's deep breaths, she knew he must have still been sleeping. She nudged him, saying, "Get up. It's time to meet with the Newcombs."

He muttered something inaudible as Jenny sat up and debated whether or not she should bother to get dressed. Was she really going to run into anyone in a parking lot at four in the morning? Pajamas seemed like perfectly appropriate attire under the circumstances.

Wiping her hands down her face, she stood up and stretched, walking around the bed and giving Zack a shake. "It's three-thirty—time to get up," she repeated.

She was met only with a groan.

After turning on the light, she went into the bathroom and got ready; she even changed out of her pajamas. When she emerged ten minutes later, Zack was still sound asleep in the bed.

Marching over to him, she shook him vigorously and demanded, "Get up."

The words sparked something in Jenny's mind. Suddenly, she wasn't in the hotel room anymore, but rather lying down on a hard floor with the back of her head throbbing. "Get up!" she heard the male voice say, feeling a swift kick to her ribs.

The room spun as she tried to get onto her hands and knees. Her head hurt so badly she felt like she could vomit, but she didn't dare. Stabilizing herself on all fours, she put her right foot flat on the floor, taking a second to get her balance. The male voice spoke again, riddled with anger. "Move faster, nigger!"

"What time is it?"

The transition into the real world took a second, but Jenny finally figured out that Zack had asked the question. "Time for you to get out of bed," she said dryly. "It's almost three forty-five."

Zack grunted as he rolled over. "Already?"

"Yes, already. But your laziness has proven to be helpful, so thanks for that. I just had a vision."

Sitting up and blinking while squinting, Zack asked, "Oh, yeah? What was it?"

"It wasn't much, but it was telling," she said. "The victim—who I assume was Ebony—was being yelled at to get up off the floor. The thing is, she was called the n-word. I'm not sure if that was just an insult, but we have to consider that may have been the reason she was kidnapped in the first place. But the other interesting part about it was that the man speaking definitely had an accent."

Zack ran is hands over his messy hair. "Russian?"

"No," Jenny replied, shaking her head. "Southern."

Jenny drove with Hailey in the passenger seat; Zack and Leslie sat in the back. The GPS gave the directions as she worked her way down the nearly deserted streets of Richmond. The ride was quiet; nobody in the car appeared to be fully awake yet.

The convenience store appeared, and the lot was empty. "It happened over there," Hailey instructed with a point, directing Jenny to the side of the building. She parked the car, and a slight buzz started inside of her.

"Are you feeling anything?" Jenny asked Hailey softly.

With a nod, Hailey said, "A little bit."

Without another word, they got out of the car and stood in the darkness. A lone car passed on the main road; the noise from it threatened Jenny's concentration, but she managed to stay focused. "Let me make this real simple," she heard a man say. "Either you get in the car, or we kill you."

Closing her eyes, Jenny saw herself next to a small car; a gun was pointed at her head. She could see two men with bandanas over their faces standing so close to her they were touching her. One opened the back door to the car, the other forced her inside.

She felt remarkably calm as all of this unfolded, almost as if it were happening to someone else. She sat in the back of the car with the man holding the gun, noticing a third man in getting in the passenger seat. The man next to her yanked the keys out her hand, handing them to the driver, who did not turn around. He simply reached back, grabbed the keys and started the car.

The gun remained pressed up against her face as they backed out of the lot and headed down the street. Somehow, she managed to not even feel nervous, optimistic that if she just kept her cool, they would ultimately take the car—and maybe her wallet—and let her go unharmed.

Removing his bandana, the man next to her spoke. "What are you doing out here at this time of night, huh, spic? Your landscaping job keep you up late tonight?"

Funny, Jenny thought. *Racial jokes.* She glanced up in time to see the passenger slip his bandana over his head, looking quickly over his shoulder toward Jenny.

"I asked you a question," the man repeated, his tone growing angrier.

Jenny heard Hailey's voice penetrate her vision. "We need to go that way." She opened her eyes to see Hailey pointing down the road, gesturing in the direction they had just come from.

Still holding the keys, Jenny paused for a moment to let her vision sink in. Then, with a fake smile plastered on her face, she said, "Well, then, let's go."

They wordlessly got back in the car. Jenny was not feeling a pull this time, so she was going to have to rely on Hailey to get her to their destination. She was confident, though, that a middle school student could do that, unlike the time she relied on a kindergartener to provide her with directions.

"Here's the issue," Hailey said with a point. "We need to go that direction, but it's a one-way street."

"That's actually not an issue at all," Jenny said softly. She turned the only direction she could go, making two more right turns to get them headed the correct way. She was becoming an expert at making squares.

Hailey led Jenny down some roads that put them in the older section of town. The buildings that had looked quaint in the daylight had an aura of spookiness when lit only by the street lamps. After a few more turns, Hailey announced that they had reached their destination, so Jenny stopped the car.

"This is it," Hailey declared, tapping the passenger window with her finger. "Mom, this is the house I was telling you about before."

Zack spoke for the first time in a while, simply saying, "Jenny..."

"I know," Jenny replied, looking at the ominous house. "It's eight twenty-two South Bayhill Avenue."

"You're familiar with it?" Leslie asked from the back seat.

The same unrest from earlier in the day buzzed within Jenny. "We were here before," she said. "I was led to this very same house." Jenny's blood ran cold as she added, "If this is related to our cases, I think we might be dealing with the same killers."

Chapter 10

A tangible silence filled the car until Hailey said, "It's awful here. The spirits are going crazy."

"Let's get out of here," Jenny replied, a chill working its way up her spine. "It's not going to do us any good to sit in front of this horrible building at four in the morning." Pressing the gas pedal, she headed back toward the hotel.

"You think the same people killed both Luis and Ebony?" Leslie asked, even though Jenny had just said that.

"I think it's possible," Jenny remarked, "and, based on the amount of spiritual activity surrounding that house, there may be some other victims."

"You felt it, too?" Hailey asked.

Jenny nodded emphatically. "Sure did, and it was terrible. Hailey, let me ask you this...did you have any visions at the convenience store parking lot?"

Hailey shook her head. "No...well, not tonight. I did earlier in the day. Tonight, I just felt the need to go toward the house."

Nodding slightly, Jenny thought about her own vision. Perhaps Luis didn't want to expose an innocent young girl to the racial slurs that were said to him.

Perhaps he was as nice as he seemed.

Deciding to honor Luis's wishes, Jenny kept her mouth shut about the s-word and the n-word that had been thrown around in her visions, simply saying, "Well, we have a Hispanic man and an African-American girl being victimized by the same people. It looks like it could be racially motivated." She shook her head. "It may not be, but we can't eliminate that possibility.

"I did get the name of the landlord of that awful building earlier today," Jenny continued. "I work with this wonderful private investigator who can tell me anything I want to know—well, almost anything. He wasn't able to find the names of any of the tenants, even though there are eight apartments there. He said it's unusual for the renters to be anonymous. I'm not sure what's going on at that place, but it's obviously something sinister. Anyway, I gave the landlord's information to Detective Spicer; I'll follow up with him a little later to see if he found out anything. Maybe has figured out the names of the people who lived there at the time—which very well may be the names of our killers.

"But, in case that doesn't work," she went on, realizing she was monopolizing the whole conversation, "I have a little something else that will help. I actually had a vision at the convenience store just now, and I saw what happened after Luis was put into the backseat of his car. The men took their bandanas off, and I was able to get a look at their faces. I'm going to try to sketch them when I get back to the hotel. I just hope I can remember them well enough and not get them confused with each other."

"You saw their faces?" Leslie asked.

"Two of them, yes," Jenny replied. "I saw the person sitting in the backseat with Luis and the person in the passenger seat."

"And you can sketch them?"

"She's a good artist," Zack declared. "She'll be able to draw them well."

"That'll help," Leslie replied.

"Maybe." Jenny shrugged one shoulder. "If they already know who it is based on the address, it may be unnecessary."

"Well, it certainly can't hurt."

Before long, the car pulled into the hotel parking lot. "I don't know about you guys, but I'm looking forward to a little more shut-eye," Zack said as they got out of the car.

"Yeah, I'm tired, too," Leslie agreed. They walked toward the building.

Jenny didn't say anything; she was tired as well, but she wanted to make the drawing before she forgot what the people looked like. However, if Zack was going back to sleep, she imagined she'd be banished to the bathroom in order to make her pictures. This wouldn't have been the first time she'd made a sketch of a murderer in a hotel bathroom.

How odd her life had become.

Susan sat with the baby on her lap in the hotel restaurant, the smell of coffee in the air. Steve was perfectly content in this stranger's arms, presumably because she had that psychic feel like his mother did.

"I am so ready for grandkids," Susan announced, kissing Steve on the top of his bald head. Holding up her hand, she added, "I'm willing to wait; I want my kids to finish college first. But I am counting the days until I get to be a Grandma."

"Trust me," Isabelle said, "it's wonderful. You get to love on them, spoil them...and then give them back when they get fussy."

That seemed awfully appealing to Jenny, too; it sounded a lot like Zack's life.

"I was a grandmother and didn't know it," Amma said dryly.

Jenny glanced at her mother out of the corner of her eye. Jenny had been conceived during a brief affair between Isabelle and Amma's son, Rod, but she had kept the true father's identity a secret to save her marriage. Even Rod didn't know he was a father. Isabelle looked down at her lap, softly muttering, "Sorry about that."

"I'm not," Amma replied, in typical Amma fashion. "You gave me a granddaughter—one that carries on the family gift. I'm not sorry any of it happened."

Isabelle's relief was obvious as she let out a long exhale and relaxed her shoulders. "I'm so happy to hear you say that. I've been afraid this whole time that you were upset with me for lying all those years."

"My son got you pregnant and then didn't take care of the baby. You think I'm mad at you for that?" Amma asked.

Once again, Isabelle focused on her lap. "He didn't know he got me pregnant."

"This one," Amma replied, pointing at Jenny. "This one here was much better off being raised by your husband instead of my son. My son had nothing. He was off doing that hippie dippy thing of his." She rolled her eyes and made a dismissive gesture with her hand. "What would he have given you for child support, eh? A homegrown tomato and a couple of cucumbers?" She shook her head. "No, things happened just the way they were supposed to." She reached over and took Steve's tiny hand into hers. "And now I have this little guy, carrying on the family gift. I get to go to my grave knowing that the ability isn't going to die when my son does. That brings me comfort."

Jenny couldn't help but smile. At that moment, Leslie and Hailey came into the room, taking the two empty seats at the table. After saying hello and giving them a moment to look at the menu, Jenny asked the Newcombs, "Were you able to get back to sleep after our little midnight field trip?"

"Eventually," Leslie said.

"I had no trouble," Zack noted.

Jenny made a face, glancing in his direction. "You could sleep through a tornado." She directed her attention back to Hailey and Leslie. "I didn't even try to go back to sleep when we came back. Instead, I made the sketches of the kidnappers before I forgot what they looked like...but, of course, I didn't bring them with me. I'll show them to you when we go back up; they're in my room."

At that moment, the waitress came by and took their orders. After that, everyone shared the progress of their cases. Susan said she was making small strides, whereas Amma said the killer in her case had been arrested the night before. She had already started working on one of the fraud's cases, but she said she hadn't gotten very far on that yet.

"Did you manage to get ahold of Detective Spicer?" Leslie asked Jenny. "I'm curious to hear what he has to say about the apartment building we went to last night."

"I put in a call," Jenny said, "but he hasn't gotten back to me yet. At least, I don't think he has." She reached down into her purse and pulled out her phone to check for any missed calls. Lowering her shoulders as she looked at the screen, she declared, "I'm an idiot."

"What's the matter?" Leslie had a smirk on her face.

"I may not have brought my sketches down, but I took pictures of them when they were done." After pressing a few buttons and scrolling through some images, Jenny held out her phone for Hailey. "Here," she said. "This is a side-by-side. There are individual pictures if you scroll to the right. Do they look at all familiar to you?"

Hailey took the phone, looking at the drawings on the screen. Without hesitation, she announced, "That's Keegan and Cody."

"What did you say?" Jenny asked with awe.

Hailey shrugged. "I don't know why, but the names Keegan and Cody popped in my head." She looked at the phone a little longer, the blank expression on her face indicating she was receiving a message. After a moment, she sheepishly announced, "I saw something, but I don't know if I can describe it."

"Give it your best shot," Jenny said encouragingly. Hailey handed the phone back to her.

"I'll need to draw it," Hailey replied, "but I'm not that good of an artist." She looked around. "And I don't have a paper and pencil."

Jenny dug in her purse and found a receipt. "Is this big enough?" she asked, holding it up for Hailey to see.

Hailey only nodded in response.

Jenny handed the receipt over, and Hailey's mother gave her a pen. She soon began sketching an odd collection of circles and arrows, all attached, creating a symbol Jenny had never seen before. When Hailey was done, she handed the receipt back to Jenny, explaining that this was a tattoo that was etched into somebody's forearm, presumably either Cody's or Keegan's.

With her eyebrows down, Jenny looked at the picture. "I wonder if it means something," she muttered, handing the receipt over to Zack. "Have you ever seen anything like this?"

Zack shook his head, taking the receipt and passing it over to Susan. "No, not me."

After the picture had circulated the table and nobody claimed to recognize it, the receipt ended up back in Jenny's hands. "Well," she said, using her phone to snap a picture, "I guess I'll send this to Kyle, too. While I'm at it, I'll see if he can find out about this Cody and Keegan."

Shortly after Jenny pressed the send button on her text, the phone vibrated in her hand. Looking at the screen, she said, "Ooh...just the call I've been waiting for; it's Detective Spicer."

Chapter 11

Jenny covered her free ear with her finger as she answered the phone. "Hi, Detective Spicer. I'm so glad to hear from you."

"Hi, Jenny. Sorry it's taken me a while to get back to you. Life is crazy when you're a homicide detective in the city."

"I'm sure it is."

"Well, I talked to your friend, Andrei Petrovich, but he wasn't willing to release the names of any of his tenants. I'm positive he's hiding something, but I don't know if it's a murder or if it's a simple matter of immigration. I assured him I wasn't concerned with the citizenship status of his renters, but he was adamant about not giving me any names unless I had a subpoena, which I won't be able to get. No offense, but a judge isn't going to issue any kind of summons based on the recommendation of a psychic."

"I understand," Jenny replied, "but it's actually two psychics, now. Hailey, who has Luis Alvarez's case, also led us to that same house."

"Really?" he said, more with interest than surprise. He remained quiet for a while before adding, "That's quite a little twist, now, isn't it?"

Assuming the question was rhetorical, Jenny stayed quiet.

"Either way," he continued, "whether it was one or two of you that expressed interest in that house, I do want to get in there. If we are invited in, then there's nothing illegal about taking a look around."

"Do you think the tenants are going to invite us in?"

"Me? No. I don't think they'll take too kindly to law enforcement showing up at the door. But you? Maybe."

"Um...I'm not entirely sure I want to go in that house without you," Jenny admitted.

He let out a laugh. "I would never send you in there alone. That's not my plan. I just want you to be the front person and approach the tenants...let them know that we are not from the Department of Immigration, just in case that's the reason we're being shut out. Then, hopefully, one of them will invite us in and we can have a look around. I'll be sitting in a car just outside either way; no matter what happens, you'll be protected."

"What if nobody lives there, and it's just a place where Andrei kills people and chops them up into tiny little bits?"

"Well, if we go and it's empty, then that tells us something, now, doesn't it?"

Jenny only grunted, disturbed by the thought.

"Exactly. So, tell me...would you be able to free up some time in an hour or so to pay the house a visit?"

"I think that can be arranged."

"Great," he replied. "I'll call Leslie Newcomb and see if she can bring Hailey there, too."

"Um...I'm actually with her right now," Jenny said. "I can tell her."

"Perfect. I'll meet you there in an hour, then."

Jenny hung up the phone and reiterated the conversation to the rest of the table. Leslie looked noticeably worried about the prospect of going to the house and knocking on the door. "Are you sure that this is a good idea?" she asked. "I mean, is it safe?"

"You want my Taser?" Amma asked.

Jenny held up her hand. "We won't be needing the Taser."

"Not when you have the real deal," Zack said, putting his arm around Jenny's shoulder. "Right, Annie Oakley?"

Closing her eyes, she let out a sigh. "I will not need my gun, either. Detective Spicer will be with us. He just wants me to be the one to initiate the conversation to put the tenants at ease. We can make sure Hailey stays in the car—far away, if need be, until we know it's safe for her to come in."

With that, Leslie looked moderately relieved.

Jenny glanced at her phone to check the time. "We have to meet him in an hour. Should we all gather back down here in forty-five minutes?"

"Sounds good," Leslie agreed, "but if you don't mind, we'll drive to the house separately...just in case."

Parking was not easy to find near the house, so Jenny took advantage of a space around the corner. The Newcombs sat in their car, which was even further away, and awaited a phone call to let them know the scene was safe.

Detective Spicer conveniently parked his car along a stretch of the road that was marked with a sign stating, "No parking at any time." Jenny imagined that nobody would give him a ticket, despite the illegal parking job, and his location gave him an excellent view of the horrible house.

As agreed, Zack and Jenny stood on the sidewalk near the house, pretending to wait for someone. Or be lost. Or be there for some other legitimate, normal reason. Zack kept his phone to his ear, even though he wasn't talking to anyone, just to make their presence appear more natural.

"It's hot," Zack announced. "Hot as shit, in fact."

"Yeah," Jenny agreed, "try not to think about it."

Seconds felt like hours as they stood there, waiting for someone to go into or come out of the house. After a long twenty minutes, a pale, blond woman who appeared to be in her twenties walked out of the front door and across the porch. She strode with purpose down the steps toward the road.

"Now's our chance," Jenny whispered to Zack, relieved that the person who walked out was a woman. Somehow, she doubted this slight woman was responsible for the attacks. "Excuse me," she said loudly as she approached.

The woman froze, looking like a deer in headlights. She glanced with just her eyes down the street, appearing to be contemplating making a run for it. Jenny kept her tone pleasant and casual as she added, "I was wondering if you could help me."

The woman's shoulders lowered slightly, although she didn't respond.

Jenny walked over, her smile broad. "I'm looking for a little information." Quickly holding up her hand, she added, "I'm not with the police—I'm just trying to figure out what happened to a teenage girl a few years ago."

The woman furrowed her brow, shaking her head, indicating she didn't understand.

"Do you speak English?" Jenny asked slowly.

"Yes, but not understand every word," the woman said with a thick, eastern-European accent.

Jenny nodded, wondering exactly how elementary she was going to have to be with her vocabulary. Remembering the old adage, she pressed the button to turn on her phone, which had already been set up to reveal a picture of Ebony. "See this girl?" she asked, holding the phone so the woman could see.

The woman looked at the picture, shielding it from the sun with her hand, and studied it for a moment. "I no know her."

"She died," Jenny said loudly. For some reason, she thought volume should accompany simplicity.

Based on the concerned expression the woman wore, she appeared to understand.

Jenny pointed to the house. "I think she died here."

The woman's jaw dropped a bit as she glanced back at the house. "She die here?"

Making a gun with her thumb and forefinger, Jenny put her fictitious weapon to her temple. "Someone shot her." She moved her finger quickly to mimic the motion of the gun going off.

The woman put her hand over her mouth, looking back toward the house one more time.

"I want to go inside," Jenny said, pointing to the horrible building. Holding up the phone, she added, "To find out what happened to her."

"You police?"

"No, I am not the police." Feeling the need to be honest, she confessed, "I am working *with* the police to find the man who killed her." She pointed to her phone again. "But they don't care if you are a citizen." She made a dismissive gesture to accompany her words. "We just want to find the man who did this."

The woman looked as if she was contemplating Jenny's words. Eventually, she asked, "You need go inside?"

"Please."

The woman looked in her purse for her keys.

"Do you have time to answer some questions?" Jenny asked. "I want to know who else lives here."

Finally fishing her keys out of her pocketbook, she nodded. "I help if I can."

Jenny didn't want to ambush this woman too quickly, so she followed her into the house alone. She was hit by both the cool air and the wall of angered spirits all at once, nearly overwhelming her on both accounts. With a calming exhale, she addressed the woman one more time. "My name is Jenny." She held out her hand.

"Alina," the woman said, shaking Jenny's hand daintily. As Jenny suspected, she didn't burn from the contact; Alina had nothing to do with the murders.

"Nice to meet you, Alina." Trying to think of a simple way to explain it, Jenny simply said, "I am a psychic. I hear words from the dead."

Once again, Alina shook her head to indicate she wasn't following. Jenny determined that maybe Alina did understand but simply didn't believe what she was hearing.

Holding up Ebony's picture, Jenny repeated, "I can hear her."

"But she died."

Nodding emphatically with wide eyes, Jenny said, "And I can hear her."

Alina seemed to finally grasp what Jenny was saying. "You can hear her? Now? After she die?"

Jenny smiled sympathetically, realizing she was asking Alina to believe the impossible.

"But how?"

With a shrug and raised hands, she admitted, "I don't know how. My family can hear her...my grandmother, my father and me."

Alina appeared as if she was formulating a thought. Eventually, she pointed at the phone and asked, "And she say she die here?"

"Yes. So I want to look around. I have other people with me. Can they come in?" Alina seemed nervous, so Jenny placed her hand on her shoulder. "One of them *is* with the police, but he is not here for you. I promise." She pointed to the phone screen. "We are here for her."

Looking shaken, Alina thought for a long time. Eventually, she nodded and said, "They can come in."

Jenny held up one finger, asking Alina to wait. She poked her head out the door, hollering, "Zack, can you get the others? It's okay."

Once that technicality had been handled, Jenny was able to focus on the horrible aura that filled the house. She felt as if she had walked through the gates of Hell when she came through the front door. If she could trust her instincts, she would swear that more than just two spirits were roaming these halls—and they were angry.

If these walls could talk, the story they would tell would surely be nightmarish.

Hailey and Leslie walked in first, followed by Zack and, finally, Detective Spicer. Jenny introduced them all to Alina, placing one hand on Hailey's shoulder. Holding up Ebony's picture again, she said, "Hailey can hear her, too."

Jenny looked at Hailey's face; this poor girl could apparently feel the same awful tension as Jenny. She looked as if she was barely keeping it together. Leaning in, Jenny quietly whispered, "When this is over, you should just go back to the hotel and swim for a while or something."

Hailey appeared to be blinking back tears as she agreed with a nod. This whole episode must have been overwhelming for her. Even Jenny wanted to run and hide, and she was an adult. Poor Hailey must have been horrified.

Although, Jenny had to acknowledge this must have been horrifying for Alina, too. Assuming she wasn't in the country legally, she was risking a lot to help Ebony. Despite being overwhelmed with agitation and negative energy, Jenny felt admiration toward Alina for her kindness.

Detective Spicer pulled a notepad from his suit pocket. "How long have you lived here, Alina?"

Not surprisingly, Alina looked like she wanted to run. Perhaps having the detective there was going to be more of a hindrance than a help.

Trying to do damage control, Jenny held up her phone and said, "Ebony—that's the girl—she died five years ago. Were you here then?"

Alina nodded. "I live here during seven years."

"Do you know the other people who live here?" Detective Spicer asked.

"Some of them. Some friendly. Some more quiet."

Jenny scrolled through her pictures on her phone to find her sketches from earlier in the morning. Handing the phone over to Alina, she asked, "Do you know either of them?"

Lowering her brow, she investigated the screen closely. Turning the phone around and pointing to the picture on the right, she replied, "That look like Cody."

Chapter 12

Cody—that was one of the names Hailey had mentioned earlier. "You know him?" Jenny asked.

Alina nodded. "He live here before; not now. He very nice."

"Do you know his last name?" the detective asked.

"No," Alina replied, "I only know he Cody."

"What about the other one?" Jenny pointed to the phone. "Do you know his name?"

"I no know his name," Alina confessed with a shake of her head. "He did live here—with Cody. He quiet. He not say much."

"How long ago did they move out?" Detective Spicer asked.

Alina seemed to think about it, ultimately declaring, "I no remember. I can show you apartment where they lived. You can ask new people how long they live here."

"That would be great," Jenny replied.

Alina remained in place, not appearing to move toward the apartment. "Actually, the new people might be…um…not wanting to talk to you. I can ask them instead if they like that better."

"We may want to go into the apartment to look for evidence," the detective replied.

Shaking her head, Alina looked like she didn't understand his words.

"I may want to go inside, too," Jenny told Detective Spicer. "I think I have a better chance of getting invited in than you do—no offense. That suit of yours would be a little intimidating to someone who is trying to stay under the radar." She referred to his suit, although his ultra-professional demeanor may have been the bigger problem.

"Agreed," the detective said.

Jenny turned her attention back to Alina. "Can you bring us upstairs? Not him," she added, pointing to Detective Spicer. "Just us." She gestured to herself, the Newcombs and Zack. "We don't need to go into anybody's apartment. I just want to see if Ebony leads me somewhere." She held up her phone again.

Alina still looked confused.

"Can we go upstairs?" Jenny asked slowly. "We will stay in the hallway."

This time, Alina nodded. "In hallway."

Jenny turned to the detective. "Don't leave, just in case."

"I don't intend to," he replied.

Without another word, Alina turned and headed up the old, wide staircase, with Jenny following suit. The others trailed behind. Jenny found herself growing nervous—not just for herself, but for Hailey. If they encountered some terrible things upstairs, she hoped the young girl would be able to handle it. Or, at least, she prayed the spirits would spare Hailey from the worst of the images.

Before she knew it, she was upstairs, feeling herself drawn to the apartment marked 2A. The door seemed to serve as a thin barricade between herself and a horrible flood of activity. Should she ever go into that apartment, she was sure she would be overwhelmed with images that she would rather not see.

Clearing her head of that thought, she pointed to the door and announced, "It's this one. Something terrible happened in this apartment. Do you know who lives here?"

"Two people," Alina began, "about my age. A man and a woman."

"How long have they lived here?"

She shook her head as she thought. "I no know. Two or three year?"

"Is this where Cody lived before?" Jenny asked.

"No," Hailey said, causing everyone to look in her direction. "Cody lived in 2C."

Jenny froze, wondering what Hailey had seen to make her say that.

"That's right," Alina said with wide eyes. "Cody live there."

"Did the spirits tell you that?" Jenny asked Hailey, fearing the answer.

"Not in words," Hailey replied, her shoulders sinking. "I can just feel it. It's awful in there."

Running her hand through her hair, Jenny announced, "I get the same feeling from 2A." After taking a moment to regroup, Jenny turned to Alina again. "Do you know who lived in 2A five years ago?"

"Man," she replied. "One man. Friend with Cody, but live alone."

"Do you know his name?"

Alina shook her head. "He have dark hair and beard. Tall."

"Was he white?" Jenny asked.

"White skin?" Alina clarified. "Yes."

Hailey's mother spoke up. "There were three men who jumped out of the car and ambushed Luis that night. Could this be our third man?"

"I would think," Jenny replied. "I would *hope*. I hate the thought that there were two, separate, unrelated sets of killers in this house. I have to think they worked together."

"You think Cody kill that girl?" Alina asked; the look of betrayal on her face was heartbreaking.

Jenny's tone reflected the compassion she felt for this poor woman. "I don't know for sure if he was the one who killed her, but I think he may have helped."

"But he so *nice*," Alina protested.

Lowering her head, Jenny replied, "Sometimes people who seem nice do some very bad things. I've seen that before."

A moment of silence took over before Jenny eventually asked Alina, "Do you think the people who live here will let us come in and look around?"

Alina furrowed her eyebrows and drew her lips into a circle, shaking her head rapidly with fear. "Oh, I think no."

Jenny made a fist and placed it against her forehead. She took a deep breath as she tried to figure out if her next statement was going to be appropriate. Ultimately deciding the words needed to be said, she spoke kindly, barely above a whisper. "I know you are here illegally. I don't care. The police don't care. We just want to catch these killers."

Tears formed in Alina's eyes; she tried to blink them away, but she couldn't. Her voice was shaky as she said, "I no want to go back to Russia."

Feeling terrible, Jenny reached out and hugged Alina, who began to cry into her shoulder, adding, "It bad there."

Jenny rubbed her hand up and down Alina's back, saying, "We are not sending you back to Russia. I promise. You are safe with us."

Jenny only hoped she could keep that promise.

Pulling out of the embrace, Alina wiped her tears, gathering her composure. "Sorry. I try not cry. I just see terrible things in Russia. It not like America. It not safe for young woman there."

"Listen," Jenny began softly, "why don't we go out and get some lunch? We can sit down and have a nice talk..."

With her tears stopping, Alina shook her head and said, "I no have lots money."

"We will pay for you," Jenny assured her. "I just want to talk to you about what you may have seen and learn as much as I can about Cody and the other men."

After a little thought, Alina said, "I must call sister. We clean houses, and she waiting for me."

"Go ahead," Jenny said sincerely. "Take your time."

Alina dialed her phone and began a conversation in Russian. During that time, Jenny switched her focus over to Hailey, hoping she wasn't being exposed to anything too horrible. Looking over at the young girl, she asked, "How are you doing?"

"Better than I thought I would be," Hailey admitted. "The upstairs isn't as bad as I thought."

"For me, either," Jenny said. "Although, I have the feeling that I'll get bombarded if I go into that apartment."

"Me, too," Hailey said, "except for me, it's 2C."

Without warning, a name echoed through Jenny's mind. It was little more than a whisper, but she clearly heard the name *Lizette*.

No sooner than the voice went away, Hailey announced, "I just heard the name Lizette."

"Oh my Gosh," Jenny replied. "You heard that, too?"

Hailey's eyes grew wide. "You heard it?"

Jenny nodded. "Loud and clear." Looking worried, Jenny added, "I haven't come across that name before. We'll have to ask Alina about it when she gets off the phone."

The group waited in uncomfortable silence while Alina finished her conversation. Once she hung up, Alina announced, "I go to lunch. Katya say she clean alone."

"Great," Jenny said with a smile. They started to walk toward the stairs when Jenny asked, "Do you know anyone named Lizette?"

"Lizette?" Alina repeated. "No."

"Huh," Jenny muttered, "I wonder who she could be."

Hailey's mother spoke as they worked their way down the steps. "How are we going to find out?"

Jenny smiled as she said. "It looks like it's time for Kyle again."

Chapter 13

"Kyle," Jenny began, talking through the car speakers, "I've got something for you."

"You shouldn't have," he replied dryly.

"I just can't help myself sometimes. I'm wondering if you can find out about a woman named Lizette—or maybe a girl. I don't know how old she is."

"You got a last name?"

"Sure don't."

"Well, at least this is an unusual first name," Kyle noted. "If you told me you needed information about a Kim, you'd be out of luck."

"If the first name was Kim, I'd hope the spirit would have given me the last name instead."

"A spirit gave you this name?"

"Yup," Jenny replied. "It was creepy, actually. I'm here with another psychic—a very young one—and we both heard the name at the same time."

"I swear, even after all this time, you still fascinate me." Papers shuffled in the background. "Okay, so what do you think this 'Lizette' is in connection with? Any context to go with the name?"

"It's still the same address as before," Jenny said. "We were at the house on South Bayhill when we heard it."

"This must be quite a house," Kyle replied.

Jenny let out a grunt. "I can't even begin to explain it."

"Same time period as the others?" Kyle asked.

"I would assume so, but I can't be sure."

"Alright," he said, pausing as if he were writing notes. "Got it. Now, I haven't had any luck with that symbol you asked me to look into. I've enlisted the help of some other folks; none of them immediately knew what it meant, but they promised to do a little research. Some guys are really into this cryptology stuff, so I'm leaving it up to them."

"Sounds good to me," Jenny replied. "I wouldn't have even known where to begin. Have you found anything out about Cody and Keegan?"

"No, not yet. I've looked into guys with those names who have criminal records, but I haven't gotten anywhere. I have found some Keegans and I've found some Codys, but their cases aren't related and their pictures don't match the sketches you sent. It may be that these two have flown under the radar until now, and I'll need to take a different approach."

"Thanks, Kyle. I know I give you some difficult tasks."

"Well, that's what I'm here for. Alright, let me start looking into this Lizette person, too. I'll let you know as soon as I find anything out."

"Perfect. I appreciate it."

Jenny hung up the phone as she continued toward the restaurant. She then called her mother, asking her to bring the baby and meet them out for lunch. She did the same with Susan and Amma, but they were both busy working on cases.

The Larrabees and the Newcombs arrived at the restaurant shortly before Isabelle came with the baby. Jenny and Detective Spicer had agreed that he shouldn't come along; Alina would have felt more comfortable without him there. She hadn't even developed enough trust of Jenny to ride in her car; Alina had insisted on taking the bus and was the last to arrive.

The group sat in a long booth with Steve in a wooden high chair at the end. Alina seemed enamored with the baby. "He so cute," she said, smiling broadly. "I want to have baby someday." With a laugh, she added, "Have to find husband first."

"Take your time," Jenny replied. "Be choosy."

Alina shook her head, indicating she didn't understand the word.

"Make sure you pick somebody really nice," Jenny explained.

"That hard to find," Alina replied.

"Yeah," Zack interrupted, exaggeratedly puffing out his chest. "Good men like me are hard to come by."

After rolling her eyes, Jenny turned to Alina. "Ignore him." Making her tone more serious, she took a sip of water and added, "I hope by now you know we're not trying to deport you."

Alina looked down at her lap and nodded.

"Both Hailey and I were led to the house where you live," Jenny continued slowly, "but we weren't able to find any information about who lives there. Actually, what we're looking for is information about people who lived there five years ago, but there is no record of that, either. I imagine that your landlord, Andrei, is allowing people to rent apartments without giving their full names?"

Her face grew solemn. "Andrei is a good man. He save my life. I no want to get him in trouble."

"You won't get him in trouble," Jenny assured her. She wasn't sure he wouldn't *face* trouble, although Jenny was pretty sure her hefty bank account could shield him from the worst of it.

Alina took a moment, wringing her hands and blinking away tears. Eventually, she confessed, "He part of, um, what you call *underground system.*"

When nobody responded, Alina continued, "You must understand that horrible things happen in other countries. People are very poor. My family live in village that have no money. The people there farm for food, but we had no rain for long time, and food did not grow. Many people hungry.

"Some men came into village and say they have jobs for us," she went on. "They say that young women can go with them and be nanny or clean houses for rich people in city. They say we make enough money to send the extra back to our family. The men leave and tell us they come back in two days with truck, and they take with them the women who want to go.

"My sister, Katya, and I talk about it with parents, and we decide we should go. The village have no future, but the city—lots of opportunity in city. So, when truck come back two days later, Katya and I get in." Tears filled Alina's eyes as she added, "That was last time I see my parents."

After taking a moment to wipe her eyes and take a deep breath, she said, "We know very fast that men not there to help us. As soon as truck leave village, men show they have guns, and they tell us not to run or scream or try to be free."

"How many women were in the truck?" Jenny's mother asked.

"There eight of us," Alina replied. "We all very scared. We all hold hands and hug each other. Some start cry. We not know what men want to do with us.

"We drive long time. Days. We not given food. We get very little water. The men laugh—it funny to them that we scared." She closed her eyes and shook her head. "We know getting in the truck a mistake, but nothing we can do. It horrible.

"After long time, I fall asleep. I wake up when the truck stop and the men start yelling. They very angry. The other girls and I not know what going on. We look out window to see more men with guns. Lots of men. All guns pointed at truck. We all start crying. We thought we going to die.

"The men outside come on to truck and start to take us away." Alina's hands were shaking as she told the story. "We did what men said. There were more of them and more guns. And we knew the men we were with were bad. Nothing good would happen to us if we stayed. So we got into different truck and drive off. I still so scared. I have no idea where I am or where I go or who these men are.

"One of the men spoke Russian, but not very good. He told us that we safe with them. They give us water and food, and they not angry. They speak different language—English, but I not know that then. I feel better with them, but still scared. I not know where I am or where I go, or if I ever see family again."

She released a long sigh, indicating the worst part of the story was over. "We drive long time. The men give us pillows and blankets and food. They speak kind to us, even though we not know what they say. I relax little, but still scared. We get out of truck after two days. We stay in house where woman make us hot food. They have beds. We take shower. A woman who speak Russian explain to us that we are saved. The men who came to village wanted to sell us as slaves. They take lots of young women and sell them. We lucky—we get rescued. Many women do not get rescue."

Jenny made a grunting sound as she shook her head.

"The woman tell us we go to America. It not safe to go back to village. Men would only come back, and they be more angry. She say the trip to America be long, but we be safe there. I ask if I ever see family again..." Alina had to stop talking due to the tears that had welled up in her eyes. Jenny's mother reached over and rubbed Alina's back as she wiped her tears. "The woman tell us no," Alina managed to say, "but she say we lucky ones. The other girls not see family, either, but they live awful life. Forced to do awful things." Her voice became shaky as she cried freely. "I so lucky. I not know why I get chose to be so lucky and other girls not."

"You can't feel bad about that," Jenny told her. "It was out of your control."

"I tell myself that," Alina replied with a nod. "It still hard." She sighed again, this time quickly, resuming her story. "After few days in house, we go on boat. We stay on boat long time, and we reach land at night. We sneak into van again and drive off. I ask if we in America, and they say 'not yet.' We land in Canada.

"After another long drive, we spend night in different house. The next day, they tell us we go into America. We have to get in trunks of cars to cross border. I very scared. I not know what happen if get caught. The trunk is hot and the car spend lots of time not moving. I not know what going on. Finally, car start moving and stay moving for while, and then car stop. The man let me out of trunk and into seat, and he tell me, 'Welcome to America.' I never been so happy.

"I go to farmhouse, where Katya and I meet Andrei. He say he has place for us to stay and job for us. We clean houses." She let out a sarcastic laugh. "Funny—I get job cleaning houses, which is job I thought I get in Russia. But this time, job is real.

"Andrei drive me and Katya to Richmond, where he have apartment house. He have friends who get houses cleaned. Katya and I have key; we go in and clean during day, and people leave cash on kitchen counter. We never meet people—just clean house. We give some cash to Andrei, who give us phone and place to stay. We use extra cash for food and clothes. I feel safe here, except I worry about being caught and sent back. I not know what happen to me if I go back to village." She shook her head.

"Your story is absolutely incredible," Hailey's mother noted with awe. "You are an amazing young woman."

Alina shook her head. "I am not amazing. The people who send me here—they are amazing. So many people went through so much troubles to help us, and we do not know them. They risk so much. They are hero."

"All the more reason we will not get Andrei in trouble," Jenny said, hoping her words were true. "So," she continued, "this apartment house he runs is like a safe house for people who need to flee their home countries?"

"Yes. He save people."

"But Cody and his roommate...I get the feeling that they were from the United States."

"Not everyone from other country," Alina replied. "Not everyone work for Andrei. He say he use money from apartments to help pay for...uh...transport. Apartments cannot be empty, or he make no money and cannot help people."

"How long have you lived there?" Zack asked.

"Seven year."

Zack followed up with, "How long has Andrei been doing this?"

After giving the notion some thought, Alina concluded, "A few year before I move in. So, maybe ten year? Twelve year?"

"Wouldn't the house eventually become full?" Zack asked again. "I mean, I imagine that once you move into that house, you have to stay there if you are here illegally."

"Not everybody stay," Alina said.

Zack seemed confused. "Where do they go?"

Alina shrugged and shook her head. "I not know. Not everybody there from same country, and not everybody speak same language. I came here not knowing a word in English, but I learn over time. Some new people have not learn English yet, so I cannot speak to them. We just wave hello. If they move out, they not tell me where they go."

"So," Jenny began, pulling a pen and a receipt out of her purse. Putting the cap on the other end of the pen so she could write, she asked, "Were Cody and his roommate living there when you moved in?"

"Yes. I see them in stairwell."

"And what about the other man...the one in 2C?"

"He live there also."

"Do you have *any* idea when they may have moved out?"

Releasing a sigh, Alina replied, "If I had to say, I guess three year."

"Are the apartments furnished?" Zack asked.

"Furnished?" Alina apparently didn't understand the word.

"Do they already have furniture in them when you move in?"

"Oh...yes, they do."

Jenny squinted at Zack. "What are you getting at?"

Zack leaned his elbows on the table. "Well, you and Hailey have both said there's a buttload of spiritual activity coming from that house."

"Yeah," Jenny said, still not seeing where this was going.

"And you have your suspicions that these killings might be racially motivated," Zack added. "So, I'm thinking that some of these people from other countries may have different colored skin…"

Zack's point became clear in an instant; suddenly Jenny felt ill. "Oh, dear."

"Exactly," Zack concluded. "If illegal immigrants had been hooked up with a job and a place to stay, why would they leave? And where would they go? No, I don't think they moved out—and you wouldn't be able to tell if they didn't actually move any furniture out. It's not like there'd be a van getting loaded up out front." Zack's expression was serious as he added, "Unfortunately, I think these people fled their dangerous home countries, only to come here and be murdered by three racists living in their own apartment building."

Chapter 14

Jenny closed her eyes and allowed the disturbing notion to sink in for a moment. "Alina," she said slowly, "those people who moved out...what did they look like?"

The poor girl sat frozen for a long time. Eventually, she put her hand over her mouth and replied, "One man short, dark hair. I think he say he from Colombia."

"What about the other people?"

"One man look like Middle Eastern, and a woman come from Africa." After a pause, she added, "That all I can think of."

"And those people," Jenny asked, "they just disappeared?"

"I no know about *disappear*, but they stop living in apartment."

"Like I said," Zack reiterated, "where else would they go? It sounds like they were most likely undocumented; it's not like they could easily find another place to live."

Sucking in and releasing a long breath to steady herself, Jenny calmly said, "Alina, I really need to talk to Andrei. Do you think you can arrange that?"

Nodding, Alina pulled her phone out of her purse. "I see what I can do." Alina dialed, and soon she began a conversation with Andrei in Russian.

Jenny also pulled out her phone, dialing it quickly, explaining, "I need to call Detective Spicer." As soon as he answered, she said, "Hi, it's Jenny. I've got a question for you."

"Sure. What's up?"

"Do you have any John Does from around the same time period as Ebony and Luis?" She ran her hand through her hair. "And maybe a Jane Doe?"

"Why? What are you finding out?"

"We're just guessing at this point, but we believe there may be more victims associated with this house. I can fill you in on the details later, but the John Does I'm talking about would be a Hispanic male, a Middle Eastern male and an African American female."

"Shit," he whispered.

"Does that sound familiar?" Jenny asked.

"It sounds very familiar. We had a spell a few years back where we had three murder victims within a short span, and none of them had IDs. None of them had missing persons reports filed on them, either. We went public with pictures, but nobody called in saying they recognized them."

"According to Alina, they all lived in those apartments," Jenny explained. "And suddenly, they just stopped living there."

"Jesus."

"Exactly. Considering Keegan and Cody seemed to target minorities, this makes sense."

"If I send you pics of our John and Jane Does," Detective Spicer began, "do you think Alina would be able to positively identify them?"

"Uh...how gruesome are the pictures?" Jenny asked.

"They're not. They're sketches of what we believe they looked like in life."

"Then, by all means, send them. Maybe if we can get Alina to confirm that the victims came from that apartment building, the landlord will be willing to cooperate."

"I'm working on granting him immunity, by the way," the detective said. "I'm hoping we can get the big wigs in Immigration to officially overlook the whole illegal immigrant thing if he is willing to cooperate with us on the murder investigation."

"Good, because I've kind of been promising that anyway," Jenny confessed.

"Um, you may not want to make promises like that until we get official word."

Jenny shook her head. "I won't let it happen. Although," she continued, "based on what I just heard, you wouldn't want to arrest the guy anyway. He's saving people by allowing them to live there."

"Well, I'm working on it. Okay, let me get those pictures sent to you so you can let me know if she recognizes them. Everyone in the department will be thrilled if we can put names to those faces."

They concluded their call, and Jenny turned to Alina, who was also off the phone. "What did Andrei say?"

Alina looked heartbroken. "He say he know they dead."

"What?" Jenny said with dismay.

At that moment, the food arrived, causing a diversion. Once the meals had been handed out and the waitress walked away, Jenny turned to Alina and asked, "Andrei knows they are dead? That's what you're telling me?"

She nodded slightly. "But he say Cody not the one who kill them."

Jenny's phone chirped, but she ignored it. "Who does he think did it?"

"People," Alina replied. "Bad people."

"Which bad people?" Jenny's tone was more impatient than she had wanted.

Alina rubbed her forehead with her hand. "Everyone who live there run from something. Andrei say past catch up with them."

A million thoughts swirled around Jenny's head, but she focused on the need to get detectives into that apartment building. Somebody had to figure out what was really going on. "Did he say if he was willing to meet with us?"

Looking apologetic, Alina replied, "He say there no need."

Jenny's phone dinged again; this time she looked at the screen to find a black and white sketch of a Hispanic man staring back at her. Holding up the phone so Alina could see it, she asked, "Is this one of the men who lived in your building?"

Alina studied the picture for a moment. Biting her lip, she nodded. "That him."

With one more alert, the third picture arrived. Jenny scrolled through the images; Alina recognized all three of them to be her old neighbors. The poor girl was on the verge of tears, but Jenny was less sympathetic than she should have been. Her mind was preoccupied with getting this investigation rolling.

Tapping out a text to Detective Spicer, Jenny wrote, *She identified all three of them. Does that merit a subpoena? We need to get inside that house.*

Almost, was the reply. Jenny didn't know what that meant.

Her phone chirped again, and she assumed it was going to be an elaboration about that last statement. However, this message was from Kyle. "Good grief," she said. "There is too much going on at once."

The text from Kyle read, *This is the only Lizette I could find from that area, but it makes sense. She was murdered four years ago. Her name is Lizette Micheaux.*

Jenny looked at the image below the words, and confusion set in. "Huh," she said, still fixed on the screen, "this is interesting."

"What is it?" Zack asked.

"It's a message from Kyle; he sent a picture of a murder victim named Lizette."

"He found her?" he posed.

"I guess," Jenny replied.

"You guess?"

"Yeah," she said. "I can't imagine that more than one Lizette would have been murdered in the Richmond area in the past few years, but look." She spun the phone around so everyone could see. "She's white."

The table was silent for a moment before Jenny showed her phone to Alina. "Do you recognize this woman?"

Alina looked at the picture, shaking her head. "I no know her."

Next, she handed the phone to Hailey. "Does this picture trigger anything in you?"

Hailey took the phone and stared at the screen. After focusing for a while, she got a nervous look on her face and said, "I am seeing a bathroom. It's small and is solid green on the bottom with, like, ivy wallpaper on the top half." She lowered her eyes and added, "I feel like she was scared while she was in that bathroom." Hailey handed the phone back to her.

Jenny sat back in the booth, contemplating the new information, when her phone chirped again. Another text from Kyle read, *Lizette's case was solved. Her boyfriend was given a life sentence.*

Jenny held up a finger, announcing to the table, "I might have good news. Lizette's murderer was caught; it was her boyfriend. Hopefully this was one of our killers." She immediately saw a hole in her own theory. "Although, Kyle said he couldn't find a Cody or a Keegan with a criminal record around here—at least, not one that matched our guys."

"Maybe it's the third guy," Hailey's mother suggested.

"Let's hope," Jenny replied. Messaging Kyle, she asked, *What was the boyfriend's name? Can you send a pic?* She then turned and said, "Alina, if I showed you a picture of the guy in 2A, would you be able to recognize him?"

She nodded wordlessly.

After a moment, Jenny's phone chirped and she looked at the screen. "Oh, my."

"What's the matter?" Zack asked.

"Her boyfriend is clearly not the third guy," she announced. Jenny looked up, her eyes circulating around the table. "Lizette's boyfriend—the guy who got arrested for her murder—was black."

Chapter 15

"This could explain a few things," Zack said.

At the moment, Jenny's mind was too overwhelmed to grasp anything. "What do you mean?"

"Well," he replied, "it could be that Lizette was a friend of Keegan and Cody and her murder is what triggered this rampage."

Leslie chimed in, "Do you think they would target all people of color because they were upset with one African American man?"

With a shrug, Zack said, "They're obviously not completely sane. Who knows what is going on in their heads?"

"While that's a good theory, the math doesn't add up," Jenny noted, shaking her head. "Lizette was killed four years ago, which is after Luis and Ebony. Her murder couldn't possibly have been the trigger."

Everyone at the table sat silently for a few moments before Zack suggested, "You could call Rod."

"I *could* call him," Jenny repeated excitedly. "That is a very good point. I have a picture of Lizette, and that's probably all he'd need." She looked up at the Newcombs and Alina. "Rod is my father. He lives out on the west coast, and he couldn't make it out here to work on the cases, but he has the gift, too—kind of. His ability works differently than ours. He can get a sense of what the spirits are currently feeling." She focused her attention on Hailey. "You and I can see snippets of the person's life, and we feel what they felt at the time that event was unfolding. My father can't do any of that, but he can sense their state of mind now." She began to scroll through her contacts on her phone. "It's quite fascinating, really."

As Jenny pressed the button to call Rod's number, she heard Leslie mutter, "This just gets stranger every day."

Her father answered after three rings. "Jenny! Great to hear from you."

"Hi, Pop."

"Is everything okay back east?"

"Sure is. We're just working on some cases, and there's a particular element that has us stumped. We were wondering if you could clue us in on what a victim has to say...and maybe others, if you have the time."

"I think I can spare a little time for my favorite daughter."

"Thanks," she replied with a little laugh, knowing she'd won that accolade by default. "I don't want to tell you anything about these people; I just want your unbiased take on them. Maybe you can let us know how these people fit in."

"I'll do my best."

"Thanks, Pop. I know you're at work, so I don't want to hold you too long. I'll text you their pictures in just a minute, if that's okay."

"Sounds good."

They concluded their call, and Jenny sent pictures of all of the victims. "I'm actually testing something here," she announced to the group.

"You're testing your father?" Zack asked.

Jenny shook her head. "No, there's no need for that; I don't doubt my father's ability. I'm sending pictures of Keegan and Cody, though, to see if he can get a reading from them." She looked up with her eyes. "If he can get something from them, then we know they're dead. Since we're dealing with cases from several years ago, there's always the possibility that we are trying to find two people who don't exist anymore."

"Wouldn't that be great?" Zack asked.

Jenny thought about it for a moment. "Sadly, it would be."

"So," Leslie began, "when you say your father gets a sense of what the spirits are currently feeling..." She shook her head, signaling she didn't know how to proceed with her question. "Does that mean their emotions still change, like ours do? Almost like they're still alive?"

"It does," Jenny replied. "They can feel anger and fear; if someone they love—or even a stranger—is too close to their killer, for instance, they can get scared. But they can also feel happiness and pride." Jenny smiled. "I'm sure they enjoy weddings just as much as they did in life."

"Wow," Leslie said, "that's amazing."

Holding up her hand, Jenny added, "Now, I can only speak for the spirits before they cross over. Once they go to the other side, I have no idea how aware they are of what's going on down here or if they have emotional ups and downs. The one thing I do know is that there's an overwhelming sense of peace and happiness when someone is in the process of crossing. It's like...going home. There's a feeling of belonging. But then, after that, I lose contact."

"So, every spirit who has contacted you and Hailey has not crossed over yet?" Leslie asked.

"Correct," Jenny said with an emphatic nod.

"And what would prevent them from doing that? Is it just murder victims that stick around?"

"No, not at all. I remember talking to one man—a police officer, actually, whose older brother was lingering to keep an eye on him. The police officer had been a bit...*rebellious* in his youth, and I guess the brother wanted to make sure he stayed on the straight and narrow."

"I'm going to do that to you," Leslie said to Hailey with a smile.

"Mom," Hailey replied. Once again, the young girl was embarrassed, which seemed to be an almost permanent state of being for her.

"I am," Leslie continued, unfazed. "So don't get any big ideas, even after I'm gone."

Jenny's phone rang, so she signaled to the rest of the group with a raised finger. "Hang on," she said. "This is my dad...Hello?"

"Hey, Jenny."

"Were you able to find out anything?"

"Yes and no," Rod replied. "I got an overwhelming sense from the woman with the red hair. She's upset."

"Upset? How so?"

"Desperate. That was her predominant emotion. I got a sense from her that something needs to be pulled in a different direction. She is positively mortified that something has gone wrong."

"Interesting."

"Yeah, she was eager to get through. She overshadowed everyone else, although I got a feeling of betrayal from the Hispanic man."

"Unfortunately, that's accurate," Jenny said.

"The middle eastern man held some anger, and the African American woman felt fear...but again, those feelings were dwarfed by the despair from the Caucasian woman."

"What about the two Caucasian men?" Jenny asked with apprehension.

"From them I got nothing," he replied. "My guess is that they either crossed over or they're not dead. Either that, or I'm losing my knack."

"No, you're not losing your knack at all. Your answers are perfect."

"Well, I'm glad I could help, if that's what I did."

"You did," Jenny assured him. "I promise."

She got off the phone with her father and turned to the group at the table. "Okay... it seems that Lizette is feeling desperate because something has gone in the wrong direction."

"Do you think her boyfriend in jail is actually innocent?" Zack asked.

"That sounds like a logical conclusion to me," Leslie affirmed with a worried expression on her face.

Everyone was quiet for a moment before Zack added, "Wouldn't that be a bonus for them? Keegan and Cody killed a woman who engaged in an interracial relationship, and then the black man she was dating got a life sentence for it? It would be like a two-fer."

Jenny closed her eyes. "If that's true, this whole situation just got uglier." She thought about the implications for a moment before shaking her head, freeing herself of that terrible thought. "In other news, my father wasn't able to get a reading from Keegan or Cody's pictures."

"Does that mean they're alive?" Leslie asked.

Jenny looked her in the eye. "I believe that means they're very much alive."

"It's not that easy to find," Zack announced while sitting at the desk in the hotel room. "Since there are no names to look up, I'm having trouble finding information about the three unidentified victims."

"I will just ask Detective Spicer about that," Jenny replied softly from the bed, Steve asleep in her arms. "I'm sure he'll know. In the meantime, can you look into Lizette's murder? That might have been in the news." She picked up her phone with her free hand and scrolled through Kyle's texts. "Her last name was Micheaux." Jenny spelled out the name.

As Zack looked through old articles, Jenny thought about the situation. It broke her heart to know that three people were murdered, their pictures got circulated, and nobody claimed to know them. She wondered how that could have happened. Wouldn't *somebody* have recognized them? She considered Alina's story—the sisters earned their money because friends of Andrei left cash on the counter; Alina and Katya cleaned their houses while the owners weren't home. Alina admitted she never saw her clients. Perhaps a similar arrangement had been made for those other three tenants. Maybe the others did yard work or walked dogs or also did cleaning, never seeing the people they worked for.

Jenny understood the need for secrecy in this arrangement. In order to protect his friends, Andrei had to ensure that none of them ever saw Alina or Katya. If immigration came by and showed the homeowners a picture of the Russian sisters, they could honestly say they didn't know the girls. Jenny also considered what Alina had told them in the diner—everybody who lived in that apartment building was running from something. The more people who saw their faces, the more danger they would have been in.

However, Andrei knew them, and Andrei knew they were dead. He must have seen their sketches on the news, acknowledged that they had met a terrible fate, but didn't call in a tip. She could understand why he wouldn't contact the police with their identities—that could have potentially ruined his whole operation.

Unless there was something a little more sinister going on with Andrei...

"I found some information," Zack said, interrupting Jenny's thoughts. "Lizette Micheaux was forty-five and worked as a secretary for a construction company. Her boyfriend, Gordon Cox, was one of the construction workers. They'd been dating for about six months when she went missing. Authorities found her body about an hour and a half outside of the city. The gun was found in a crawlspace under a lake house that belonged to a friend of Gordon's. Apparently, Gordon used to hang out there quite often. The case was circumstantial at best, but he was convicted anyway. He apparently lived alone and had a lot of time with no alibi, and some of the construction workers had seen the two of them arguing shortly before she went missing. I guess that was enough to convince a jury of his guilt."

Jenny hung her head. "Anybody could have planted that stuff there. Whatever happened to reasonable doubt?"

"Hey, I wasn't on the jury. I didn't convict him."

Jenny's phone buzzed next to her. Softly, she answered, "Hello?"

"Hey, Jenny, it's Detective Spicer."

"Hi," she said with surprise. "What's going on?"

"I caught up with Alina and got her to admit that she knew the unidentified victims."

Jenny's blood ran cold; she hoped the detective hadn't scared the poor girl to death. "You *caught up* with her?"

"I waited outside her building for her to come home. It wasn't enough for you to tell me that she knew the vics; I had to hear it for myself. But now that she has admitted it to me, I'm applying for a search warrant for the house, and I expect to get it. Soon. Are you available this afternoon if we can get in?"

"Yes, of course," Jenny whispered.

"Good. Because I want to get tangible evidence, but I also want to know what you and Hailey have to say."

Jenny nodded, even though the detective couldn't see it. "While I have you on the phone, can I ask you to elaborate on the three unidentified victims a little bit?"

"Um...yes...but I may need to hold off on that for a while. I've got to get this paperwork in. Can I fill you in later, while we're at the house?"

"No problem," Jenny said. "I won't hold you."

"Thanks," he replied. "Sorry—it's just crazy around here."

They said their goodbyes and hung up. "Okay," Jenny said to Zack, "it looks like we may be getting some answers in just a few hours."

Jenny drove herself and Zack, as well as the Newcombs, to the house on South Bayhill Avenue. Detective Spicer said he was already there, as was a crew from the forensics team. While Jenny assumed they had all gotten close to the house by parking in the illegal spots, she didn't want to risk it. She chose to park a good distance down the road and walk in the heat.

As they approached on foot, the nervous buzzing that surrounded the house grew stronger. She turned to Hailey, asking, "Are you okay, sweetie?"

Hailey nodded but didn't respond. That was an unconvincing reaction at best.

Jenny put her arm around the young girl's shoulder and said, "If it gets to be too much, you can always leave and wait in the car."

Again, Hailey only responded with a nod. Jenny couldn't help but feel that the poor girl was on the verge of tears.

Rounding the corner, they saw a swarm of activity in front of the house. Alina was nowhere to be seen; Jenny could only assume she was at an entirely different location, hiding from the policemen.

Detective Spicer saw them appear from around the corner and approached them. "I'm glad you're here; thank you for coming." He glanced up at the intimidating stone house, noting, "They're getting ready to go in there with luminol; that should tell us once and for all if anything happened in here." Turning back to the group, he said, "Luminol is a spray that we use that can detect the presence of blood. Even if someone cleaned a crime scene, and even if many years have passed, luminol can still determine if blood is present. You'd be surprised at how clean an area can look, only for the luminol to show that there are actually lingering blood cells everywhere."

Jenny had already known this, but she didn't say anything. She was unsure how familiar the Newcombs were with police procedure. Instead, she simply said, "Well, a good place to start would be apartments 2A and 2C."

"That's the plan," he replied.

At that moment, a car sped around the corner and pulled to an abrupt stop in one of the illegal parking spots. A short, balding man emerged from the car, approaching the house quickly. "What is this?" he demanded. His English was better than Alina's, but Jenny could still detect a Russian accent.

This could only be Andrei.

Detective Spicer walked calmly toward him. "Are you the owner of the property?"

"Yes," he said angrily.

"We have a warrant to search for evidence. It has come to our attention that three of your residents have been found murdered, and we want to get to the bottom of it."

Andrei wiped his hands down his face, glancing back at the house. He looked as if he contemplated arguing with the officer for a moment, only to lower his shoulders and pitifully ask, "Can I talk to the people inside first?"

"No," the detective said emphatically, "you may not go in ahead of us." Holding up his hands, he added, "I can assure you that we are only interested in blood evidence. That is all the warrant entails. Here," he said, pulling out the piece of paper, "you can take a look at it for yourself."

Andrei read the paper, hanging his head a bit with relief.

"I am not concerned with who lives here, or their immigration status," Detective Spicer said more compassionately. "That isn't even my department. I'm Homicide."

Andrei raised his eyes, looking at the taller detective. He knew his secret was out, and that was probably one of his worst fears.

A police officer approached Detective Spicer; she held a spray bottle in her hand and wore gloves. "You ready?" she asked.

"I was born ready," the detective said.

Jenny wasn't quite sure she was as prepared.

The group walked into the lobby of the apartment building, and Jenny was hit with the same level of spiritual activity as the last time. Currently, however, it was more about excitement than anger. Perhaps the victims knew what was about to happen. She turned to Hailey, asking, "Is it different for you this time?"

Hailey nodded again, but this time she appeared much more relaxed. "It's happier."

"I agree," Jenny said. *Happier* was a good way to explain it.

They walked up the stairs to the second floor hallway with Andrei following. As the detective was about to knock on the door of apartment 2A, Andrei grabbed his hand. "Let me knock," he said with a pleading look on his face. "Please."

The detective paused for a moment before nodding and stepping out of the way. Andrei knocked, announcing that he wanted to come in, but there was no answer. "They must be at work," Andrei said, producing a ring of keys from his pocket. After finding the correct one, he unlocked and opened the door.

As Jenny had feared, a flood of activity poured through the open door. She stood still and sucked in a breath, grabbing onto Zack's arm for support. It felt almost as if a giant gust of wind had barreled through the opening, strong enough to knock her over, but Jenny was the only one who could feel it.

Spoken phrases pinged around her head.

I just want to do God's will.

Please don't.

I have children.

Why are you doing this?

Beg, nigger!

I'm not fearing any man.

That last sentence jarred Jenny back into the moment. *I'm not fearing any man?* She felt a sense of calm defiance as those words echoed in her mind, although she had no idea what it was about.

"Are you okay," Zack asked her.

She nodded with determination. "Yes, I'll be fine." She wasn't sure how honest she was being, but she was inspired by the resolve she felt with the last comment. "Let's do this."

The technicians were busy lowering the shades and closing the curtains. The apartment became dark as a result, making it seem much more intimidating.

"Go to the bathroom," Hailey said quietly. "That's where you'll find the blood."

Jenny whipped her head around quickly, addressing the young girl. "What?"

"They killed people in the bathroom with the shower running to drown out the noise," Hailey explained with tears welling in her eyes. Her mother wrapped her arm around her shoulders. "It's going to be green in there," Hailey added with a shaky voice, "and have ivy wallpaper."

Jenny looked at Detective Spicer, who, in turn, was focusing on Andrei. "Where's the bathroom?" he demanded.

Andrei led them to a bathroom that was indeed green with ivy wallpaper. Jenny glanced in quickly but then stepped away, trying to be as unobtrusive as possible.

"You were right about the bathroom," Jenny told Hailey softly. Hailey had hung back, probably because she didn't want to be anywhere near that awful room. "It looks just like you described it."

"Lizette was killed there," Hailey whispered. "She let me know that."

Jenny looked up at the ceiling, wondering how many people had died in this very apartment. That ivy wallpaper was the last thing they had seen. She also thought about how many years Lizette's boyfriend had been sitting in prison for something he apparently didn't do.

This whole scene was a nightmare.

"Spray in here," the detective told the young woman with the bottle. "Don't miss anywhere."

"Yes, sir," she replied and got to work.

A tension-filled silence permeated the room as everyone waited for her to finish applying the luminol. Soon, she walked out of the bathroom and announced, "It's ready."

Detective Spicer headed into the bathroom with determination, reaching over to shut off the light. He stood back as he looked in the room, disbelief evident on his face. "Oh. My. God."

Chapter 16

"Haines, get this," the detective ordered.

"Yes, sir." A man with a camera went into the bathroom and started taking pictures.

Detective Spicer came out into the living area and addressed Andrei. "It's lit up like day in there. There's enough blood to account for several murders."

Jenny looked over at Andrei, who lowered himself in slow motion onto the couch. Any suspicion she had of him disappeared when she saw the color drain from his face. He placed his hand on his heart, looking as if he was having trouble breathing. Jenny wondered if he was about to have a heart attack.

The detective continued to speak to Andrei. "We're going to need to ask you some questions."

A wave washed over Jenny in an instant. She saw the man she knew to be Keegan very close to her with a gun pointed at her face, muttering through gritted teeth, "Nigger, I told you to beg."

She held her chin up and spoke clearly. "And I've looked over, and I've *seen* the promised land." Her eyes remained locked on Keegan's, her defiance remaining intact.

The image disappeared just as quickly as it came. Jenny was spooked, but there was so much going on that she remained quiet.

Hailey's mother had gone into the kitchen and returned with a glass of water for Andrei; she apparently had the same fears that Jenny did about his wellbeing. Leslie placed it on the coffee table in front of him.

"Who has lived in this apartment?" Detective Spicer asked urgently, pulling a notepad out of his suit pocket.

Andrei seemed like he couldn't even say his own name at that moment. He looked up at the detective, his eyes pooling with tears, asking, "The murders happened here?"

"What murders?" the detective demanded, even though he already knew the answer to some degree.

Andrei covered his face with his hands and spoke slowly. "Diego, Syed and Ngula."

The detective's expression showed a mixture of emotions; while he was still serious and determined, he appeared to be relieved to finally have names to go with the unidentified victims. "You're going to have to spell those names for me."

Andrei obliged and then took a sip of water; his hands trembled so badly that some water spilled onto the floor.

"What are their last names?"

Shrugging hopelessly, Andrei said, "I don't even know."

"Those are the three people who lived here, I assume?" Detective Spicer asked. "The ones whose bodies were found but never identified?"

Andrei nodded slowly. "Oh my God," he muttered as a tear leaked out. "This is horrible."

"If you knew these were the victims, why didn't you identify them when we put their faces on the news?" the detective asked.

"Do I really need to spell it out for you?" Andrei asked, looking up helplessly at Detective Spicer.

"Where did they come from?"

Releasing a breath, Andrei slowly said, "Diego came from Colombia; Syed was from Syria, and Ngula came from Uganda."

"This man does wonderful things," Hailey's mother said with a shaky voice. "Please don't punish him for it."

Detective Spicer shook his head. "I'm not interested in that; I'm from Homicide. I only want to find out about the murders that apparently took place here."

"I never imagined they had gotten killed *here*," Andrei whimpered. He shook his head, looking distant. "The first one to be killed was Syed; I remember you asking for the public's help in identifying him. My heart was broken. I thought the bounty hunters that were after him had gotten to him." His eyes regained their focus, and he looked at the detective. "Telling you wouldn't have done any good. It would have only drawn attention to this house and the people hiding in it, so I kept quiet."

"Alright, I get it," the detective said. "Let's get back to who lived in this apartment."

"At the time?" Andrei asked. "I think it was Randy."

"Do you have a last name on this *Randy?*"

"I don't have a last name on any of them."

"Where was Randy from?"

"Here," Andrei replied. "The United States."

"Was he running from something?"

"Not that I know of."

"Then why did you rent to him?"

"Empty apartments yield no money."

"Where is he now?" the detective asked. "Do you know?"

Andrei shook his head. "I have no idea. He moved out when Keegan and Cody did. I assume they left together, but I don't know where they went."

Jenny tapped out a quick text to Kyle. *Keegan, Cody and Randy. See if that helps.*

The officer taking the pictures exited the bathroom.

"Swab it," Detective Spicer demanded with a point. Some more officers entered the bathroom with a kit.

"Um, Detective Spicer?" Jenny began with absolutely no confidence in her voice.

He looked at her, making his tone more civil. "What is it?"

"I think you will find Lizette Micheaux's blood in there mixed with the others."

"Lizette Micheaux?" He sounded like he didn't believe his ears.

"I'm afraid so," Jenny said. "It doesn't appear that Keegan, Cody and Randy took too kindly to her being in an interracial relationship."

"But her boyfriend..." The detective stopped midsentence, walking away. He rubbed his forehead with his hand, taking a moment to gather himself. None of this could have been easy for him.

Jenny was about to make it worse. "And I think you will find Ebony Carter's blood, too."

Hailey, whose voice sounded smaller than usual, added, "Luis Alvarez's blood will be in apartment 2C."

Just when the detective looked like he was ready to lose his mind, Jenny remembered something. "Oh! Wait! I have drawings of Keegan and Cody."

Detective Spicer spun around with optimism. "You have what?"

"Sketches," Jenny replied as she swiped her phone, "of Keegan and Cody. At least, I think they are Keegan and Cody." She approached Andrei with her phone screen facing outward. "It this them?" she asked.

Glancing up at the screen briefly, Andrei replied, "Yeah, that's them." He looked away in disgust.

"Send them to me," the detective said to Jenny. He pulled his phone out of his pocket, dialed, and didn't even bother to say hello when someone answered. "I'm going to send you the pictures of two people named Keegan and Cody. I want you to put an APB out for them *now*. And when I say now, I mean yesterday. They are wanted for questioning in connection with several unsolved homicides." He hung up the phone without saying goodbye.

Jenny sent the pictures to the detective, who, in turn, sent them to someone at the station.

Addressing the forensics team, Detective Spicer raised his voice and said, "Okay, people, I want you to process every inch of this apartment. Do you hear me? Every. Last. Inch."

Several of the officers replied with a "Yes, sir." Others just continued to work.

Looking at Andrei, the Larrabees and the Newcombs, the detective spoke more calmly. "I guess it's time we go have a look in apartment 2C."

Chapter 17

Everyone remained motionless for a moment, until Andrei said, "Let me go see if they're home." He looked up at the detective, adding, "That's where Keegan and Cody used to live."

"I gathered," the detective replied curtly.

The group went the short distance down the hall to apartment 2C. Andrei knocked and announced himself, but again was met with no response. Keying his way in, he opened the door—an act that seemed completely harmless to everyone, although Jenny wondered just how much of an impact that had on Hailey.

If Hailey was overwhelmed, however, she didn't show it. She exhibited remarkable poise as she walked into the apartment, looking around, declaring, "Luis has definitely been here."

Jenny stayed back, allowing Hailey to do her thing. It felt strange to be the observer, knowing this is how she must have appeared to other people when she had visions. The process was remarkable to watch, but it had an element of hopelessness to it as well. All she could do was stand there and pray the necessary information came through.

"He had something balled up in his mouth. It was taped there," Hailey added, "and his hands and feet were tied." She scrunched her face and closed her eyes, "Or maybe they were also taped." Heading slowly toward the back of the apartment, she pointed downward. "They made him drag himself along the floor...at gunpoint." Ultimately, Hailey stood in a short hall, at the entrance of a room that Jenny couldn't see. "It happened in here," she remarked with a point. "Luis was also killed in the bathroom."

The glossy-eyed look she'd had while reciting the facts had disappeared, signaling the vision was over.

After a moment of silence, the detective said, "I have a lot of questions for you."

Smiling sheepishly, Hailey nodded her consent.

"You said, '*they* made him drag himself along the floor.' Did you see who was with him?" Detective Spicer began.

"It was Cody and Keegan."

"Did they say anything? Anything that might lead us to exactly who they are?"

Hailey winced apologetically, announcing, "Um...they didn't actually *say* anything in the vision; I just had a quick flash of them being there."

Although Jenny understood that, she wondered if the others would. "Not every scene unfolds like a movie," Jenny explained. "Sometimes, you just get a sense of something that happened—little snippets here and there."

"Exactly," Hailey agreed, seeming grateful for the interruption. "It was more like some random scenes blending together, so I'm not sure how much I'll be able to tell you. But there is one thing..."

"What is it?" the detective asked.

"Well, it was the gun," Hailey replied with a confused look on her face. "It didn't look like a normal gun. It had, like, an extension on it."

"A silencer," Detective Spicer said. "I'm sure that's what you're talking about. I don't think they would have been able to get away with shooting someone in an apartment complex without one."

"They ran the shower," Hailey added, "and played music real loud. And, wait..." She made a concerned face as she froze for a moment.

Nobody else spoke as she headed over to the couch. Removing the cushions, she placed them on the floor, looking around amongst the crumbs that had accumulated underneath.

"What are you doing?" Detective Spicer asked.

Hailey didn't say anything; she just ran her hand along the crack that spanned the back of the sofa. After a moment, her eyes grew wide, and she pulled out a gold chain with a cross on it. "This," she said, holding up the necklace. "I was looking for this."

Leslie gasped, apparently knowing the significance of the chain. "You found it," she declared with awe.

"This was Luis's," Hailey said, walking over to the detective. "He wore it everywhere."

The detective took the chain and inspected it. "The clasp isn't broken," he noted. "It's just undone."

"Luis left it there on purpose," Hailey told him. "His hands were tied in front of him; he could have easily spun the necklace around and undone it. I think he wanted to have some kind of proof that he'd been here so Cody and Keegan could be connected to the crime."

Jenny had seen this once before; one of her other victims left a ring behind for the same reason. The notion had upset her then, and it had the same effect now. These people knew they were going to die—their goal went from surviving to making sure the killers were caught. Jenny couldn't imagine the fear that went along with the realization.

So I'm happy tonight. I'm not worried about anything.

The words echoed through Jenny's mind, and with them came the same sense of defiance she had felt before. It seemed at least one of the victims refused to be scared, and that gave Jenny an incredible sense of joy. She bit her lip to prevent herself from smiling.

"His family will be so happy to have that back." Leslie's shaky voice interrupted Jenny's thoughts. "They have a little shrine set up in their house, and the chain is missing from it."

"We'll make sure they get it...eventually. For now, it needs to be treated as evidence," Detective Spicer said. "Unfortunately, I'm pretty sure Luis left more than just this necklace behind as a calling card. If what you say is true, Hailey, we'll find his blood all over that bathroom."

Hailey hung her head as Jenny's phone buzzed from within her purse. Glancing quickly at the screen, Jenny saw that Kyle was calling. Sensing that it could be important, she walked away from the crowd, placed a finger over her free ear and whispered, "Hello?"

"Hey, it's Kyle. It sounds like I caught you at a bad time."

"No, it's okay. What's up?" She kept her voice barely above a whisper.

"Well, I've got a hit on that symbol you sent me. It turns out it's from a white supremacist group called Purify America."

"Purify America? I've never heard of it."

"I hadn't either," Kyle admitted, "so I looked into it a little bit. They've got little factions all over the country. Unlike some other groups that live all on one compound, or others that hide out in remote areas, the members of Purify America live within society, and their goal is to eliminate any and all people who threaten the sanctity of this country."

Jenny felt an intense rage bubble up from deep inside her. "What—people whose skin isn't white? That's what ruins the *sanctity* of this country?"

"Apparently, according to these folks, yes."

"Oh my God." Jenny tilted her head back toward the ceiling and closed her eyes. "How many people are in this...group?"

"It's hard to say an exact number," Kyle replied, "but it looks like it might be a couple hundred. Some are in jail, but they could be recruiting new members, too, so who knows?"

"Anything else you can tell me about them?"

"Not at the moment." Kyle shuffled papers in the background. "I did get your text about Randy, though. I'll look into that and see if it helps me figure out who Keegan and Cody are, but I'm not optimistic. I've hit nothing but dead ends with those names."

Jenny sighed and glanced back at Detective Spicer, who was placing Luis's chain into a plastic bag. "I should probably tell the detective about Purify America while I still have his attention. They just found a lot of blood evidence in the house on South Bayhill, so I imagine he's going to be busy processing this place for the rest of the night."

"Okay," Kyle replied, "sounds good. I don't really have anything else to report at this point, anyway. I'll keep digging, though."

"Thanks, Kyle," she said genuinely. "I owe you, like, a million."

She ended her call and walked back over to the group. "What was that about?" Zack asked when she approached. "You looked troubled."

"I am troubled," Jenny replied. "That was Kyle; he was able to figure out what those tattoos mean. They're apparently the symbol for a white supremacist group that call themselves Purify America. Their goal is to *eliminate...*" She made finger quotes. "...anyone who threatens the sanctity of this country. They don't have a home base like a lot of radical groups do, but rather the members live in society with everyone else and carry out their plan that way."

"Purify America..." Detective Spicer muttered. "I've never heard of them before." He sucked in a long, deep breath. "But I guess I have now."

"This infuriates me," Jenny exclaimed as she gripped the steering wheel on the way back to the hotel. "The whole concept behind Purify America makes me crazy."

"Agreed," Leslie said from the back seat.

Jenny was nowhere near done with her rant. "They want to *purify America* by killing fathers who volunteer as soccer coaches and brilliant young girls who want to become doctors? That's how they plan to purify America? It's completely absurd. I mean, how can they be filled with so much hate for people they don't even know?"

"You hate *them*," Zack said calmly.

"What?" Jenny asked with passion still in her voice.

"You hate them," he repeated, "and you don't know them."

"But I have a *reason* to hate them," Jenny contended.

"They would say the same thing."

Jenny looked incredulously at her husband. "Are you telling me you support what they are doing?"

"No, of course not," Zack replied. "What they're doing is obviously horrible. But what I'm saying is that you should be able to at least understand hating someone you've never met because you hate them."

Before arguing, she took a moment and thought about what he said. Yes, she did hate those assholes. No, she had never met them.

But it wasn't the same

"Okay, see, I hate those guys for what they *did*," Jenny explained, "not for what they look like. It's entirely different. What is it that Martin Luther King said? He wants to live in a country where people are not judged by the color of their skin but rather the content of their character? I'm judging these guys by the content of their character—or lack of character, in this case."

"Let me ask you this," Zack began, "could you shoot one of them?"

"Could I *shoot* one of them?"

"Yeah."

"You ask strange questions," Jenny said.

"And you seem to be dodging my strange question," Zack replied. "So, tell me, if Keegan or Cody was standing right here in front of you, and you had your gun...and you thought about all the horrible things they've done to innocent people...could you shoot them?" He whacked her on the arm with the back of his hand. "I'll even throw in a guarantee that you'd never get caught. Would you be able to go through with it?"

"That depends," Jenny replied, "could I just call the cops and have them get arrested?"

"Nope," Zack told her. "You either shoot them dead or they carry on."

"Carry on and kill other people?"

"That's what they do," he remarked.

Jenny let out a long sigh of defeat as she turned on her blinker for the hotel parking lot. "If that's the case, and it's either I shoot them or they go on to kill other people, then yes." She glanced at her husband. "Yes, I could shoot them."

Chapter 18

"This says you need an application to go visit," Zack remarked as he looked at his laptop. "You can't just show up there and see an inmate."

Jenny nursed Steve on the hotel bed. "Well, that can put a damper on things, now, can't it? I wonder how long the application takes to process."

"I'm thinking we can potentially get around that if we tell them our visit is related to his case and not just a personal visit."

"We're not law enforcement, though," Jenny noted. "Can we get away with that?"

"It's worth a shot," Zack replied. "Let me make a phone call and see what I can do." He pressed a few buttons and walked over to the window, looking outside as he began his conversation.

Jenny leaned her head back against the propped pillows and allowed her mind to wander. She recalled the defiant words that she had heard while at the house. *I'm not fearing any man. I've looked over, and I've seen the promised land.* Jenny picked up her phone, and with a quick search of 'I'm not fearing any man,' a speech by Martin Luther King instantly popped up on her screen. She froze for a second, aware that she had most likely found the source.

The speech was called *I've Been to the Mountaintop*, and it was delivered on April third, 1968…the day before Dr. King was killed.

Opting to play the video instead of reading, she turned up the volume on her phone and listened.

All we say to America is to be true to what you said on paper. If I lived in China or even Russia, or any totalitarian country, maybe I could understand some of these illegal injunctions. Maybe I could understand the denial of certain basic First Amendment privileges, because they haven't committed themselves to that over there.

But somewhere I read of the freedom of assembly.

Somewhere I read of the freedom of speech.

Somewhere I read of the freedom of press.

Somewhere I read that the greatness of America is the right to protest for right.

So just as I say we aren't going to let any dogs or water hoses turn us around, we aren't going to let any injunction turn us around.

Well, I don't know what will happen now; we've got some difficult days ahead. But it really doesn't matter with me now, because I've been to the mountaintop. And I don't mind. Like anybody, I would like to live a long life—longevity has its place. But I'm not concerned about that now. I just want to do God's will. And He's allowed me to go up to the mountain. And I've looked over, and I've seen the Promised Land. I may not get there with you, but I want you to know tonight that we, as a people, will get to the Promised Land. And so I'm happy tonight; I'm not worried about anything; I'm not fearing any man. Mine eyes have seen the glory of the coming of the Lord.

Jenny watched Dr. King walk away from the podium with determination. Goosebumps covered every inch of her skin as the enormity of it all sank in. Based on what Ebony's mother had said about her affinity for Martin Luther King, Jenny believed those words to be Ebony's. It seemed that brave young girl knew she was about to die. From the sound of it, Dr. King was aware that his enemies would eventually get to him, too. The grace with which those two faced their mortality was awe-inspiring. Chin up, shoulders back. No begging, no pleading. Just pride.

Jenny could only mutter one word at the thought of it.

"Damn."

Zack got off the phone and immediately looked over at Jenny. "What was that about?" he asked. "I heard you playing something over there."

"It was a speech," Jenny explained, "by Martin Luther King—his last one, in fact, given the day before he was shot."

"It sounded powerful," Zack said.

"It was." Jenny still had goosebumps. "That man could surely fire up a room. Not only was he one of the best public speakers *ever*, but his message was incredible, too."

"Why were you playing it?"

"I searched some of the phrases I heard at the house, and it led to this speech. Ebony was apparently quoting some sections from *I've Been to the Mountaintop* while she was staring down the barrel of a gun. She was being told to beg, but she didn't. She recited parts of the speech instead...parts about not being afraid and going to the Promised Land."

"Wow. And how old was she?"

"Exactly."

Zack shook his head. "I don't think I would have been able to do that. I probably would have wet myself."

"I'm with you."

"I bet it was effective, though," Zack said. "They wanted her to beg and die without dignity, but she didn't give them the satisfaction."

Tears suddenly stung the back of Jenny's eyes. Blinking them away, she asked, "So...what did the people at the prison say?" She needed to change the subject before she started bawling.

"Well, I told them that we'd been hired to look into his case, and they said we could talk to him."

"We'd been *hired*?"

"It was the easiest explanation."

"But it's not true."

With a shrug, Zack said, "It's close enough. I doubt they'll ask for a pay stub or anything. Either way, they said we could visit, so I'm calling this a victory."

"Did they say when we could come?"

"Since we're working on his case, we can swing by anytime. We don't have to wait for visiting hours."

Jenny glanced down at the heavy-eyed baby in her arms. "How about first thing in the morning?"

"Sounds like a plan," he replied with an emphatic nod. "Tomorrow we can go let Donald Cox know that, soon, he might be a free man."

Thursday

Jenny sat alone at a table in an otherwise empty room. Unsure of what else to do and aware that she was most likely being filmed, she interlaced her fingers on the table and sat with rigid posture. After what seemed like an eternity, Donald Cox walked in, dressed in orange and escorted by a guard. His ankles and wrists were shackled, causing him to take baby steps. He eventually sat in a chair on the opposite side of the table as Jenny, and the guard affixed his ankle restraints to a pair of hooks on the floor.

That seemed like awfully rough treatment for an innocent man.

He looked up at Jenny with big, brown eyes, splitting her heart in two. She couldn't help but think he had the look of a sweet, enthusiastic puppy who had been beaten one too many times. She forced a compassionate smile, even though she wanted to look away. His broken face was too sad to see.

"Hello, Mr. Cox," she began with resolve. "I suppose you are wondering why I'm here."

He raised his lips into a half-smile. "Are you here to tell me I'm free to go?"

Glancing over at the guard who hadn't left, Jenny chose her words carefully. "Not yet, but I'm working on it."

For a fleeting moment, Gordon's face showed optimism, but that quickly passed. The expression of skepticism returned, although he didn't say anything.

Keeping her voice quiet, she added, "I happen to know that you did not kill Lizette."

"I've been saying that for years," he replied. "The trouble is, nobody listens."

"I'm sure everyone here claims to be innocent," she noted.

"Ain't nobody guilty in here."

A strange feeling came over Jenny; she knew what was about to happen. By now, she'd experienced it a million times before. Placing her elbows on the table and leaning in slightly, she whispered, "I have an unusual gift."

"For me?" he asked.

Jenny hung her head and giggled. After a moment, she said, "Not that kind of gift. I have...wait a minute." She closed her eyes, allowing Lizette to interrupt her conversation. After absorbing the vision, she opened her eyes and continued, "It's probably better if I tell it to you this way. I just heard a little something in my head. If I say you are 'bear bait,' does that mean anything to you?"

Gordon looked confused, and rightfully so. "What?"

Jenny smiled knowingly and gave a slight nod. "That's what I was trying to tell you when I was saying that I have a gift." Looking at the guard again, she made sure she spoke softly enough for him not to hear. "I have the ability to receive messages from the deceased. I have been contacted by Lizette, and so has a friend of mine with the same ability. Just now, I heard her tell me that you were bear bait..." She held up her hand, signaling for him to wait another moment. "Not because you're fat and slow," she added, "but because bears love honey."

Gordon didn't say a word; he just stared at her with awe.

Continuing the silence, Jenny looked at him in return. Eventually, she asked, "Do you believe me now? Have I convinced you that I have the ability?"

Raising both shackled arms, he scratched his chin with his right hand. "I've got to admit, I don't know how else you would know about the bear bait."

"Was it an inside joke between the two of you?" Jenny asked.

"Well, we were alone when we said it, and I don't think we ever told anyone about it. We were at a cabin, going fishing for the weekend." For a brief moment he got lost in his memory, even taking a second to smile. "She was walking through the woods in front of me, and we heard rustling in the trees behind us. Not just squirrel rustling; *big rustling*. I said to her, 'If that's a bear, I'm done. I'm fat and slow. I'm bear bait for sure.' That's when she told me that if a bear does attack me, it's not because I'm fat and slow, but because bears love honey." His distant look turned sad, and he once again raised both hands to wipe his face. "She was good to me," he added solemnly. "I sure do miss her."

Agonizing. That's the only word Jenny could think of to describe this whole scenario.

"Well, I know she's still thinking about you, too," Jenny explained. "She has to be. See, there's something interesting about the gift that my friend and I have. We can't hear from just anybody; we can only hear from the spirits who are lingering. Most folks cross over when they die—there is something beautiful on the other side, and people who are at peace go over there immediately when they pass. Spirts who are troubled, though, stick around." She leaned back in her chair but still kept her voice down. "Lizette is clearly troubled, or else we wouldn't be hearing from her. I think what's troubling her is that you are sitting in here for something you didn't do—and the person who did do it may still be out there on the streets."

"I didn't do it," Gordon repeated with a shake of his head. "I swear on my life that I didn't hurt her—ever. Her family doesn't believe me. The jury didn't believe me. Hell, I'm not even convinced my own defense attorney believed me. But, you know, I'm not bothered by that anymore. Nobody has to believe me. *God* knows I didn't do it, and when this life is over, I will go to heaven where I belong." He leaned back in his chair. "I just have to bide my time here on earth until I get there. I take one day at a time here in this hell hole." He snorted bitterly. "One minute at a time."

"Well, I'm going to try to get you out of this place so you can enjoy your time on earth as well."

"Good luck getting the system to listen to you. Guilt or innocence doesn't seem to matter all that much to them. They hear what they want to hear. Once they decide you're guilty, that's it. It don't matter what the evidence says."

Jenny wiped her eyes; she didn't blame Donald for being bitter. She certainly would have been angry under the same circumstances.

"You know what landed me in here?" Donald continued. "You know what was the most damning piece of evidence against me? Two of my coworkers heard me and Lizette bickering one day. That's all it was—bickering. All couples do it. Shit, when you work together and are dating, you're together all the time. It's bound to happen once in a while. Well, the way those guys testified, you would have thought it was World War Three. They made it sound like I was threatening violence toward her. I was *never* violent toward her." He shook his head with disgust. "It didn't matter how many people testified that I've never raised a fist to a woman in my life—and I never would. The jury heard those two, plain and simple." Looking off to the side, he added, "I have no faith in this system. At all. And I'm not counting on the fact that I'll ever get out of here."

"Well, I might have some indisputable evidence up my sleeve—something they have to listen to." When he didn't respond, Jenny leaned in and added, "I'm talking blood evidence."

"Blood evidence?"

"Yup. In the bathroom of the house where her killers lived."

"You know who did this to her?" Donald asked. Jenny could tell by his expression that he was more angry than relieved—he wanted to know who had killed his girlfriend, not the names of the people who could get him out of jail.

"Yes, sir, I do," Jenny replied. "I don't have last names, but I know their first names were Keegan and Cody."

"Keegan and Cody?"

"Yes."

"Keegan and Cody." This time, he said it like a sentence.

"Yes. Do you know them?"

"Yeah, I know them," he replied with disgust. "Those are the two motherfuckers who testified that I fought with Lizette."

Chapter 19

"Wait," Jenny said with dismay. "What?"

Daggers shot out of Gordon's eyes as he gritted his teeth. "You're telling me that Keegan and Cody killed Lizette? That's why they lied in court—those little bastards were framing me."

There were so many puzzle pieces swirling around Jenny's brain, she had trouble focusing. Shaking her head rapidly, she closed her eyes and held up her hand. "Okay, you knew them? What were their last names?"

Tearing himself away from his anger, Gordon looked intently at Jenny. He appeared to be piecing things together in his own mind as well. "I don't know what their last names were, and that's some bullshit right there. Everybody on that crew was called by their last name, except those two. I should have known there was something sketchy about them just from that alone."

"Well, they testified in court." Jenny spoke, but she was mostly thinking out loud. "They had to give their last names there. And your boss should know their last names."

Gordon shook his head. "Not necessarily. There was a lot of under the table work being done on that team. I don't think all the guys were legal, and they got paid in cash."

A frightening thought hit Jenny. "Were some of those guys Hispanic? Or from some other minority group?"

"Yeah," Gordon said, "lots of them. Why? Does that matter?"

Ignoring the question, Jenny sucked in a breath and braced herself for Gordon's response. "Did any of them go missing? Like, did they ever just stop showing up at work one day?"

The similarity between this and what happened to Steve O'Dell, the man the baby had been named after, was not lost on Jenny. She desperately hoped the situation hadn't repeated itself.

Gordon shook his head and frowned, apparently giving the notion some thought. "Not that I know of. But Keegan and Cody quit the crew just after testifying. A buddy told me that."

Jenny closed her eyes. They could have been anywhere by now; this murder happened years ago.

"I thought that they quit because they were scared of what my friends might do to them," Gordon added, interrupting her thoughts, "but maybe they quit because they were afraid of the truth getting out." He shook his head, his anger resurfacing. "I can't believe they did this to her. Tell me…why would they kill her? I mean, what did they have against her? She'd never done anything to them. She'd never done anything to anyone."

Hanging her head, Jenny felt reluctant to answer him. How could she look this man in the eye and tell him that their relationship was what sealed his girlfriend's fate? She clenched her hands into fists, remembering what Susan had said to her when she first discovered her ability: it was her job to tell the truth, no matter how awful that truth might have been.

She just wished the truth could have been different.

Clearing her throat, she looked down at her lap. "Keegan and Cody were part of a hate group called Purify America. They were white supremacists, and they were…opposed…to interracial relationships." Glancing up with only her eyes, she saw Gordon's expressionless face. "I guess by killing her and framing you, they were able to punish both of you at the same time."

Jenny studied him for a moment, concerned by his lack of reaction. He sat frozen, looking like he could explode at any moment.

"That's why I asked about your minority coworkers," Jenny continued calmly, hoping her logical words would dismantle the time bomb. "I was worried for their safety. Those two have killed some other undocumented immigrants, and I was afraid they may have done it again. It sounds like they didn't, though, which is a good thing."

Gordon's face changed to anguished confusion. "They killed other people? How many are you talking?"

Remaining professional in her tone, Jenny said, "We believe they were involved in at least five additional murders at this point."

"*Five*? Before or after Lizette?"

"The ones that we know of all happened before."

He turned to the side, sticking his jaw out into an under bite. "So you mean to tell me that if they solved any of those other murders, Lizette would be here today?"

"I know it's disheartening," Jenny said sincerely, "but we're hoping to put an end to this now so it doesn't happen to anyone else. What you have to understand, though, is that some of Keegan and Cody's victims were undocumented, so nobody came forward to identify the bodies. It's hard to solve a murder when you don't even know the name of the victim. The other people they killed were strangers to them. Even though those people had families who missed them dearly, stranger killings are the most difficult to solve. Their victims were just minding their business when they were abducted off the streets. Where do you even begin in an investigation when it appears the person just dropped off the face of the earth?"

"You begin with me, apparently," Gordon replied bitterly. "You get in your head that I'm the one who did it, and you don't listen to reason after that."

Jenny's stomach sank; Gordon had every right to be angry, but it was still painful to see. "I'm sorry that happened to you, and I'm doing my best to right that wrong. It actually should be easier now that I know where I can find out Keegan and Cody's last names." Flashing a broad smile in Gordon's direction, she added, "Actually, it should be *a whole lot* easier. It might even be the key to getting you out of here. But there is one other person who appears to be involved in this; his name is Randy. Does that ring any bells?"

"Randy?" Gordon looked around as he thought. "I guess you don't have a last name."

"We sure don't."

Shaking his head, he replied, "I don't know a Randy outside of work, but there may have been one *at* work. Like I said, we always called each other by last name."

"Well, I can find that information out from your boss. What's his name?"

"Dave O'Brien from Regency Construction."

Jenny closed her eyes to focus. "Dave O'Brien, Regency Construction." After taking a moment to commit that to memory, she announced, "Got it." Leaning forward onto her elbows, she smiled genuinely at Gordon. "I am so glad I came in here to talk to you today. I really only wanted to let you know that I was aware of your innocence and was working to prove it; I had no idea that you could tell me where to find Keegan and Cody..."

"I don't know where to find Keegan and Cody," he replied with a scoff. "I bet them guilty motherfuckers are long gone by now."

Holding up her hand, Jenny shook her head. "I said that wrong," she replied. "You have given me enough information so I can at least figure out who they are. We only had first names before, and that wasn't getting us anywhere."

"Let me ask you something," Gordon began. "How is it you knew the killer's first names, and that's it."

"That's all the spirits told us."

Gordon's expression flattened. "You are basing all of this on what some spirits told you?"

"Oh, but it led to some solid evidence," Jenny said emphatically. "The spirits led us to Keegan and Cody's apartment, where, like I said, the detectives found a ton of blood evidence. It's obvious that some murders occurred in that apartment. They don't officially know who the victims were at this point, but I guarantee you that some of that blood is Lizette's."

"I hope there's DNA," Gordon said. "That's what I need. They convicted me on bullshit. I need some good, hard evidence to show I didn't do it." After that moment of defiance, sadness seemed to sink in. His girlfriend's DNA was spattered all over the walls in her killer's apartment. With a much softer tone, he added, "They need to punish those bastards for what they did to Lizette. She deserves that much."

"Well, let me not waste any more time here, then," Jenny said, patting the table. "Let me get in touch with Dave O'Brien at Regency Construction and see if he has last names. Then, hopefully, we will be able to find this Keegan and Cody and put them away."

"I'd prefer if you'd let me at them instead. I could save the taxpayers some money by taking care of them myself."

"I'd love to," Jenny replied genuinely. "But, unfortunately, that's not how I operate."

"Keegan and Cody testified at Gordon Cox's trial," Jenny said into the phone. She hadn't even reached her car in the parking lot.

"Really?" Detective Spicer replied with interest.

"I just talked to Gordon Cox, and he recognized the names—not just from the trial, but from his job at Regency Construction. It seems that Keegan and Cody worked with Gordon and Lizette, and their testimony was what put him away. They said that Gordon and Lizette had been fighting, when that was a huge exaggeration...maybe even a lie."

"So, I assume Gordon knew their last names?"

"Sadly, he didn't," Jenny replied. "But I'm sure their names are on record somewhere. Wouldn't they need to give their full, legal names in order to be part of a trial?"

"They sure would. Okay, let me get on that," the detective said. "It shouldn't be too hard to find."

Jenny hung up with Detective Spicer as she reached her car. Plopping down in the driver's seat, she put on the air conditioning. The humidity was out of control, and a storm looked like it was about to roll in. She hoped she made it back to the hotel before the sky opened up, but she looked forward to the lower temperatures the rain would bring.

Once the car became a little cooler, she pressed a few buttons on her phone.

"Regency Construction." The woman who answered had a monotonous voice; Jenny wondered if Lizette had been more animated when doing that very same job.

"Hi, my name is Jenny Larrabee. I'm looking to speak with Dave O'Brien."

"He's on a job right now; can I take a message for you?"

"Um, it's kind of an emergency. Is there any way I can get in touch with him?"

"Please hold."

"Please hold," Jenny repeated once the music started. She used the same lackluster tone the receptionist had. Somehow, she was bitter about the woman's nonchalant attitude.

Lizette should have still had that job.

The receptionist returned to the line. "Let me give you his direct number." She rattled off the first few digits of his number.

"Wait a minute," Jenny said, searching her purse. "I'll need to write this down. Let me get a pen."

She was met with silence.

"Okay, got one," Jenny continued. "I'm ready."

The woman repeated the number and insincerely told Jenny to have a good day.

"You, too, Little Miss Sunshine," Jenny muttered after she'd hung up.

After a quick dial, she heard, "O'Brien."

"Hi, Mr. O'Brien, my name is Jenny Larrabee; I'm looking into the death of Lizette Micheaux."

"Lizette Micheaux?" He remained quiet for a moment before adding, "That was solved years ago."

"Well, I'm not sure it was solved correctly."

Releasing a breath, O'Brien sounded like he was in shock. "Wow. Uh, that's good to hear. I never did think they got it right."

"So, you don't think Gordon Cox did it?"

"He didn't have it in him," he replied.

Jenny knew that statement was going to make her sad later, but she couldn't afford to let it get to her now. "I am under the impression that you also employed a Keegan and a Cody during that time period," Jenny added professionally. "Can you tell me a little something about them?"

"They haven't worked for me in years. What do you want to know?"

"It's my understanding that they testified against Gordon and then quit shortly afterwards."

"Yeah, that's right. Hang on." He shouted something to a crew member and then said, "Sorry, I'm at work."

"It's okay. What were they like, Keegan and Cody?"

"They were good workers, I guess. Quiet. Kept to themselves quite a bit."

"You don't happen to remember their last names, do you?"

He cleared his throat, which Jenny took as a sign of guilt. "I don't."

She debated questioning whether he forgot their last names or never knew them to begin with, but she decided against it. Detective Spicer could determine their names; she needed to find out the less tangible information, and putting this guy on the defensive was not going to help that cause.

"Did you ever see any signs of violence in them?" she asked instead.

"In Keegan and Cody? I don't think so." Before Jenny had the chance to ask her next question, he added, "Wait a minute...are you telling me..." He didn't finish the sentiment.

Letting out a sigh, Jenny said, "We think so. Do you know where they went after they quit?"

"No, no idea. They just asked for their final pay up front and said they weren't coming back."

"They didn't tell you where they were going?"

"Nope. They just said they weren't coming back here. But what makes you think it was them? I can't see any reason why they'd kill Lizette. They hardly interacted with her at all."

"I'd rather not say at this point," Jenny replied honestly. "I'm sure you'll find out soon enough. I do have one more question for you, though; around that same time period, did anyone named Randy work for you?"

"I don't think I've ever employed a Randy."

Jenny could physically feel her disappointment. She was hoping to end all of this in one fell swoop. "Okay," she said, "thank you. But, please, do me a favor; if Keegan and Cody happen to get in touch with you, call the police right away. Although, I'm sure the police be paying you a visit sooner rather than later."

"Wait, you're not the police?"

"Not officially," she replied, "but I'm a consultant, of sorts."

He grunted, appearing to question his decision to say anything at all to Jenny. "I haven't heard from those two in years. I'm willing to bet they won't be contacting me in the next few days."

"I don't know," Jenny replied. "Their pictures are about to go national—who knows where they may try to hide."

Chapter 20

Jenny enjoyed the feeling of accomplishment as she drove back toward the hotel. Granted, nobody had been caught, and Randy's true identity was still a mystery, but they were on the right path to finding out the whereabouts of the elusive Keegan and Cody. Perhaps those two would be put behind bars soon, before they had the chance to hurt anybody…

A tug.

The familiar feeling grew stronger inside Jenny's belly, causing her to free her mind and allow her instincts to lead the way. After a series of turns down the one-way streets of Richmond, her car found its way to a brick building that didn't stand out from the houses surrounding it. Based on the overwhelming sense of peace she felt and the sign out front, however, she knew this was her destination—First Baptist Church. Even without being told, Jenny was sure that this was Ebony's church.

She parked in the small lot behind the building, where signs reminded her that parking was for church-related business only. This qualified, at least to Jenny, so she got out of the car and was met with an ominous gust of wind. The fear of the impending storm affected her only for a moment; soon she was filled with delight and optimism, taking the route Ebony had walked so many times before, headed to a place she loved more than anything in the world.

Considering it was a weekday, Jenny wasn't sure if she'd be able to get inside, but the large, wooden doors parted when she turned the knob. Inside, she was greeted by a simple layout—an aisle with a hardwood floor led to a pulpit; the pews were the same dark wood as the floor. The podium in the front was flanked by a stage with risers, and stained glass windows let in minimal light. Jenny eased the front doors closed so they would latch quietly behind her, and once fully inside, she sniffed in the scent that invoked a million memories that didn't belong to her. The building smelled beautifully old, like a cherished hardcover book, and the familiarity embraced her like a hug.

Taking a few steps in, Jenny allowed her fingertips to touch the pews. They were smooth, just like Ebony had remembered. She patted one affectionately as the empty seats filled with people and the silence was broken by a deep, masterful voice. "We will *all* go home someday."

"Go 'head!"

"And we will be welcomed into the arms of the Lord."

"That's right!"

"And while the people we leave behind may be hurting, death is not a time for mourning. Death is a time for celebration. When we die, we get to *leave* the strife."

"Uh-huh!"

"We get to *leave* the hardship."

"Amen!"

"When we die, we get to walk with God and *all* his glory."

The cheers of the crowd faded in Jenny's mind as the people disappeared and the sheen of the wooden pews could be seen again. Jenny smiled at the message she'd just gotten, quite certain that Ebony hadn't chosen that particular sermon at random.

She took several steps down the aisle, the sound of her shoes echoing through the church. She felt herself drawn to the stained glass windows; while they were small, they were beautiful and intricate. Her eyes made their way to a colorful mosaic that didn't depict anything in particular, but she knew that had been Ebony's favorite as a child. It looked like a kaleidoscope, with every color of the rainbow in a random but symmetrical pattern. Walking further, she found herself inexplicably attracted to another window, knowing there was something she was supposed to understand about it. This window featured a simple candle with a flame. Standing still, she studied it, trying to absorb the message Ebony was trying to send. What was it about this candle that she was supposed to understand?

"Can I help you?"

The echoing voice caused Jenny to jump a foot and let out both a squeal and a little pee. Turning around, Jenny saw the friendly face of the large man behind the voice—that same voice she had recognized from the sermon. Still shaken from the startle, she placed her hand on her heart, let out an exhale and said, "My goodness, you scared me."

"Sorry, young lady," he replied with a smirk, "I didn't mean to."

Despite his towering size and broad frame, he was not at all intimidating. Jenny could feel his friendliness and kindness from across the room. "Reverend James," she found herself saying, suddenly aware of his name.

He looked puzzled, and rightfully so. "Have we met?"

Deciding this was not the time to explain, Jenny simply said, "Indirectly."

"Well, it's a pleasure to see you here today. What can I do for you?"

Thunder rumbled outside; Jenny wondered if lightning was going to strike the church because she—the woman who conceived a baby with Zack while very much married to Greg—was sitting inside. Ignoring that thought, she took several steps toward Reverend James and smiled. "I'm here because I'm an acquaintance of Ebony Carter."

His jovial expression immediately turned to sadness as his shoulders slumped. "Oh, Ebony." He shook his head. "I'm sorry for your loss."

"I'm sorry for yours. She was a lovely girl."

"Indeed she was. It's such a shame." Reverend James shook his head with disgust. "I still can't wrap my head around what happened."

"Neither can I," Jenny confessed.

The reverend looked at Jenny with an expression of utter confusion. "I mean, really...what did that person have to gain by taking Ebony? Was it fun for him? With all the things a person can do with their spare time, *this* is what he chose? He could have been feeding the homeless or mentoring a child, but instead he murdered a beautiful and promising young woman? It just doesn't make sense."

Jenny remained quiet as a disturbing thought popped into her head. All of those things Reverend James had mentioned would have made the world a better place. However, in their own sick, twisted minds, Keegan, Cody and Randy thought they were improving the world by *purifying America* into one single race. Unwilling to say that out loud, however, Jenny just sighed and said, "I can't explain it either."

Thunder roared outside, and the sound of driving rain could be heard hitting the roof, even though the stained glass windows prevented it from being seen. The reverend looked up at the ceiling, acknowledging the storm, but didn't say anything about it. Instead, he remarked, "I'm sorry. I shouldn't be going on about that. Would you like to have a seat?"

"Sure, that'd be great." Jenny worked her way over to him, and the two sat next to each other in the front row of the pews. She looked around, her eyes catching that stained-glass candle again. "It's lovely in here."

"It's nothing extravagant, but, I agree, it's beautiful—although, that has more to do with what goes on *inside* these walls. A wonderful group of people attends this church; we're like family here at First Baptist."

"I'm happy to hear you say that," she replied. "I have to admit, I often drive by these amazing churches that look like they cost a ton of money to build, and I think, 'wouldn't that money have been better spent feeding the hungry? Or clothing the poor?'"

"We do a lot of that around here," Reverend James replied, shifting his position. "In case you haven't noticed, there are plenty of folks in this area who need a little help."

With her exorbitant bank balance flashing in her mind, Jenny's eyes made their way to the floor. "Yeah, I did notice."

"We do what we can. As proverb 19:17 says, *one who is gracious to a poor man lends to the Lord, and He will repay him for his good deed.*"

More thunder rumbled outside as Jenny nodded with a smile, contemplating what a great influence this place must have had on Ebony.

At that moment, a wave washed over her. It was brief, and she didn't get the chance to gain anything from it, but she knew that Ebony was there with her, trying to get her to understand something. "Reverend James, I actually have a confession to make, of sorts."

"Oh, yeah? What is that?"

Clearing her throat, Jenny didn't look at him while she spoke. "I am here because I was led here...by Ebony."

Although she waited a long while, a response never came, so she continued, "I didn't ever know Ebony when she was alive. I can only hear from her now—now that she's gone." Playing with her fingers, Jenny added, "I don't know if you believe that or not, but I've been asked to work on Ebony's case because I have that gift. I can hear from the deceased."

Again, more silence led Jenny to say, "She's led me to several places, and we're on the right track to finding out who killed her. But now she's brought me here, and I want to figure out why." She finally looked up at the reverend, adding, "It may be just to say hi, but I can't help but feel like there's more than that." She glanced back at the flame in the stained-glass window before returning her gaze to Reverend James. "I don't suppose you know why I would have been led here."

He furrowed his brow and looked at her, his expression revealing he had a million questions swirling around his head. After remaining quiet for a while, he eventually said, "Before I begin, I'll start by saying no, I don't know why she would have led you here. Not specifically. I do know that she loved it here. But..." He paused, apparently to formulate his words. "You're telling me you can hear from those who have passed on?"

Jenny nodded. "Some of them, yes."

"But...how?"

"How do I have the ability or how does it sound when I hear from them?"

Letting out a deep, hearty laugh, the reverend replied, "Both."

A sudden crack of thunder filled the room, inspiring another short wave inside Jenny. It left her body before she had the chance to absorb the message, but she decided she wouldn't leave until she figured out what she was supposed to know. "It sounds like it's getting bad out there," Jenny noted.

"I'm grateful for it, honestly, as long as nobody gets hurt," Reverend James replied. "Maybe it will cool things down a bit."

And maybe it will burn the church down because I'm sitting inside it. Ignoring her thought, Jenny simply replied, "I hope so. It's been so muggy and hot the past few days. Anyway, you asked me a question. I have the ability to hear from the deceased because it runs in my family. An ancestor of mine had a near death experience when she was a child; actually, I think she technically was dead and was brought back to life. Ever since then, she was able to hear from the dead, and so have some of her descendants."

"My goodness," he whispered, looking off into space. Turning to Jenny, he asked, "Did she ever say what it was like...being dead?"

"I've only heard the story second hand, obviously, but from what I was told, it was peaceful. She and her brother had fallen out of a boat into icy water, and they held hands—in a spiritual sense—as they rose up toward the sky. She could look down and see her family frantically trying to get her and her brother back into the boat. Her family was upset, but she wished they wouldn't be." Jenny smiled as she added, "I remember this part of the story specifically—she said that if her family knew how peaceful and happy she felt, they wouldn't have been so upset by what was going on."

The reverend leaned back into the pew, looking awestruck. "That's how I envision it," he muttered softly. "When you're with the Lord, it can only be peaceful. Did she see the Lord?"

"She never got that far," she replied. "Her family was able to get her back into the boat. Before she knew it, she was being pulled back down to earth."

"What about her brother?"

Jenny shook her head. "He didn't make it."

The reverend's expression reflected sadness.

"I remember that my great-great-great-you-get-the-idea-grandmother said she felt conflicted. She had been close to her brother, and she didn't want to come back to earth without him. He assured her that she should go and that he would never leave her. With that, she let go of his hand and returned to this life, but her brother kept his promise. She was able to hear from him—and other deceased family members—after that."

"This is absolutely fascinating to me," he replied. "I have..."

A loud boom from outside interrupted his words. The wave returned, and Jenny heard screams inside her head. Frantic screams. Lots of them. They disappeared as quickly as they came.

"Wow," the reverend said. "It's getting close."

"I fear I'm the target," Jenny confessed. "I don't think the man upstairs takes too kindly to me being in a church. I've done some...questionable...things in my day. I apologize in advance if your church gets struck."

With bouncing shoulders, the reverend let out a laugh. "You think this is about you?"

Looking down at the floor, Jenny playfully said, "Possibly."

"My guess is that it has more to do with the cold front they predicted days ago. If the Lord struck down every church that a sinner walked into, there would be no churches. Besides, He isn't vengeful."

Jenny smiled. "I know. The timing is just pretty ironic."

The lights flickered, causing both of them to look around. "Uh oh," Reverend James said. "This may be shaping up to be a long afternoon. It gets hot in here with no air conditioning."

"I'll bet," Jenny replied, noting the windows didn't open.

"Whatever," the reverend said, returning to the topic at hand. "I have always wondered what it was like after you pass. I mean, the scripture tells us, but I've still thought about it."

"From what I understand, there is something beautiful on the other side," Jenny assured him.

"That's what I've figured. I've thought about that since I was a child. My grandfather died of ALS; it's an awful disease. I was close to my grandfather; we lived right around the corner from him while I grew up. But that disease stripped him of everything. It started out mild—his legs were stiff, and he'd fall sometimes. But then it took over. He ended up in a wheelchair, with so little control over his muscles that he was unable to speak. The sad part is, from what I understand, he was still fully aware of what was going on. His mind was fine; his body just wouldn't work. And he stayed that way for months."

Jenny winced, imagining what it would be like to be a prisoner inside her own body.

"When he finally passed, my mother rejoiced. Nobody loved him more than my mother did, so it was a bit strange to see her so happy when he died. But she explained to me that there is no ALS in heaven. He was free of the body that had been failing him. He could go back to being his old self in heaven, and he'd be there waiting for us when it was our turn."

"I believe that's true," Jenny said softly. "I've experienced the feeling of reunion when two souls get to see each other again. It's absolutely beautiful." She smiled as she remembered the warmth that encompassed her body when Elanor saw Steve again. Even though that had been a sad moment for Jenny, Elanor and Steve were delighted. "Although," she began, returning to the present, "for some, it's not a direct trip. Some souls—like Ebony—stick around because they have an unresolved issue."

"What do you mean, they 'stick around?'"

"They don't cross over. Eternal peace is waiting for everybody..." Jenny thought about some of the murderous monsters she'd dealt with in the past. "Well, maybe not *everybody*...but for those who deserve it, a wonderful place awaits us after we die. However, you have to go there. You have to walk through that door, so to speak. Most people go right through; they have no reason not to. But for murder victims whose killers haven't been caught—they tend to linger. I guess they're waiting for justice."

"They know?" the reverend asked. "I mean, they are aware that their killer hasn't been caught?"

"I'm sure of it," Jenny replied, "and I know they are aware of when the killer *does* get caught. A lot of times, the spirits have let me know who the killer is, and as soon as the person gets arrested, they cross over. I can feel it. It's an overwhelming feeling of satisfaction, for both me and them."

"So, let me get this straight. The spirits can see what's going on?" He raised his hands and gestured all around him. "Like, Ebony could be watching us right now?"

"I'm pretty sure she is, actually. Every time there's thunder, I get a wave over me. I know it's her, trying to tell me something. I just can't figure out what."

Putting his hand over his mouth, Reverend James looked like he could cry.

"I've also seen things before, from their perspective," Jenny continued. "I have had flashes in my mind—memories, in a way—that are messages from the spirits. But some of the scenes I'm seeing happened after the person had died. It's from their point of view—like, from above—and the image is foggy, but I can still see what's happening."

The reverend spoke in a mumble, "This is fascinating."

Thunder filled the room, although not as loudly as it had before. Jenny sat still, waiting for the wave, but it was milder than it had been before. The intensity of the feeling seemed directly related to the thunder's volume.

"I've actually seen a couple of sprits save people, too," Jenny continued. "I'll suddenly get the urge to go somewhere, and when I get there, I see someone is in trouble. My own father-in-law was saved by a young man who had died three decades earlier."

"Wow," Reverend James declared, "if only everyone had your ability. Could you imagine that?"

With a sheepish smile, Jenny tucked her hair behind her ear. She was about to disclose something she rarely talked about. "Everyone might, to some degree. I actually saw it happen a couple of weeks ago. I brought my baby to the community pool on a perfectly sunny day. There was, like, maybe one cloud off in the distance, but that was it. It was right around lunch time, and the pool was crowded. I think a lot of moms had the same idea—get the kids tired so they'll take good afternoon naps. Anyway, out of the blue, there was a single clap of thunder. We all looked around, but we couldn't figure out where it had come from. It didn't matter—once they hear thunder, the lifeguards close the pool for thirty minutes. The moms were upset about it, too—it takes forever to get kids ready for the pool, and now they couldn't swim. Not only that, but the kids had to sit outside in the hot sun for the next half hour. There was a lot of grumbling among the parents and very whiny children.

"I had a funny feeling, though, when that happened. It was that feeling of a spirit sending a message. My eyes were drawn to one little boy in particular, way on the other side of the pool. He was about four, I guess, and he was dripping wet because he'd just gotten out of the water. He looked positively exhausted. His mother was dealing with a fussy baby at the moment, and I suddenly understood." Jenny looked Reverend James in the eye. "Someone saved that boy from drowning.

"I don't know who it was, but someone was obviously watching the situation, realizing that boy was too tired to be in the water. It was clearly someone who loved that boy enough to be able to conjure up thunder on a sunny day. That can't be an easy task. But anyway, while all the parents griped about having to chase toddlers around the pool deck in the heat, I felt nothing but joy. What those other parents didn't realize was that a disaster had been averted. There wasn't a drowning that day. Thirty minutes of toddler-chasing was *nothing* compared to what would have been. But I'm sure a lot of people went home and complained to their spouses, talking about how dumb the thirty-minute rule was and how their morning got ruined." She shook her head. "It's a perspective changer; that's for sure."

The reverend pointed his finger. "You know, I had something similar happen to me once. This was when I was younger and a little less patient. I was running late to something, driving faster than I should have been down a windy back road, when a car pulled out in front of me like a bat out of Hades. Now, mind you, he pulled out like he was in some sort of hurry, but then he proceeded to go fifteen miles an hour below the limit in front of me. I was so mad. My temper was *flaring* as I drove behind this guy. A few minutes later, we approached an intersection where a car had run off the road and crashed into a tree. The accident had apparently just happened. The driver was okay, but he said his brakes went out. He mentioned that he was glad nobody was in the intersection at that moment, because he definitely would have hit them.

"I did a little calculation in my head, and I figured that I may have been in that intersection at that time if the guy hadn't slowed me down. I couldn't help but wonder if someone upstairs had been looking out for me that day."

"Your grandfather, maybe?" Jenny asked.

"That's what came to my mind, too," the reverend confessed, his eyes directed toward the floor, "but I thought that may have just been wishful thinking." He raised his eyes to look at Jenny. "I loved that man. It would be amazing to know he could still see me and was protecting me. He was a man of God, and I know he'd be thrilled to see that I've become a pastor. One of my biggest regrets is that he didn't live long enough to see that happen."

"I'm sure he knows," Jenny whispered.

"It'd be nice if he could give me some kind of sign…"

The lights went out as deafening thunder echoed throughout the room. The darkness around Jenny erupted in chaos. People were running and screaming. Flames billowed through the air. Smoke filled the room at an alarming rate. The image was hazy but unmistakable.

A whisper of a word bounced around Jenny's mind. *Middletown.*

The lights came back on, and silence returned. Jenny sat motionlessly, aside from her shaking, overwhelmed by the vision she'd just had. She knew exactly what it meant.

"Reverend James," she began slowly, "Are you aware of any church bombings at a place called Middletown?"

Chapter 21

"Church bombings?" Reverend James asked, stunned. "I-I-I don't know."

"I think we need to look into it." Jenny looked him in the eye. "And now."

She pulled out her phone and began to type, quickly noticing a huge problem. "It appears that just about every state in the union has a Middletown, but none of them have had a church bombing."

"You'll have to forgive me, but..."

Even though he didn't finish the statement, Jenny knew what he was getting at. The lights flickered again as she said, "That last clap of thunder triggered a vision—a horrible one. The sound must have been like the noise the bomb made when it went off. I saw the left side of a church destroyed immediately, with fire and flames shooting up and spreading quickly. Smoke filled the room, and people were scrambling to get out. They were screaming—blood curdling screams." Jenny shook her head as she shuddered. Taking a second to regroup, she added, "I saw the vision from above, so it wasn't from anybody when they were alive. It had to have been from a spirit, and I'm assuming it was Ebony's."

The reverend remained quiet for a while, seeming to absorb what she was saying. Eventually, he whispered, "Why would she show you that?"

Jenny looked at the floor as she answered. "I think it must have been the work of the same people who killed Ebony." She shifted her feet and cleared her throat. "What I haven't told you is that I believe Ebony's murder was a hate crime. She was targeted for the color of her skin—and she wasn't the only one. We've been able to tie her case to several other cold cases around here, and the common thread is that all of the victims were minorities."

The reverend stumbled over his words. "H-h-how do you know that—that her case is related to others?"

"The spirits are telling us," Jenny whispered. "Another psychic and I have both been led to the same house, where…" A rumble of thunder caused Jenny to freeze, but no frightening messages came through this time. It seemed Ebony had already gotten her point across. "We've been led to the same house where three men lived…men with tattoos that signified that they were part of a white supremacist group called *Purify America*. And that's not the worst of it." She went on to describe the long list of victims attributed to Keegan, Cody and Randy. "And now—if I'm interpreting this vision correctly—it seems they have taken this murder spree to the next level. Instead of killing their victims one at a time, they went after an entire church full of people."

Jenny heard the words as they came out of her mouth. *They went after an entire* church *full of people.* A church. They targeted people who gathered on a Sunday morning to celebrate the good in the world. Her level of hatred for those men instantly multiplied.

"The parishioners in my vision were all African American," Jenny continued. "It would make sense that the bombing would also be a hate crime."

"If what you're saying is true," the reverend began, "these people need to be stopped. Immediately."

"I know," Jenny replied. "The only problem is, this last vision doesn't completely make sense. When I looked up Middletown church bombings, nothing came up. I'll have to call my friend Kyle and have him look into it. He's a private investigator, and he's awesome."

"You have his number?" Reverend James asked.

"It's in my phone."

The look on his face was intense. "Call him now."

Jenny sat still for a moment, entranced by the reverend's serious expression. That man remained calm on the outside, but he clearly wanted these people caught as soon as humanly possible. "Got it," Jenny said with a nod. She called Kyle quickly and gave him the information, hanging up and returning her attention to the reverend.

Although his intensity had gone down a notch, it was clearly still high. Softening her tone and speaking compassionately, Jenny asked, "Are you okay?"

The words roused him out of his trance, causing him to shift his position and hang his head. "Yeah, I'll be alright," he muttered. "This is just so difficult to hear. So many innocent people."

"I know," Jenny agreed. "It's unimaginable." The prevailing theme of the past few days popped into her head, and she thought for a moment about the person she was sitting next to. If anyone would have insight on the matter, it would be him. "You know what astounds me, though?" she asked.

"What's that?"

"Ebony's mother," she replied. "I can't believe the grace and dignity she has regarding her daughter's death."

"I know. She's an amazing woman."

"She told me she was just living by Ebony's example...that Ebony lived by the words of Martin Luther King and tried not to hate anybody."

"Ebony didn't have a hateful bone in her body."

"But..." Jenny began, trying to formulate her words carefully. "Now she has a legitimate reason to be hateful."

"Who—Ebony or her mother?"

"Both," Jenny replied with a snort, "but I was actually referring to the mother."

"Yeah, well, you got that right. Those people wronged her in the worst imaginable way. They took her only child."

Jenny thought about her baby, and then forced herself to stop. If she made this too personal, she wouldn't have been able to function. "My husband pointed out something to me, and—while it makes sense—I've been struggling with it."

"What's that?"

Jenny took a moment to formulate her words. "I can honestly say I hate the three men responsible for this. The thought of them makes my skin crawl." She turned to look at Reverend James. "But does that mean I'm no better than they are? They do what they do because of hate—hate for people they've never met. And that's exactly what I have for them." She shook her head. "I'm not saying this well, but do you get what I'm saying?"

"Loud and clear," the reverend replied. "It's a tricky thing. I can stand up here and preach all day that people shouldn't hate, but those are hard words to live by, especially in situations like this. What you have to do, though, is separate the actions from the people. You can hate what they've done, but you shouldn't hate *them*." He shook his head. "But, like I said, that's hard. Even I struggle with it, and I'm a man of God."

In an unexpected move, he smiled slyly, looking over at Jenny. "But the bible does say a little something about an eye for an eye, a tooth for a tooth. So we should be looking to punish these guys; we just shouldn't be doing so out of hate. We should be motivated by our desire for justice...and our love for Ebony."

Jenny nodded as she thought about his words. It wouldn't have been too hard to switch her focus—it wasn't about hate for Keegan, Cody and Randy; it was about love for Ebony. She could have been just as motivated doing the latter as the former, and it would have made her feel better inside. "Thank you," she said. "I needed to hear that."

"My pleasure," the reverend replied.

A quiet rumble of thunder filled the room. "It sounds like the storm is passing," Jenny noted, patting her thighs with her hands. "Maybe I should get out of here and start looking into this new information. I will do better on a laptop than my phone."

"By all means," Reverend James said, standing up. "These men need to be caught—for Ebony's sake." He gave her a knowing smile.

"That's right." She returned the smile.

"Let me see you out," the reverend began, gesturing for Jenny to lead the way.

She walked down the center aisle, wondering how many newly married coupled had made that same trek, smiling from ear to ear as they went off to start their lives together. The thought warmed her.

"It was a pleasure to meet you, Jenny." Reverend James said as he hurried around her, opening the large, wooden door to let her out.

"I can certainly say the same..." She froze as she caught a glimpse of the outside, and an unmistakable feeling took over. "Um...Reverend James?"

Looking concerned, he asked, "What's the matter?"

"Nothing. But you know how you said you would like to see a sign from your grandfather, letting you know he's out there?"

"Yes."

Jenny pointed to the sky, where a brilliant rainbow spanned the horizon. "I do believe your grandfather says hello."

Chapter 22

"I'm hungry," Zack declared as they sat in the restaurant, waiting for the Newcombs.

"Tell me something I don't already know," Jenny replied.

"I'm glad Susan took the baby?" he said like a question.

"Oh, that goes without saying, too." Jenny's tone was emphatic. "Steve was seriously grouchy today."

"Yeah, that was rough. I know you say he's crying because he's teething, but does it really hurt that bad to grow teeth? I got teeth in elementary school, and I don't remember it being painful. They just kind of...appeared."

Jenny shrugged and shook her head. "Apparently, it's rough on babies."

"Well, then, babies are wimps."

At that moment, Leslie and Hailey approached the table. "Is it just us four tonight?" Leslie asked as they sat down.

"Sure is," Jenny replied. "My mom ate dinner with Amma earlier, and Susan is with the baby." She shook her head. "Steve has been fussy all afternoon; we think he's cutting teeth. He was driving us a little bonkers, so Susan said she'd take him."

"Susan begged, actually," Zack clarified.

Jenny laughed. "She did beg. I've never seen anyone beg to take a fussy baby before."

"Oh, I would," Leslie said without a moment's hesitation. "A fussy baby is better than no baby at all—especially when you can give them back after a couple of hours."

"That's what Susan said," Jenny replied. "She told me that since she doesn't have any grandkids yet, she needs to get her baby fix with Steve. If that means I get to have a peaceful dinner, then who am I to argue?"

"You got that right," Zack muttered.

Hailey's mother clasped her hands together. "Well, we had a productive afternoon."

"Really?" Jenny asked. "Do tell."

"First we went to see Luis's wife again to update her. That was sad, but at least we got to tell her that we found Luis's necklace."

"She must have been happy about that," Jenny noted.

"She was. It made up for the fact that we had to inform her that her husband was the target of a hate crime." Hailey's mother shook her head and continued, "While we were there, Hailey felt the need to get in the car and go somewhere else. The place we ended up was this lake house where the gun used to kill Lizette Micheaux was found."

"You're kidding," Jenny said with awe.

"We didn't know that at the time, though," Leslie added. "All we knew was that she was led to this house—the crawlspace, specifically. She found some blood on a crossbeam under the house, and we figured it must have been related to the cases somehow, so we called Detective Spicer. He let us know that the murder weapon had been found in that crawlspace, but he had to have another detective come out and investigate it. Since it was outside city limits, it was a different jurisdiction.

"Anyway," she went on, "it was raining cats and dogs outside, so we waited until the storm passed to go under the house. While we waited, the owner of the house came out, so we got the chance to talk to him. Long story short, Hailey was able to determine the blood belonged to Cody, who hit his head on the crossbeam while hiding the gun in the crawlspace. When she mentioned Cody's name, the owner of the house, Edward Williams, knew exactly who that was. Edward, Gordon, Keegan and Cody had all worked on the same construction crew together, and Lizette had been their secretary."

"Regency Construction," Jenny said with a knowing smile.

Leslie's eyes grew wide. "You already know this?"

"Some of it," Jenny replied, "but I want you to keep going."

"Keegan, Cody and Randy had apparently killed Lizette and then hid the gun under the crawlspace, knowing the cabin was a place where Gordon had hung out many times. Then, they phoned in a tip, telling the police that's where the gun could be found."

"They phoned in a tip?" Jenny asked.

"Somebody did," Leslie clarified. "We can only assume it was them. Who else would have known the gun was there?"

"I assume that was an anonymous tip," Zack added.

"I'm sure it was; otherwise, they would have been questioned. As it was, they testified against Gordon in court, saying they saw Gordon and Lizette fighting shortly before she went missing."

"That much I knew," Jenny replied.

"How do you know this?" Leslie asked.

"I visited Gordon in prison this afternoon. He told me that Keegan and Cody testified against him and then quit shortly after. Where they went, nobody knows."

"Well, the good news is that the detective that came out to the cabin took a sample of the bloodstain; she's going to submit it for DNA analysis. If it can be identified as Cody's blood, that would put him at the place where the gun had been found. The detective said that if Cody's blood can be found at the lake house and Lizette's blood can be found in Cody's neighbor's apartment, that's pretty good evidence that he's guilty."

"That's spectacular," Jenny said genuinely. "I will be so happy when Gordon can get out of jail, and evidence is what we need to make that happen."

"You visited him today…" Hailey's mother began. "How are his spirits?"

"Broken. It's such a shame, too, because he seems like a nice guy. But I don't blame him, really. I couldn't imagine spending all that time in jail for something I didn't do—especially right after losing a loved one." Jenny shook her head. "Did they give a time frame on that DNA analysis of the bloodstain?"

"No, they didn't," Leslie replied, "but we didn't ask, either. The detective did say she wanted to get it processed as soon as possible. Cody and Keegan have already shown they are capable of killing more than once, and she wanted to make sure we got him before they did it again."

Jenny lowered her head and released a big sigh. "Apparently," she began slowly, "they've even started killing more than one person at a time."

"There are more?" Hailey's mother asked with horror.

Jenny closed her eyes. "I get the impression that Keegan, Cody and Randy are responsible for a church bombing. It seems they targeted a church with an African-American congregation."

"A *church bombing*?" Leslie also hung her head. "Please tell me the church was empty when it happened."

"I wish I could," Jenny said solemnly.

Leslie let out a sound that expressed her disgust. "How many people were killed in that?"

"I don't know," Jenny confessed. "I only saw it happen; I think it was through Ebony's eyes."

"Do you know when or where...?"

"No, I don't know any details. I heard the word *Middletown* in my head, but do you know how many states have a Middletown? I'm not even sure that helps us narrow it down. And when I researched church bombings in Middletown, I came up empty."

"Huh," Hailey's mother remarked. "Strange."

"I know," Jenny replied. "I gave the information to Kyle, the private investigator, and I'm hoping he can come up with something." She rubbed her temples and added, "And I hope he tells us that nobody was killed in the blast."

Jenny's phone rang from inside her purse, so she raised her finger to the table, implying they should hang on a minute. She saw that Detective Spicer was calling, so she eagerly said, "Hello?"

"Hi, Jenny, it's Detective Spicer. Listen, we got a last name on Keegan and Cody."

Jenny felt her eyes grow wide. "Wow. That's huge."

"They're brothers, and their last name is McDermott. We got that through the court records from when they testified. I just found this out a second ago, so we haven't done anything with that information yet. I just wanted you to know in case it triggered something."

"Thank you," Jenny replied. "That's good information."

"Now, if you'll excuse me, I have some assholes to find."

Jenny smiled and said goodbye. Looking up at the rest of the table, she announced, "McDermott. Keegan and Cody are brothers, apparently, and their last name is McDermott."

"Have they found them?" Zack asked.

"No," Jenny replied with a shake of her head. "That was Detective Spicer. He was just letting me know they were able to determine their last name from the court records. Now I can at least pass that information along to Kyle, whose chances of finding them have just gone way up."

"Unless they're using aliases," Zack pointed out.

Jenny flashed an unhappy look in Zack's direction. "Don't rain on my parade."

Zack just shrugged and looked around. "Are we ever going to get served? I'm starving."

Ignoring her husband's comment, Jenny added, "I'm going to call Kyle right now. The sooner he has this information, the better."

Without waiting another minute, Jenny dialed Kyle. "I've got some good information for you," she said the moment he picked up.

"Oh, yeah? Hit me."

"A last name. Keegan and Cody McDermott. They're brothers."

"Excellent," Kyle replied, sounding as if he was writing that down. "That should point me in the right direction."

"I certainly hope so."

"Well, I've been doing my best to tie church bombings to the name Middletown, and, try as I might, I just can't do it. I decided to take a different approach and just look into church bombings. I've got some information about ones that have happened in the last few years. Now...you say you saw this bombing in a vision?"

"Yes, that's right."

"What did the church look like?"

Jenny closed her eyes tightly as she recalled the image. "I saw it from the inside...from above, like I was on the ceiling looking down. I knew what was about to happen, and I desperately wished I could have gotten everyone out of there...especially the people closest to where the bomb was." Jenny shook her head rapidly, realizing she wasn't answering his question. "Anyway, the church had red carpet, and it must have been tall, because I was high up. It had a big stage area with three giant wooden crosses behind it."

"You can stop now," Kyle replied. "I know which one you're talking about."

Jenny felt a nervous buzz throughout her whole body.

"Eastwood Baptist in Falmouth, North Carolina," Kyle replied.

"Eastwood Baptist in Falmouth, North Carolina," Jenny repeated, mostly in an attempt to remember the name.

"Yes, ma'am. It was subject to a bombing a year and a half ago." He lowered his tone. "It was a bad one. The bomb went off during services."

Jenny put her elbow on the table and rested her forehead in her free hand. She didn't say anything, simply because there was nothing to say.

"Six dead, thirty-seven injured," Kyle went on.

Hate bubbled under Jenny's skin. These people were in a *church*. There was no act more decent than that. And yet, they were brutally murdered for being there. "Okay," Jenny said slowly and deliberately. "I want you to get off the phone with me, and I want you to find Keegan and Cody McDermott...*now*."

"On it," Kyle said. He hung up without saying goodbye.

Jenny pressed the end button to the call, reluctant to tell everybody what she'd just learned. She paused, dropping her phone back into her purse, unable to bring herself to say the words.

"I'm assuming, based on your reaction, that the news wasn't good," Leslie said.

"No," Jenny said slowly, "it most definitely was *not* good." She glanced over at Hailey, who had busied herself with her phone and appeared to be oblivious to the conversation around her. Jenny was glad to see that; Hailey didn't need to hear something quite so horrible. "The bomb went off during services," she added softly, trying to keep Hailey in her technology trance. "Something like six dead and thirty-five injured."

"Wait a minute," Leslie replied, "I remember that. It was on the news. Wasn't that at Christmas time a couple of years ago?"

Christmas time. Jenny hadn't thought about that. But if Kyle said it was a year and a half ago, and it was currently June, that math added up that way. Suddenly, the unthinkable became even more tragic. "Yes," Jenny replied, "that's the one."

Leslie shook her head. "It was awful. I remember seeing the story and thinking, 'Who on earth would do such a thing?' I guess now I know."

"Some people have no souls, I guess," Jenny muttered.

"There is some good news in this, though," Zack said.

Jenny flashed a strange look at her husband. "What do you mean?"

"Well, we have a last name, we have a location and we have a time frame. Shouldn't that make Keegan and Cody a lot easier to find?"

That sounded good, but Jenny could see a hole in the theory. "They didn't necessarily have to live in the area of the church bombing. They could have planted it there and driven away."

"No," Hailey said, "they lived there." Glancing up from her phone, she added, "In fact, they lived very close to the church."

Chapter 23

"Wait," Jenny said to Hailey. "What?"

"They lived close to the church," Hailey explained. "Close enough for their house to shake when the bomb went off."

"How do you know this?" Jenny asked.

"Look," Hailey replied, handing the phone over to Jenny. "This picture was taken from the scene of the bombing."

Jenny glanced at Hailey's phone screen, which had zoomed in on Keegan and Cody's faces among the crowd. Her eyes went wide, but she didn't reply.

"The article also quoted some neighbors who said they wanted to remain anonymous," Hailey continued. "Why would anyone refuse to give their name unless they had something to hide? I figure it has to be them."

With her eyebrows down, Jenny scrolled through the article, which did quote anonymous neighbors describing the blast. "Good find," she eventually said. "Very good find, indeed." Handing the phone back to Hailey, she once again grabbed her own phone. "Let me call Kyle back. This is good information. And then I'll tell Detective Spicer—he needs to know this, too."

"And I'm going to go find a server," Zack said as he stood up. "I'm about to eat my arm." He disappeared around a corner.

After filling Kyle in on the latest news, she dialed Detective Spicer, who asked her, "Any chance you'd be willing to head down there and see what Falmouth has to offer? We've apparently got six new victims who might have something interesting to say."

Zack returned with a waiter who was saying something to the table, but Jenny kept her attention focused on the phone conversation. "I think that can be arranged," she told the detective. "I'm not exactly sure where Falmouth is, other than North Carolina, but no matter where it is in that state, it can't be too far from Richmond." She pointed at the menu, showing the waiter what she wanted, nodding and smiling to express her gratitude.

"Thanks," the detective replied. "The sooner we catch these bastards, the better. I'm going to call the police department down there and have them circulate the pictures of Keegan and Cody. Hopefully, somebody will have some information on their whereabouts. But in case that person with the information is not currently alive, I want you down there as well."

"Got it," Jenny replied. She said goodbye to Detective Spicer and got off the phone. Turning to the Newcombs, she asked, "How do you feel about going down there tomorrow? To Falmouth, I mean, to check out the church and the area around it."

Glancing over at Hailey, Leslie replied, "That's okay with me. Are you up for that?"

"I'm fine with it," Hailey said with a nod.

"Good." Jenny held up her hand and spoke to Hailey. "As always, if it gets to be bad, you can leave…but I have the feeling you'll get spared the worst of it. I'll be there with you, so if there's anything gruesome to relay, I imagine the spirits will save that for me." Directing her attention toward everybody, she added, "Detective Spicer said he'll get some officers in Falmouth to circulate the pictures of Keegan and Cody right away, and hopefully that will lead to their capture. But there are six people who can't tell the detectives what they know, and that's where we come in. One of those six might hold the key to finding them, and we are the only ones who can hear what they have to say."

"Do you think Keegan and Cody still live around there?" Leslie asked.

"I tend to doubt it," Jenny reasoned. "They seem to travel around. They stay in an area long enough to do some damage, and then they move on to the next unsuspecting place."

"How are we going to figure out where they've gone?" Leslie added. "Some people in Falmouth might be able to recognize them, but that won't do any good if they've moved on to a new place without telling anyone."

A horrifying thought hit Jenny all at once. She looked off in the distance with wide eyes, declaring, "They've gone to Middletown."

Nobody at the table said anything, so Jenny continued, "Ebony said the word 'Middletown' when she clued me in about the church bombing. I thought she was trying to tell me that the bombing had been in Middletown, but that clearly wasn't it." She rested her elbow on the table and rubbed her forehead. "I think she was trying to tell me the *next* church bombing will be in Middletown."

"Oh, dear," Leslie muttered.

After a long sigh, Jenny closed her eyes and asked, "Do you think we can leave for Falmouth tonight? I'm not sure we have much time to waste."

"I'm worried about the baby," Jenny told Zack as they drove into Falmouth.

"Why, because three adult women fawning over him is not going to be enough attention?" Zack replied. "He'll be fine."

The GPS spit out some instructions, which Jenny followed. "I'm just wondering if we should have brought him."

"He was half asleep. He's much better off spending the night uninterrupted with your mother than he would be with us, driving all over the place. Besides, we shouldn't be gone too long."

Jenny didn't say any more about it. In her mind, she knew he was right. Her heart, however, was a different matter.

"There's the church," Jenny told Zack after a few minutes. "Thank goodness. I'm tired and ready to get out of this car."

"It looks like the pastor is already here," Zack replied as they pulled in the parking lot. "Think the Newcombs will be here soon?"

"It shouldn't be too long," Jenny said. "They were right behind us for a good part of the trip."

Jenny pulled into a space and the couple got out of the car. Less than a minute later, a second car pulled into the lot. Everybody gathered in between the cars, where a tall man extended his hand and introduced himself. "I'm Mike Huff, but everyone just calls me Pastor Mike."

The rest of the group introduced themselves as well, and Pastor Mike continued, "Thank you all for coming down here. I know it wasn't a short drive for you."

"We're just happy to help," Jenny replied. "What happened here was horrific, and we want to make sure it never happens again."

"You got that right," Pastor Mike muttered. "It was, by far, the worst day of my life."

"You've rebuilt, though," Zack said, causing Jenny to look over at the church. With flood lights aimed at it from every direction, the building was lit up so well she could see every detail. "It looks good. This couldn't have been quick or easy."

"It was neither," Pastor Mike confirmed.

"It looks similar to the old church, but not exactly the same," Jenny noted.

"We modernized a bit," the pastor replied. "We, as a congregation, decided we should honor the old church by keeping the look, but we also decided to show we are stronger than ever. We didn't just rebuild—we rebuilt better."

"That's awesome," Zack said.

"You know what else is awesome?" Pastor Mike began. "The fact that you all drove down here because you can hear from the dead, and the dead have been telling you who did this. I saw the sketches of the two individuals you think are responsible; unfortunately, they didn't look familiar to me."

"Hopefully, someone will recognize them," Jenny said, "and 'that someone' will know where they are now."

"They do need to pay for what they've done," Pastor Mike replied. "They shattered the lives of some amazing families." He shook his head. "And they best not do this to anyone else."

A quick, undefinable wave came and went; it didn't tell Jenny anything other than she was capable of receiving messages here. "I just got something. I'm not sure what, but somebody is trying to tell me something. That's often how it starts," Jenny informed Pastor Mike. "Give me a little time, and I will hopefully get the message more clearly."

"Well, would you like to come inside?" Pastor Mike asked. "Maybe that will help."

"That'd be great," Jenny said.

Pastor Mike led them up the steps and in through the massive front doors. What was dark, at first, became illuminated with the flick of a switch, revealing a beautiful room with high ceilings and an elaborate stage—with a flat-screen TV behind it.

"You've gone high-tech," Zack said.

"I told you," Pastor Mike replied, "similar, but better. I have power points to accompany my sermons now, which I post after the service for the people who can't attend. Some of the older parishioners like that, since their health doesn't always allow them to come." He playfully nudged Hailey with his elbow. "Although, they usually need somebody about your age to play it for them."

Hailey simply smiled awkwardly.

Feeling a sudden urge, Jenny wordlessly walked away from the crowd and toward a shrine that had been set up on the left side of the church. Having seen the explosion through Ebony's eyes, she knew this was where the bomb had detonated. The three rows of pews closest to the explosion were shorter than the rest, meaning nobody could sit where the victims had sat. Instead, a beautiful, giant—and presumably fake—flower arrangement was where the seats would have been. Six statue angels flanked the stained glass window; one of the statues was wearing a small fancy hat that somebody had clearly made specifically for that angel.

Warmth encompassed Jenny like a blanket. Gesturing toward the shrine, she said, "I feel happiness here. Somebody clearly approves of this." She closed her eyes, adding, "It's spec-tacular," saying it as if *spectacular* was actually two words.

"What did you just say?" Pastor Mike asked.

"I said, it's spec-tacular," Jenny repeated with a smile. Based on his reaction, she had clearly struck a nerve with those words.

Pastor Mike said something too softly for Jenny to hear, his eyes blinking away tears.

Jenny approached the group again. "I assume that means something to you."

Clearing his throat, Pastor Mike pulled himself together as he replied, "Miss Evelyn. Evelyn Wright. She was one of the six victims." With a point, he gestured toward the statues. "See that one over there with the hat? That one's Miss Evelyn. She was always here, every Sunday, always in a beautiful hat. And then she'd have half the congregation over to her house after the service for some good old fashioned southern cooking." He looked off into the distance as he added, "She was everybody's honorary Grandma, and she could sure make some mean biscuits." He shook his head quickly as he appeared to return to the present. "Anyway, she used to say spec-tacular all the time, and she'd say it just like that. Spec-tacular. Everything was spec-tacular." With an awestruck expression, he asked Jenny, "Can you talk to her?"

"Well, I mostly just listen," Jenny replied.

"You listen," he repeated. "And you heard her say spec-tacular?"

"Heard it, felt it, just kind of knew it," Jenny said. "It's difficult to explain. But what I can say for sure is that she's pleased with the shrine over there. You've saved her seat." With a smile and a soft tone, she added, "I do believe she's still here every Sunday, in that very same spot."

After sucking in and releasing a long breath, Pastor Mike replied, "That was her seat. She was one of the first ones here every week, and she always took that seat by the window."

"Is it the same spot?" Zack asked. "Like, the exact same spot? Did you rebuild on the same foundation?"

"We sure did," Pastor Mike said with a mixture of pride and defiance. "We didn't move an inch. Someone clearly wanted us to leave, but we won't let fear dictate where we go. This is our space—our place to worship." His smile grew broad. "Nobody even left the congregation."

"How long did it take you to rebuild?" Zack asked.

"Fourteen months. This building is quite new, actually. In between, we were graciously offered space in the local high school to conduct our services."

Looking around, Zack added, "This must have cost a pretty penny."

"We had insurance," Pastor Mike replied with a smirk. "But we also had donations pouring in from all over the country. We had enough money to rebuild with improvements, give some money to the school for letting us use their facility and give some extra to charity. See, through all this ugliness, some beauty came through. We saw the hateful act of one or two, but then we saw the love of many. Love definitely wins."

"I'm impressed by how you're handling this," Jenny noted.

"Well, you have to consider their motive," the pastor explained. "Yes, they wanted to kill us...and for some of us, they did. But I'm sure they wanted the rest of us to move away. To disband. To become consumed with hate and negative feelings. No, we can't give them the satisfaction of watching all that come true. In fact, what happened was the opposite. The Sunday after the bombing, we all stood in the parking lot and worshipped. We needed God more than ever that day. We prayed for the injured. We prayed for the deceased. We prayed for the bombers—that they would see the light and not do this to anyone else. We are a stronger congregation now than we ever were before." He raised his eyebrows and added, "And now we have outdoor lighting, security cameras and an alarm system."

"Good call," Zack noted.

"We won't let them stop us, but we're also not foolish," the pastor remarked.

"So," Jenny began, speaking to Hailey, "are you feeling anything?"

"I did outside, but not so much in here," Hailey replied.

Jenny nodded. "Me, too. I mean, I got the message from Miss Evelyn, but the closest thing I had to a lead was outside." She smiled at Pastor Mike, adding, "You may not know this, my friend, but you have an angel on your side."

"I believe I have six angels on my side," he replied.

Jenny shook her head. "Seven. There is a young woman from Richmond named Ebony Carter—a beautiful, gifted seventeen year old who fell victim to these same monsters—and she's looking out for you."

"She's looking out for us?" Pastor Mike asked.

"Very much so," Jenny replied. After a pause where she gathered her thoughts, she eventually added, "Ebony is the one who tied this all together. She was here when the bombing happened." She gazed and pointed toward the high ceiling. "She was up there, knowing the bomb was outside. The poor girl was aware of what was about to happen but was helpless to do anything about it. She could only watch as the chaos unfolded." Jenny shook her head. "But now she's not helpless anymore. She has people who can hear her, and she's led us here to you. She must be keeping tabs on the people who did this, trying to stop them. She has clued me in on the name 'Middletown,' which I believe is their next destination—and by destination, I mean target. We've got police and private investigators trying to figure out which *Middletown* that refers to; of course, there are many. But we're down here in the middle of the night trying to get any information we can about the people who did this, hoping Ebony and the others can clue us in on something that the living can't."

"Wow," Pastor Mike said. "And what happened to Ebony?"

"She was ambushed—attacked from behind," Jenny replied, "and taken to a house where she was killed. That same house was the scene of many more murders; all of the victims were minorities. We are under the impression that the people who lived in that house are the same ones responsible for this bombing." Jenny reached in her purse and pulled out her phone. After a couple of taps and swipes, she handed it over to Pastor Mike. "These two. There was a third accomplice, but we don't know what he looks like yet, and we don't know for sure if he was tied to this incident or not. But do these guys look familiar to you?"

"I saw this picture earlier today," the pastor replied with a shake of his head. "No, they don't look familiar to me."

"Wait," Jenny said, suddenly feeling dumb. "You said that earlier, didn't you?"

"That's okay," Pastor Mike replied. "I'd rather see the picture twice than not at all."

"Sorry." Jenny shook her head as she put her phone away. "It's been a long day."

"No need to apologize. So, should we go back outside?" Pastor Mike asked. "You say that's where you felt something."

"Sounds good to me," Jenny said. They all headed back out the front door. "We should go to where the bomb was. I think that will give us the best shot at tracing their steps."

"There's a little memorial garden at the spot," Pastor Mike replied as they descended the steps. "You can't miss it."

With the outdoor lights illuminating the church like day, it wasn't hard to navigate the grounds to go around to the side. Just as the pastor had described, there was a small garden with plants and six plaques in the ground, right up against the building. As Jenny took a moment to admire the shrine, she felt a pull coming from the direction of the street. At about that time, she heard Hailey say, "That way." Looking up, she saw Hailey with her finger pointed toward the main road in the darkness. "Whatever it is we're looking for is that way."

Chapter 24

"I feel that, too," Jenny agreed. "I'm not sure what we'll find there, but that's the direction to go."

"I know what's down there," Pastor Mike said. "You're pointing in the direction of the abandoned barn where the bomb was apparently built or temporarily stored. Dogs were able to trace the scent from this spot to the barn, but then after that, they got confused. It appears whoever used the barn was familiar with the ways to throw off scent dogs."

"How do you throw off a scent dog?" Hailey's mother asked.

"Forgive me for saying this," Pastor Mike began, "but detectives believe he urinated all around the barn in a circle so that his scent was actually everywhere. He didn't try to disguise his scent, but he made it impossible to follow a path back to him. He may have also used pepper or pepper spray; that throws off dogs as well."

"It may throw off dogs, but I doubt it will deter Ebony," Jenny said. "You've got a ringer on your side now. Is that barn within walking distance?"

"It's within walking distance, but I'm not sure it's good walking terrain. It's set back off the road quite a ways, and I'm not sure what we'll encounter in the tall grass in the dark."

"Maybe we can just stand along the road in front of it," Hailey suggested. "That may be good enough."

"I agree," Jenny said. "I am definitely feeling a pull to go that direction. I have to follow it and see what it shows me."

With Hailey and Zack turning on their flashlights on their phones, the group headed toward the source of the tug. They walked along the main road for only a short time before Hailey announced, "This is where it ends for me. Well, at least the road part."

The same was true for Jenny, but she didn't feel the need to repeat it.

"Yeah, it's almost a direct shot across the street," Pastor Mike explained. "You can see the barn from the church, although it's distant."

"You never saw anyone walking in and out of it?" Zack asked.

"Nope," Pastor Mike replied, "but I never looked, either. It was just an old, abandoned barn. They're everywhere around here. I also never saw anyone parked along the road. We would have noticed the cars sitting there. This road isn't designed for parking, so that would have seemed out of place."

"So, it could be that the bombers accessed the barn from a different direction, or the bomb was just stored there temporarily," Zack said more like a statement than a question. "I imagine that once you have a completed bomb made, you wouldn't want to keep it in your house."

"Could be," Pastor Mike agreed. "Like I said, the dogs went from the church to the barn, and then they started going in circles. They weren't able to figure out where the bomb was before that."

"Did it look like a workshop in there?" Zack asked.

"No," the pastor said, "it looked like an abandoned barn in there."

"Um…" Hailey began in a tone that lacked confidence. "I want to keep going, but I don't know how far."

A brief moment of silence was followed by Leslie asking, "Keep going…you mean into the field?"

"No, I mean along the road," Hailey clarified, "but I don't know if we should walk or drive."

This time, Jenny wasn't feeling the same sensation, so she wasn't able to add any insight.

"Driving is probably safest," Zack said. "I can run and get the car real quick if you want."

"That'd be great," Jenny replied. "Thanks, hon."

Zack trotted off and returned with the car a moment later. Getting out, he handed Jenny the keys and suggested, "You should probably drive."

"That's a small car," Pastor Mike noted, "and I'm a tall man."

"You get shotgun, then," Jenny said, getting into the driver's seat.

The others climbed in with Hailey taking the middle seat in the back. "Go straight, Hailey?" Jenny asked with a turn of the key.

"Yes. I don't know how long, but straight for now."

The car moved forward, and Jenny began to feel the tug. "Wait, I've got it now." They drove toward an intersection; Jenny put her left blinker on, knowing that was the direction to go.

After another left turn, they were on a road that ran parallel to the street the church was on. Headed back in the direction of the church and barn, Jenny eventually saw a lone house with its porch light on. She knew this was her destination.

At about the same time, Hailey's finger came through from the back seat. "Up there," she said, pointing to the same house Jenny just saw. "The brick one on the left."

"One step ahead of you," Jenny replied.

They pulled up along the house and sat in front of it. "Check this out," Zack said from the back seat. He showed Hailey his phone, noting, "It's a direct shot from this house to the church and the barn. You've just got to head through the woods a little bit, and you're at the barn."

"Wow," was all Hailey said.

"Think this is where the lovely McDermott brothers stayed?" Jenny asked, looking out the window at the house.

"I imagine so," Zack replied. "If this was their house, it would have been easy for them to plant the bomb and head back home on foot."

"It would also explain why there were never any cars around the abandoned barn, even though it appeared the barn had something to do with it," Pastor Mike added.

"Wouldn't the police have looked here?" Leslie asked. "I mean, it's so close and obvious."

"The police looked everywhere," the pastor explained, "and I do mean everywhere. There just wasn't a whole lot to go on."

"Who worked on this case?" Jenny asked.

"The local police worked with the FBI. This was considered a hate crime, which qualified it for federal investigation."

"Well, we can start with the local police and let them know they should look into this house a little more," Jenny decided. "I'll also shoot Kyle a text with the address and see what he can find out about it. Hailey and I both felt pulled here, so there must be something to it."

"This is Strathmore Street," the pastor said. "It looks like the house number is 5547, according to the mailbox."

"Got it," Jenny said as she typed a text to Kyle. Quickly setting it down after hitting send, she asked, "Now, how do you get to the police station?"

"Go straight up here until you get to the stop sign," Pastor Mike told Jenny with a point, "and then you'll take a right."

"No," Hailey said mechanically, "go straight through the stop sign."

"What?" Jenny asked.

"We need to go straight and stay straight for a while," Hailey told her. "There is something else we need to see."

Chapter 25

"Do you have any idea what?" Leslie asked.

"No," Hailey replied with a shake of her head. "I just know it's something."

Jenny wasn't feeling the pull, so she looked up into her rearview mirror and focused on Hailey. "Just let me know which way to go, okay?"

"Okay," she replied awkwardly.

The rest of the car remained silent as Hailey guided Jenny through the outskirts of town. Jenny didn't feel any tug at all, so she was entirely reliant on Hailey. Eventually, Hailey made the declaration, "Here. It stops here."

They were in front of a lone house surrounded by trees. "This house?" Jenny asked with a point.

"Yes, that's the place."

"Any idea what significance this has?" Jenny asked. "This time, I'm not feeling it."

"None," Hailey replied apologetically.

"I guess the best we can do is note the address," Jenny said. "Zack, have you been following this on a map?"

"Yup. We're on Bugler Trail, it looks like."

They jotted down the house number and turned around, this time following the pastor's directions to the police station. By the time they arrived, it was after midnight, and station looked largely deserted. They all got out of the car and shuffled through the doors, where an officer who was younger than Jenny sat behind a desk.

Younger than Jenny. This was happening more and more lately, and she didn't like it.

"Hello," the officer said with a smile, "what brings you in here tonight? Oh, hi, Pastor Mike."

"Hi, Officer Bradley," the pastor replied. "They've got you on the night shift, now?"

The officer shrugged. "Whatever pays the bills."

"Don't I know it," Pastor Mike said. "Well, you may not believe what I'm about to tell you, but these people have come down from Richmond, Virginia to help us identify the bomber…or bombers, as it appears in this case. They're psychics," the pastor continued. "Well, at least, two of them are. I have to say, it's been fascinating to watch them in action."

He looked at the pastor skeptically but didn't say anything.

After introducing the group to the policeman, Pastor Mike explained, "Officer Bradley worked on the bombing, as did every cop on the force, if I'm not mistaken."

Finally speaking, Officer Bradley said, "You got that right. It was by far the biggest crime Falmouth has ever seen, and I hope we never see one that big again." He folded his arms and leaned back in his chair. "So, two of these people are psychics?"

"Jenny and Hailey are the psychics," Pastor Mike continued, pointing them out. "And they both think there's something to that brick house on Strathmore. Who lived there at the time?"

"The two guys from the sketches," Officer Bradley replied, causing a chill to go up Jenny's spine. He pulled up a printout of the drawings, adding, "Keegan and Cody McDermott."

"Wait…" Zack said, "McDermott?"

Officer Bradley shifted his gaze toward Zack. "Yeah…you know them?"

"Yeah, we know them," Zack replied, "but we know them by a different name. We know them as Keegan and Cody Lewis."

"They testified in court under that name," Jenny added. "I would assume that means their real last name has to be Lewis, doesn't it? Wouldn't that information be verified?"

The young officer just shrugged, asking, "So, if you guys know the Lewises or the McDermotts or whoever they are, can you tell us where they are now?"

"We don't know," Jenny said. "That's what we're trying to find out."

"Okay, forgive me for asking this," the officer began, "but where does the psychic ability come in? I mean, you know the guys from the sketches and you know where they lived. That doesn't require ESP."

"I drew the sketches," Jenny explained. "I made them back in Virginia, before I ever knew that the brothers lived here or had anything to do with the bombing. These two are responsible for some terrible things in Richmond, and we're just following their trail—which, so far, ends on Strathmore Street."

Still looking skeptical, Officer Bradley said, "Let me call the chief. I'll see what he has to say." Picking up the phone, he turned his back to the group, leaving everyone to themselves in the lobby.

"He doesn't seem all that warm to us," Leslie whispered.

"Hopefully the chief will be more receptive," Zack replied.

They waited in silence for a short moment before Officer Bradley returned his attention back to them. "Chief Renkin said he's coming. He asked you all to wait in the meeting room." He pointed to a door on the side of the lobby. "I'll let you in over there; just give me a second."

After disappearing from behind the desk, the young officer reappeared in the doorway. With a sweeping gesture of his arm, he said, "If you'll follow me..." He led them down a narrow hallway, around a corner and into a sterile, white room with a long mahogany table down the middle. "Go ahead and have a seat; the chief should be here in about ten minutes."

The group all sat down in the office chairs that surrounded the table; some sat more gracefully than others. Jenny's motion was more of a plop; her fatigue was getting the best of her. She folded her arms onto the table, resting her head on them, hoping she could sneak in a power nap while they waited.

She did feel herself start to doze just as the chief walked in. He was an older gentleman with white hair surrounding a bald spot on the top of his head. He looked rather tired himself, like he'd been woken by the phone call asking him to come out.

"Good evening, everyone," he announced as he entered. Slipping his phone out of his pocket and checking the time, he added, "Actually, good morning. Thank you all for being here."

The group all muttered hellos to the chief as he took a seat at the head of the table. Jenny nonchalantly wiped a spot of drool from the corner of her mouth.

"I'm Chief Renkin," he said, dropping a manila folder on the table in front of him. "I appreciate you making the trip down from Richmond. I understand you are responsible for the sketches we received earlier today?"

"Yes, sir," Jenny said.

"I'm glad you're here, actually," Chief Renkin replied. "I want to find out a little more about these sketches. Can you fill me in on how they came to be?"

Jenny recounted the story, which included the brother's affiliation with Purify America and ended with Ebony's vision from inside the doomed church. "We were able to figure out that the bombing she saw was the one here in Falmouth, which is what brought us here tonight. Hailey—who is also a psychic," Jenny explained with a point, "and I were both led to the house on Strathmore Street, without us knowing that the brothers had lived there. And then Hailey got pulled to a house on Bugler Trail; we don't know what that's about yet, but it's clearly something."

"Hmmph," the chief said with his eyebrows down. "I don't think Bugler Trail ever came up in the investigation, but the house on Strathmore certainly did. We looked into the brothers," he added, holding up the folder, "but they obviously didn't rouse too much suspicion, based on how thin this is." He opened the folder and pulled reading glasses out of his shirt pocket, sliding them onto his face. "We combed through this earlier today when we saw the sketches. A set of scent dogs led to their house, but there was a plausible explanation for that." Holding up his hand, he said, "I should back up. The first set of scent dogs led from the church to the barn. Are you all familiar with the barn?" He peered over his glasses.

"They are," Pastor Mike said. "They were led there first."

"Excellent. Well, then, the first set of dogs went to the barn, but they couldn't follow a trail after that. A second set of dogs started at the barn the next day, and they went through the woods to the house on Strathmore. We questioned the two brothers who lived there, and they explained that they often brought their dog to the barn and let him run loose in the field that surrounds it. They didn't deny that their scent would be all over the place back there, and it would lead right to their back door—which it did. We brought in some bomb sniffing dogs, who followed a trail from the barn through the woods, *past* the house on Strathmore and to the street itself. We concluded that the people who planted the bomb parked on Strathmore and carried it into the barn for storage until they were ready to use it. The brothers had reported seeing a red Mazda parked on the road a couple of times, but we never could find a car matching that description, despite an exhaustive search."

"There was no car matching that description," Jenny found herself saying in at tone more bitter than she had intended. She was simply too tired to use her politeness filter.

"What do you mean?" Chief Renkin asked.

"There was no car," she repeated. "They were just saying that to throw you off, I'm sure. Those two are notorious for being witnesses to things that didn't occur."

The chief remained silent for a moment, tracing his finger back and forth along his lip. "If there was no Mazda," he began slowly, "and the brothers were responsible for building the bomb, why didn't the dogs lead us to their house?"

"Because," Hailey began in a tiny voice, "the bomb was built in the house on Bugler Trail."

"How do you know that, honey?" Leslie asked her.

Looking apologetic, she replied, "I just do."

The adults at the table exchanged glances. Chief Renkin removed the glasses from his face, placing them upside down on the table. Rubbing his eyes, he softly said, "Tell me about this house."

Zack pulled up his phone, announcing, "It's 13702 Bugler Trail. Give me a second, and I'll tell you a little more about it." He pressed and swiped, ultimately saying, "It was purchased by a Mr. Jason Lattimer in January of last year. Prior to that, it was owned by a construction company for eight months." His eyes circulated the table. "Looks like maybe it was flipped?"

"Who was the construction company?" the chief asked.

"KC Construct…" Zack stopped himself. "KC. As in Keegan and Cody, perhaps?"

"They worked construction in Richmond," Leslie noted, "with Lizette and Gordon, so they certainly had the skill."

Silence filled the room until the chief eventually spoke. "First thing in the morning, I'm going to talk to the landlord that the brothers rented from on Strathmore, and I'm going to see if I can get into that house on Bugler Trail. I will interview people they may have run into, too, like employees at home improvement stores. Somebody, somewhere, has to know who these two are and where they have gone."

"I have a question," Leslie began. "Where are they getting all this money from? Don't you need to have a lot of money as an initial investment to flip a house?"

"You mentioned a hate group," Chief Renkin began, referring to that portion of Jenny's backstory. "Purify America, right?"

Jenny began to feel uneasy; somehow, she knew she wasn't going to like where this was going. "That's correct."

"That name came up in the investigation as possibly being affiliated with the bombing," the chief continued. "The FBI knows a thing or two about that group, although they weren't able to make a connection to this particular case. If the brothers are members, it would explain a few things. That operation is big—bigger than any of us would care to admit—and it's funded."

"Funded?" Zack asked. "What does that mean?"

Letting out a sigh, Chief Renkin replied, "Not everyone is willing to do the dirty work. Not everyone is *capable* of doing the dirty work. But some people are willing to financially back those who are."

Jenny closed her eyes.

"I'm sure the brothers are able to live comfortably off donations, and that's probably how they were provided with the fake IDs as well," the chief concluded.

"Are there really that many people associated with a white supremacist group?" Jenny asked. "In this day and age?"

"Sadly, yes," the chief replied. "You'd be surprised."

Jenny wasn't sure if that made her want to scream or cry. Or both. One thing she did know for sure—it made her want to catch Keegan and Cody.

And spit on them.

"I am a little concerned about something," Pastor Mike began.

"What's that?" the chief asked.

"If these two are serial offenders, and this bombing at our church was not an isolated incident, and they haven't done anything bad in a while...doesn't that mean they due to strike again soon?"

This was Jenny's worst fear, and it didn't help to hear it said out loud.

Nobody answered the question. Instead, the chief closed the folder and spoke in a frighteningly serious whisper. "Go get some sleep," he said to them all. "We'll pick this up in the morning. Tell me your phone numbers, and I'll give you mine. And hopefully, together we can get these two before they do anything drastic."

Chapter 26

As Zack drove to the only hotel in Falmouth, North Carolina, Jenny sent a text to Kyle and put in a call to the Richmond Police Department, letting them know the latest information. Jenny hoped that with all the manpower devoted to these cases of late, they would be solved quickly, and soon she'd be back in Tennessee holding her baby.

As much as Steve drove her crazy sometimes, she didn't feel right when he wasn't with her.

Once at the hotel, Jenny hopped in bed quickly, curling into a ball, hoping Zack wouldn't come at her with that look in his eye. She was simply too tired for any of that, even though they were alone in a hotel room and, in theory, the setting was perfect. Fortunately, Zack seemed to be as tired as Jenny, and he was sound asleep within seconds of hitting the pillow. Once his breathing became heavy, she realized she was off the hook and was able to relax; she soon found herself drifting off to sleep as well.

Friday

The Newcombs and the Larrabees once again met for breakfast in a hotel restaurant, although this one was smaller and less sophisticated than the one in Richmond. The continental breakfast was good enough, however, and the coffee was excellent, so Jenny was perfectly content in the no-name hotel lobby.

"I'm going to call Chief Renkin," she announced once they were all seated. "I'll put him on speaker phone. I know it's only nine, but I am curious if he's found out anything yet this morning."

She dialed his number, placing the phone in the middle of the table. "Hello," the chief said.

"Good morning, Chief Renkin. It's Jenny Larrabee and company. You're on speaker phone."

"I'll mind my manners, then."

Jenny smiled. "Have you gotten anywhere since we saw you last night?"

"I did speak to the landlord of the house on Strathmore. He said the brothers paid cash for the rental, up front. They wanted a nine month lease, which the landlord didn't normally do, but when they offered to pay in cash in advance, he made an exception."

"Wasn't that at all suspicious?" Zack asked.

"In hindsight, sure," the chief replied, "but at the time, no. The brothers said they made their living flipping houses, and they only needed nine months in town to flip the house on Bugler Trail. They always dealt in cash because, unlike most people, they didn't get paychecks. They got lump sums when they sold houses, and then they'd use that cash to fund the next venture."

"Nine months seems like an awfully long time to flip a house," Zack commented.

"Well," the chief replied, "when you're splitting your time between flipping houses and making bombs, I guess it takes a little longer."

"So, when did they move out again?" Jenny asked.

"January," Chief Renkin replied, "and, again, in hindsight, that looks suspicious. But the house on Bugler Trail was done and sold, so they wouldn't have had a reason to stay."

"Any luck on figuring out where they went?" Zack asked.

"I've been trying to find that out," the chief said, "but nobody seems to know. I sent some detectives to every home improvement store in the area. They went nice and early, too, during the hours where contractors usually get the stuff they need for the day. We got precisely nowhere with that. Several of the employees recognized them, but they couldn't tell us anything about them. Those two did a good job of keeping to themselves. They never made small talk with anyone while they were there. It was in, shop, out, done."

"Well, if it makes you feel any better, I have a private investigator working on this, too. He's exceptional at his job, and he got a few more clues to work with, based on our conversation last night. I texted him with the information, but I can give him a call and…"

Her phone made a beeping sound, so she stopped talking and glanced down at the screen. "Speaking of calls," she said, "I'm getting one from the detective in Richmond, Detective Spicer. Do you mind if I take this? It might be important."

"By all means. Just let me know if it's anything noteworthy."

"Thanks, Chief. Will do." Jenny swiped her phone, switching lines. Detective Spicer began by immediately saying, "We got a tip—a credible one—from an employee at a home improvement store in Middletown, South Carolina. She says she recognizes the two guys in the sketches. They come in often."

Jenny's eyes circulated the table. "Middletown, South Carolina," she repeated. "We'll be there as soon as we can."

Today gives new meaning to the phrase, 'Thank God it's Friday,'" Jenny noted as they approached Middletown. "If we can get these two caught before Sunday services…" She stopped talking at that point, reluctant to think about what could have happened if they didn't.

"Why don't you make that call now?" Zack suggested. "I think we're getting close enough."

"Be my fingers," Jenny told him. "I'm driving."

Zack dialed the number that Detective Spicer had given them; this was their contact person for the investigation in South Carolina. A female voice answered the call, simply saying, "Anderson."

"Hi," Jenny began, talking loudly through the car speakers, "My name is Jenny Larrabee; I was given your number…"

"Ah, yes, Ms. Larrabee," she replied. "I recognized the Tennessee area code. Are you on your way?"

"We are, but we're not exactly sure where we should be going."

"Come to the police station, for now," Anderson said. "We got an address on them, and we're devising a plan to capture them. This may not be your typical arrest, so we want to take every precaution to make sure it goes smoothly."

Jenny felt a thousand pounds lift off of her shoulders. A word echoed in her head, and she took great pleasure in repeating it. "That, my friend," she said with a smile, "is spec-tacular."

After a call to the Newcombs, who took a separate car, Zack looked up directions to the Middletown police station. They arrived within fifteen minutes, but they waited in the parking lot for the Newcombs, who were only two minutes behind them.

Getting out of the car with a stretch, Jenny turned to Leslie and Hailey and asked, "Are you ready for this? I, for one, can't wait."

Leslie wore an anxious expression. "I just want it to be over."

They walked into the station, where a woman behind the desk looked up and immediately asked, "Is one of you Jenny?"

"I am," Jenny replied, raising her hand.

The woman looked quite serious as she curtly instructed, "Come this way." She walked quickly as she led the group to a windowed meeting room, which Jenny could see was crawling with people, some of whom were dressed head-to-toe in black SWAT team attire.

This was far more intense than she had been expecting.

"Excuse me, Chief?" the woman said, poking her head into the room. "They're here."

A man who appeared to be the chief simply muttered, "Excellent." He pointed to an officer and then to the door. The chosen policeman stood up without a word and headed out to see the Larrabees and Newcombs.

Once in the hallway, the officer spoke softly. "Hi, I'm Officer Reid."

"Jenny Larrabee," she replied with an outstretched hand. The others introduced themselves as well.

"So it's you two with the ability?" Officer Reid said, pointing back and forth between Jenny and Hailey.

A tug hit Jenny with overwhelming force, as if someone living had grabbed her by the arm and started yanking. "Um, yes," she replied, "and we actually need to go somewhere. Now."

"Where?" Officer Reid asked.

"Don't know yet," Jenny told him. "I'll know when we get there."

"I feel it, too," Hailey admitted. "It's strong."

Jenny nodded. "Maybe one of the strongest pulls I've ever felt." She turned her attention back to Officer Reid. "We need to get in the car and go." Glancing at his hip, she noticed his gun. "Can you come with us?"

"Yes, ma'am," he replied.

"I don't necessarily think you should take a cop car," Zack said. "You may want to just be in a regular car."

The feeling inside Jenny was growing so intense that she was becoming physically uncomfortable. "I'd like to drive, if that's okay," she said as she started to walk. Taking steps in the direction of the pull offered her a little relief.

"I suppose that will be okay," the officer said. "This is all new to me."

"She gets led to places sometimes," Zack explained as they nearly jogged back out the door and into the parking lot. "It's always someplace significant, but she never knows where she's going until she gets there."

"Same with Hailey," Leslie added.

Jenny didn't say a word as she unlocked her car and climbed into the driver's seat. Someone clearly wanted her to get somewhere as quickly as possible.

"Take the passenger seat," Zack told the officer. The other three got into the back, with Hailey sitting in the middle.

Jenny wasted no time pulling out of the lot and heading down the road. "You can ticket me later," she told the officer as she drove uncharacteristically fast through the town. After only a few minutes, she pulled into the parking lot of a plaza, the urge inside her finally starting to settle down.

"It's that one," Hailey said with a point, aiming her finger at the grocery store that was the focal point of the plaza.

"I feel that, too," Jenny agreed. She pulled her car into a parking space and let out a deep exhale.

"You think they're in there?" Officer Reid asked.

"It's quite possible," Jenny told him. Looking over at him with a slight grin, she added, "There's only one way to find out."

"I should call for backup before I go in there," Officer Reid began.

Jenny placed her hand on his arm. "I was actually thinking I should go in there. No offense, but they probably wouldn't react too well to an officer in full uniform. They have no idea who I am; I could go in there and buy gum or something, and they wouldn't know they were being watched."

"Do you have your gun with you?" Zack asked, reaching up and tapping Jenny's shoulder from the back seat.

Jenny closed her eyes. She couldn't believe he's just asked that in front of Officer Reid.

"What?" Zack said, "You're legal. It was just a question."

"No, I don't have my gun," Jenny replied. "Do you think I brought it with me into the police station?"

"True." Zack opened the back door of the car. "Well, then, at least let me go with you. I don't want you going in there alone."

"Should we go too, Mom?" Hailey asked.

Jenny glanced in the rearview mirror to see Leslie's reluctant expression. "I guess," she said with defeat. "Here," she added, handing her phone over to Officer Reid. "We will text you if anything shady starts to happen. The ringer is on."

"Got it," the policeman said with a smirk. "I'm right out here if you need me, and I do have my gun."

Jenny gathered herself for a brief moment before getting out of the car. As the doors slammed shut, Zack noted, "We need to buy something other than gum. Four of us wouldn't come into the store for that."

"Snack food," Leslie suggested. "Like we're about to go on a long car trip. We can each pick up some sort of munchie for the road."

"Sounds good," Jenny replied as they headed through the double doors, which had an ominous feel as they slid open. Once inside, she immediately felt a pull toward the left. "Follow me," she instructed through closed teeth. "And act natural."

They walked at a casual pace in front of the registers. "Where do you think it would be?" Leslie asked.

"I don't know," Jenny replied, assuming Leslie was just making 'natural' conversation. "We'll just have to look down the aisles."

Glancing down the bakery aisle, Jenny was able to see Keegan and Cody putting a loaf of bread in their cart. She cleared her throat and quickly said, "Ooh, doughnuts. That sounds like a winner to me." The group walked halfway down the aisle to the snack food.

"Did you see that?" Zack whispered.

"See what?" Jenny said softly. Raising her voice, she asked, "What do you think? Chocolate or powdered?"

"Chocolate," Hailey replied. "They saw us," she added in a whisper.

"Does that matter?" Jenny asked.

"They *recognized* us," Zack clarified.

"Chocolate sounds good to me." Jenny picked up a box of doughnuts off the shelf. "How could they recognize us? They don't even know who we are."

"Apparently, they do." Zack spoke a little louder than before. "Look," he added with a point.

Jenny glanced up to see their shopping cart abandoned in the aisle. "They left?" she whispered.

"Cody saw us, nudged Keegan, and then Keegan looked at us," Zack told her. "Now they're gone."

"How do they know who we are?" Jenny asked. This didn't make any sense to her.

"I just texted my mom's phone, letting the officer know they're leaving," Hailey said.

"Do you think he'll follow them?" Zack asked.

"Not when I have the keys." Jenny put the doughnuts back on the shelf. "Should we leave now, too? I want to follow them, but I don't want them to know it."

Hailey's phone jingled, and she read the screen, adding, "Officer Reid just saw them run into their car and pull away."

"I guess it's safe to go, then," Zack noted as the group hurried toward the door. "It's going to be hard to follow them, though, if we don't know where they went."

"I can follow them," Hailey announced. "I think someone knows exactly where they are."

"They pulled out of the lot and took a left," Officer Reid said as soon as they all got in the car.

Jenny followed suit, driving far faster than she should have with a cop in the passenger seat, steering with one hand and fastening her seatbelt with the other.

Officer Reid spoke into his shoulder unit. "We're headed east on Davidson."

"Good," Jenny said. "Now we do need that backup."

"I want to make sure they don't skip town," the officer said. "The tipster may not be the only one who has seen their sketches."

"Take a right at the light," Hailey instructed.

Jenny could see Officer Reid turn around and look at Hailey over his shoulder, but he didn't say anything.

Doing as she was told, Jenny turned right.

"We're headed toward the highway on Commerce," Officer Reid said into his shoulder unit.

At that moment, the pull hit Jenny. "I've got it now, Hailey," she said. "Thanks, honey." Taking the westbound ramp onto Interstate 20, she quickly worked her way to the left lane and began to fly past other cars. "Yeah, about that ticket…" Jenny repeated.

"You won't get one from me," Officer Reid replied.

"What are they driving?" Zack asked.

"A gray Ford," the policeman said. "I think it was a Focus."

"I doubt they'll be speeding," Zack added. "They probably don't realize we're following them, and they wouldn't want to risk getting pulled over."

Officer Reid leaned in toward his walkie talkie. "Westbound I 20. Approaching exit 35."

"Units are assembling at exit 24," the voice replied.

"Can they be there in five minutes?" Officer Reid asked.

"One unit is there already."

With that, Jenny relaxed a bit; this wasn't entirely on her anymore. "I'm still feeling the urge to stay on the highway," she said. "Is there anywhere they can get off between here and exit 24?"

"Only one exit," Officer Reid said. "Will you be able to tell if they get off?"

"Probably." Jenny kept following the tug without saying anything else. After passing the only exit the brothers could have taken, she announced, "They stayed on the highway."

"Good," Officer Reid said. Clicking his walkie talkie, he added, "Suspects should be approaching."

After what seemed like forever, the same voice said, "Officers are in pursuit."

"I'll keep following," Jenny said, "just in case they lose them."

Soon, brake lights appeared in all three lanes, and Jenny found herself rolling to a stop. "Uh oh," she muttered.

Two police cars sped past them on the shoulder with their sirens blaring.

"I wonder what's happening," Leslie remarked nervously from the back seat.

They sat in tense silence for what seemed like forever. "I hope everyone's okay," Jenny whispered.

"Me too," Officer Reid said.

Jenny reached over and patted him on the shoulder. To her, these were simply police officers that she was worried about. To him, these were his friends and colleagues. This helplessness had to be harder on him than anyone else in the car.

A lifetime of silence followed. No cars moved. Police cruisers zipped by in the shoulder at lightning speed.

This wait was excruciating.

Then, the magical words came through the walkie talkie.

"Suspects apprehended."

The relief was palpable as cars started rolling forward slowly. "Get over to the right," the officer instructed. Jenny blinkered over and cut a few cars off in the process, but she found her way to the right lane. After a few miles, flashing lights became visible from everywhere. There must have been a dozen police cars sitting along both sides of the road. Cars inched through, most likely going slowly out of curiosity rather than safety. Once Jenny reached the commotion, she pulled over onto the shoulder.

"Stay here," Officer Reid directed as he got out of the car. The rest of the group remained still and quiet, as if they were afraid to move, until Hailey's phone chimed.

"He says it's safe to come out," Hailey told them.

Leslie let out a laugh. "I forgot he still had my phone."

With the car a safe distance from the travel lanes, they all got out and headed toward Officer Reid. He gestured to the back seat of a patrol car, asking, "These two the ones you're looking for?"

Jenny glanced in, looking at the faces of the two hideous human beings she had come to despise. "Yeah, that's them." She resisted the urge to open the door of the car and strangle them.

Cody glared back at her, the expression on his face sending a chill up her spine. His eyes threatened her from behind the glass; his message was unmistakable.

He knew who she was. She had no idea how that was possible, but he clearly knew she was responsible for this.

And he intended to make her pay for it.

Chapter 27

"Here's the house where they were staying," Officer Reid told the group. "As you can see, it's in close proximity to Fifth Baptist Church."

Jenny looked at the modest, unassuming house in front of her and then glanced over her shoulder at the beautiful church down the street. Cars were pulling into the lot of the church; Jenny wasn't sure if those were detectives or parishioners.

"Have you found any evidence against them yet?" Zack asked, pulling Jenny away from her thoughts.

"Not here," Officer Reid replied. "It doesn't appear there's a whole lot to see here. But at the other house? It's a goldmine."

"Were they flipping a house?" Zack asked.

The officer looked at him for a moment, clearly caught off guard by the notion that Zack knew that. "Yeah," he eventually said, "they were rebuilding a house on Buford. Or, at least, that was their front. It looks more like the real reason they were there was to build bombs."

"Bombs?" Jenny asked. "Plural?"

"Six, to be precise," Officer Reid replied. "All with timers."

She took a minute to absorb the information. "Six? They were building *six bombs*?"

"It looks like they didn't just want to do damage," Officer Reid said. "They wanted to destroy the whole building, and, most likely, everyone inside."

Jenny stood frozen, paralyzed by the thought. She looked over at the church, which was both beautiful and blissfully ignorant of the horrible plot against it. That building's days had been numbered, yet it stood there majestically with no idea.

More cars pulled into the parking lot. By the sheer volume, Jenny decided those must have been congregation members. "I'd like to go over there," she said. "I want to meet those people and let them know who saved them." Realizing how she sounded, she added, "I mean Ebony, not me."

"Go ahead," Officer Reid replied with a gesture of his arm. "I'm sure they'd love to meet you all."

"Do you want to come?" Jenny asked the Newcombs.

Leslie turned to Hailey. "Do you want to, honey?"

"Sure, that'd be okay."

The group headed over toward the church, which filled with more cars even during their relatively short walk. Jenny started to get choked up when she saw the people out into the parking lot—people who would have lost their lives if it weren't for Ebony. That beautiful, intelligent girl wanted to be a doctor so she could help people and save lives; it seemed she achieved her goal after all. Jenny blinked away her tears, realizing she would inevitably be crying soon, despite her best efforts to avoid it. This moment was both too victorious and too sad to remain stoic.

"I'm not sure I'm going to be able to handle this well," Leslie admitted as they approached.

"You and me both," Jenny said emphatically.

There must have been a hundred parishioners at the church by the time the group arrived. They were hugging each other and crying, painfully aware of the terrible fate they had escaped. At first, they didn't seem to notice the strangers who had approached them, but soon they were greeted by a man in a suit who said, "Hello, there. And welcome."

"Hi," Jenny said, choking away tears. *Welcome.* This was the opposite of Keegan and Cody's message, and yet, these were the people who nearly lost their lives. Jenny closed her eyes, so grateful at that moment for Ebony's determination to save all of those people.

She heard her husband say the words, "Zack Larrabee," as an introduction. She was appreciative that he took over the conversation; she was finding herself unable to speak. "This is my wife, Jenny, and this is Hailey and Leslie. Jenny and Hailey are the psychics who led the police to the bombers."

The long period of silence caused Jenny to open her eyes. The man stood in awe, looking as if he were battling tears himself, with his hand over his mouth. His emotional reaction did nothing to help Jenny keep her composure.

Gathering himself, the man spoke slowly and eloquently. "There are no words that will adequately reflect my gratitude. I'm Terrell Biggs, the pastor here at Fifth Baptist. You have saved the lives of my entire congregation."

Jenny shook her head, closing her eyes one more time, causing a tear to fall. "It wasn't me. It was a high school student from Richmond named Ebony Carter."

"And a man named Luis Alvarez," Hailey added. "And a woman named Lizette Micheaux."

Jenny opened her eyes again to see a blurry image of Pastor Biggs through her tears. He wasn't saying anything—he probably didn't know what to say.

Thankfully, Zack took over again. "Those three were victims of the same people who planned to bomb your church. They are the ones who guided Jenny and Hailey to Middletown and let them know who was responsible."

"So, you're telling me that you were guided here by the deceased?" the pastor asked.

This time, Hailey answered, which was good, because Jenny still wasn't sure if she could speak. "Yes, sir. We could see what the killers looked like, and she made sketches of them." She pointed in Jenny's direction. "We were able to figure out that they had bombed a church in North Carolina, and then one of the victims said the word 'Middletown.' When a tip came in that someone from here recognized the sketches, we knew this was the Middletown we were looking for."

"Was that the bombing I'd heard about on the news a few years ago?" Pastor Biggs asked. "The one that killed several people?"

"That's the one," Leslie said. "I'd heard about it, too, never realizing it would ever directly affect me."

"We prayed for those people," the pastor said solemnly. "And I never thought it would directly affect us, either." Changing his tone, he added, "So, let me get a few things straight...you can hear from the deceased." He said it more like a sentence than a question.

"At times." Jenny was finally able to talk.

"How...how does it sound?"

"It's visions, mostly," Jenny replied. "We can see what the people saw—little snippets of their lives. They often clue us in on the most important moments that will lead us to the people who killed them."

"They also get tugs," Zack added. "Jenny will say, 'Get in the car,' and she drives us to a place that we don't know about until we get there. Hailey was able to lead us to the house where the bombers lived and the house where they were building the bombs—in North Carolina, I mean."

The Pastor paused, appearing to take it all in. "Who are these victims again? The ones who helped you catch those people?"

Jenny provided the pastor with a brief description of Ebony, while Hailey and Leslie filled him in on Luis and Lizette.

After another long pause, Pastor Biggs said, "I want to write those names down. We will pray for them. We will pray for them at every service." He typed the names into his phone, cocked an eyebrow and added, "Is it safe for me to assume these were all minorities? When an all-black church is the target of a bombing, the motive is usually clear."

Jenny nodded, muttering a soft, "Yes, sir."

"Well, Lizette was actually white," Zack clarified, "but she was dating a black man."

"The bombers are affiliated with a hate group known as *Purify America*," Leslie told him.

"Purify America," Pastor Biggs repeated. "Well, we will pray for them, too—pray that they see the light and don't inflict harm on any more people."

Tears surfaced in Jenny's eyes again. Keegan and Cody approached the parishioners with bombs, and they responded with prayer. Jenny wanted to scratch Keegan and Cody's eyes out, and she wasn't even an intended victim. Apparently, she had a thing or two to learn about compassion. If she lived closer, she might have joined Fifth Baptist Church so she could get a few lessons.

Words popped out of Jenny's mouth before she even knew she was speaking. "Nothing in all the world is more dangerous than sincere ignorance and conscientious stupidity."

Pastor Biggs smiled knowingly. "Ah, a little Martin Luther King."

"I didn't say it," Jenny replied. "I can guarantee you it was Ebony."

"She can talk through you?" Pastor Biggs asked with shock.

"Sometimes."

"And she was the teenager, correct?"

Jenny responded only with a nod.

"Then she was a bright one," the pastor concluded, his smile remaining. "Now, would you all mind accompanying me to the front steps? I want to introduce you to everybody."

They all agreed, and the four visitors gathered on the church steps with Pastor Biggs. Jenny looked out to see the crowd of people, remembering the chaos she had seen through Ebony's eyes when the bomb went off at Eastwood Baptist. With six bombs, these people would have endured much worse. Although, there may not have been chaos this time; perhaps no one would have survived long enough to panic.

Jenny's eyes scanned this crowd of people whose days had previously been numbered, and they landed on a woman with a baby on her hip. The child appeared to be about Steve's age, wearing a blue tank top and sporting a gorgeous headful of black hair. The thought of that baby being in the church when it exploded sucked the air out of Jenny's lungs; it literally took effort for her to continue to breathe.

"May I have everyone's attention, please?" Pastor Biggs shouted. The crowd's chatter disappeared into a quiet hush. "These, my friends, are the people responsible for leading the police to the bombers."

Applause erupted from the audience. While Jenny didn't feel like she deserved it, she hoped Ebony could hear it. Considering she'd just received a message from her, Jenny had faith that she was around.

"Two of these people are psychics," Pastor Biggs went on. "They can get visions from those who have passed on. They were led here with the guidance of three people who had fallen victim to these same bombers back in Richmond: Ebony Carter, Luis Alvarez and Lizette Micheaux. Though they were not able to save themselves, they communicated through the people you see before you today, and they were able to save *us*. We owe our lives to them. Everyone here owes their lives to them. We ask that God embrace our brothers and sisters up in Heaven and bestow upon them our sincerest gratitude.

"What we have to remember is that we have been given a second chance here today," he continued, "and with this chance, we must do God's work. We must feed the hungry and clothe the poor. We must look out for our brothers and sisters in need. But perhaps, above all, we need to reach out to the enemy—to those who have decided to inflict harm upon us, simply for the color of our skin. We must let them know that we are not their foe. We are not their adversary. We are their brothers and sisters. We must win them over, not with hate. Not with vengeance. Not with retaliatory actions. We must win them over with love. I ask that you take a moment and pray for them, as well as the three people to whom we owe our lives."

Silence ensued, except for the baby, who was making noise for the sake of making noise. Jenny loved happy baby sounds.

Although, she realized she was supposed to be praying for the members of Purify America. That was a bit of a tall order for her, considering she wanted to strangle each and every one of them. She wondered if anyone she knew was a 'backer,' sending money to assholes like Keegan and Cody to carry out the dirty work. The backers probably lived ordinary lives, circulating among everyone else, and nobody had any idea they were filled with such hate.

Pray for them, Jenny told herself. *You're supposed to be praying.*

"Amen," Pastor Biggs concluded.

"Amen," the crowd repeated.

Jenny had blown it. She hadn't prayed. She wasn't sure if she was sorry about that, though, all things considered.

Pastor Biggs turned to his four guests, gesturing down the steps. "Thank you for that. I just wanted to give credit where credit was due."

They all thanked the pastor in return and walked into the crowd. Jenny immediately headed toward the woman with the baby on her hip, finding her quickly. The others followed her. "Hello," she said to the woman, "I just had to come say hi to this little guy."

"Oh, and I wanted to say hi to you," the woman replied, her eyes red from tears. "I cannot thank you enough for putting a stop to that bombing. We're here every Sunday; there's no way we would have lived through this."

Jenny smiled at the baby, who looked at the world surrounding him with wide eyes. Everything appeared to be fascinating to him, just as it was to Steve. She couldn't even begin to comprehend that baby being killed in the bombing. It was simply not a thought she could even entertain. "Well, you owe your gratitude to Ebony Carter. She's the one who made sure I got the message loud and clear."

"Well, then, I owe her everything," the woman replied, wiping her eyes with her free hand. "Literally, everything."

The baby discovered Jenny, reaching his hand out to her. She offered up her finger, which the baby took in his grasp. "I have a little one this age, too. What's your son's name?"

"James," she replied. "Would you like to hold him?"

Jenny was instantly filled with delight. "He'll let me?"

"He's my third," she replied. "He'll go to anybody; he's just happy to get attention."

Taking her finger back, Jenny held out her hands. Sure enough, the baby leaned outward and reached for her. She slid her hands under his little arms and situated him on her hip. He felt the same as Steve. Tears filled Jenny's eyes.

His attention was immediately drawn to Jenny's earring. He stuck out his pointer finger and touched it gently, just as Steve would have done. Blinking the tears away, Jenny was able to focus on his little face and see the curiosity in his eyes.

Unable to resist the urge any longer, she pulled James in close and smelled his head. All that hair could really hold in the baby scent, and she reveled in it. He managed to squiggle free from her grasp, beginning a quest to stick his finger in her mouth. She closed her lips, but he tried with all his might to pry his finger in there anyway. He made little grunting sounds as he wriggled his finger, desperate to get her lips apart. His eyes had a look of determination and he breathed heavily, his open mouth revealing two tiny teeth poking through the bottom gum.

Just like her Steve.

James had brown eyes instead of blue, darker skin and much more hair. Aside from that, he and Steve were the same. Exactly the same.

How dare anyone plot to kill this baby?

"Zack," Jenny began. The baby seized this opportunity to stick his finger in Jenny's mouth and feel around.

"Yeah?"

"We can visit for a little while," she muttered as if she was at the dentist, "but we do need to go back to Richmond. We have one more person to catch."

"Randy?" Zack asked.

"Randy," Jenny repeated. Looking into the baby's big, brown eyes, she removed his hand from her mouth and added, "He's got to pay for his role in this, too."

Chapter 28

Saturday

The Newcombs and the Larrabees—complete with Steve—were each sitting on a corner of the king-sized bed in Jenny's hotel room. Jenny held her sleeping son, unwilling to let him go; baby James's brush with death was still in the forefront of her mind.

Jenny's phone sat in the middle of the bed, with Kyle on speaker.

"Okay," Jenny began, "let's review everything we know about Randy."

"Well," Zack said, "we think he was that third accomplice in Luis's abduction, although you didn't get a look at his face."

"He lived in the apartment down the hall from Keegan and Cody," Leslie added, "and his apartment was where we think both Ebony and Lizette were killed."

"Andrei said he moved out when Keegan and Cody did," Jenny said, "but he clearly wasn't with them in South Carolina—or even North Carolina. People talk about the 'brothers,' with no mention of a third person."

"Could Randy be a brother?" Hailey asked.

Everybody remained silent as they thought about the simple, yet powerful, question. "Unlikely," Kyle said through the phone. "I've tried that angle. I suppose he could be a long-lost half-brother, with a different last name, but I couldn't find a Randy with the same last name that would be affiliated with them."

"What ended up being Keegan and Cody's real last name?" Zack asked.

"Shaw," Kyle replied. "I was able to get that far and trace their whereabouts until ages twenty-four and twenty-two. After that, they went off the grid. Unfortunately for me, though, I was working backwards, trying to find their history. You guys were able to trace them forward, thank goodness. Otherwise, who knows what would have happened."

"According to Officer Reid, their lease was up in two months," Jenny said. "I'm assuming that means they were planning to bomb the church before then."

"That's cutting it a little bit too close for my comfort," Kyle noted.

"What about their dog?" Zack asked.

Jenny made a face. "Their dog?"

"Yeah," Zack replied, "their dog. The sniffer dogs in North Carolina traced Keegan and Cody's scent from the field to their house, but they said it was because they let their dog run free there all the time. If both of them got arrested, who is taking care of the dog?"

"Are you suggesting that they gave the dog to Randy?" Jenny asked.

"No, I'm suggesting there is now an innocent dog in a pound."

While Jenny appreciated her husband's love of animals, this was a bit off topic. "Let's find Randy first, then we can make sure the dog has a home."

"Would it help to go back to the house...the one with the apartments?" Hailey asked softly.

Everyone remained quiet, waiting for her to elaborate.

"It helped to be there before," Hailey added. "We were able to see some visions. Maybe you'll be able to see his face this time and you can sketch him. It worked with Keegan and Cody—the sketch is how they got caught, really."

Jenny raised her eyebrows. "That sounds like a good plan to me."

"Or maybe we can get Alina to work with a sketch artist," Zack suggested. "Alina lived in the same building as him."

"True," Jenny said, "although, they moved out years ago. Do you think the time gap matters?"

"There's only one way to find out," Zack said.

"Also true. So, I guess we have a plan; we just need to make it happen," Jenny noted. "But before we get off the phone, though, Kyle...do you know how the brothers were able to change their identities so easily?"

"My guess would be a connection at the DMV," Kyle replied.

Jenny grunted. "A fellow member of Purify America?"

"Most likely," Kyle agreed.

Jenny didn't want to think about that. The idea that there were Purify America members running around among the general population was too disturbing. "Oh, well, I guess we should get off the phone and call Detective Spicer...and Alina."

"And I'll keep working on my end, although I make no promises. I don't have a ton to go on," Kyle replied.

They ended the conversation, and Jenny muttered as she dialed Detective Spicer, "A connection at the DMV. To think...you're there, just getting your registration renewed, and the person behind the counter is a white supremacist and you have no idea. The thought of that makes me want to vomit."

The sound of ringing phone was followed by, "Spicer."

"Hi, Detective Spicer, it's Jenny Larrabee...and Zack and the Newcombs."

"Oh." The detective sounded surprised by the fact that he was on speaker phone. "Hi, everyone."

The crowd said hello.

"We were just brainstorming here," Jenny began, "and we thought a few things might be helpful, if you can arrange them. First, we were hoping a sketch artist could work with Alina so we could try to see what Randy looks like."

"Already taken care of," Detective Spicer said. "She's coming in this afternoon to work with Maya Goodwin, one of the best sketch artists in the area."

"Sweet," Jenny replied. "Alina was willing to go into the station?"

"Well, once she found out they'd all officially been granted immunity and she wouldn't get deported, she was okay with it."

Jenny pumped her fist in victory as the group exchanged glances. "Does this mean Andrei was granted immunity, too, and he won't get arrested for smuggling people in?"

"Sure does."

Raising her eyes to the ceiling, Jenny said a quick thank you to whoever was in charge of that. "That is spec-tacular," she replied with a smile, knowing full well that Detective Spicer would have no idea what that was about. "I guess that makes the next question a little easier, too. I'd like to get back in that building—can you either arrange that with Andrei or give me his contact information?"

"Yeah, I'll give you his number. Hang on a second." The sound of papers shuffling could be heard, followed by Detective Spicer saying the phone number.

"Thanks so much," Jenny replied. "We're anxious to get Randy and make him pay for his part in all of this. I can see, though, why the spirits were more concerned with finding Keegan and Cody first. There was a lot at stake if those two didn't get detained."

"You got that right," Detective Spicer said. "Good job on that, by the way. I can honestly say those guys wouldn't have been caught without you all."

"Well, we don't work alone," Jenny replied. She always felt funny taking credit for simply being able to hear someone else give information. She ended the call with the detective and arranged to meet Andrei at the house in twenty minutes. Glancing around at the others, she asked, "Are you ready to go back to South Bayhill?"

Hailey nodded and looked Jenny square in the eye, displaying uncharacteristic confidence. "Let's get him."

Andrei pulled up in front of the building and once again parked illegally in front. Getting out of the car, his smile made him look ten years younger than the man she had seen a few days before. "Hello," he said with a cheerful wave as he headed toward the group.

The Newcombs and the Larrabees greeted him in return.

"I guess congratulations are in order," Jenny began.

Andrei responded with only a puzzled look.

"I hear you've been granted immunity," she clarified.

"Oh, yes," he replied, the huge grin returning. "You heard about that." He said it more like a sentence than a question.

"We sure did, and that's great news," Leslie said. "You do wonderful things here; you shouldn't get punished for it."

"It's nice to know I won't." Andrei worked his way to the front door. "I've spent many years fearing the day I'd be discovered, and then it came true. It turned out to be the best thing that could have ever happened to me." As he turned the key, he added, "Who would have thought?"

"Well, I'm glad," Jenny said as they all entered the cool building. "And did you hear that they found Keegan and Cody?"

"I did; that's a relief." Andrei shook his head. "I can't believe I harbored people from a hate group. That's the opposite of everything I stand for." He looked up at Jenny with guilt-ridden eyes. "Syed, Ngula and Deigo trusted me to protect them, and then look at what happened. I moved them into a building with the enemy. They were in more danger here than they were in their home countries."

"You can't own that," Zack told him. "You had no way of knowing what those three were capable of."

Andrei closed the door behind them once they were all inside. "Well, no more Americans are staying here unless they're hiding from something. From now on, it's refugees and victims only. They're the only ones I can trust."

Jenny wanted to argue against making sweeping generalizations based on the actions of a few, but she didn't say anything. She was afraid she would upset Andrei, who was doing them a favor.

"He has a beard," Hailey announced suddenly, causing Jenny to break free from her thoughts. All of the adults looked at Hailey.

"What did you say, honey?" Leslie asked.

"Randy has a beard," she repeated.

Jenny remembered that from Alina's description, but she doubted that was why Hailey was bringing it up at that moment. "Did you just see him?" she asked.

Hailey nodded. "I assume it was him. He was with Keegan and Cody, and I can't imagine it'd be anyone else."

"What was he doing?" Jenny asked.

"Just walking." Hailey pointed her finger along the lobby floor. "They were headed toward the door like they were leaving."

"That must be coming from one of the victims that lived here," Zack noted. "Ebony, Lizette and Luis wouldn't have seen them like that."

Jenny thought about that for a moment before announcing, "I have to start concentrating. I would like to get a look at the guy myself so I could draw him."

Everybody remained quiet, presumably to give Jenny the ability to focus. She shuddered exaggeratedly, shaking off all of the tension she'd been harboring, hoping that would relax her enough to receive messages.

Only time would tell if it was going to be effective.

"I just saw it again," Hailey said. "He seems to be taller than Keegan and Cody. Tall and skinny."

Jenny lowered her eyebrows, frustrated that she wasn't being exposed to any of the visions. "Should we head up to his apartment, maybe?" she suggested. "He lived in 2A, if I remember correctly. Being in his apartment might help." She thought about that some more, adding, "But here's something...when I was in Randy's apartment, I saw a vision of *Keegan* pointing a gun at Ebony." She turned to Hailey.

"When you saw Luis's vision—the one where he was being made to crawl across the floor—didn't you only see Keegan and Cody there?"

Hailey nodded.

Thinking out loud, Jenny added, "Is it possible that Randy is in on all of this but doesn't actually do the dirty work? Like, he helped kidnap Luis, and he offered up his apartment for Keegan to kill Ebony there...but could it be that he, personally, doesn't ever pull the trigger?"

"Well, it appears he didn't work construction with Keegan and Cody, either," Zack added, "so maybe he worked—or works—at the DMV?"

"The inside connection," Leslie muttered.

That made sense to Jenny. "Maybe he doesn't have the stomach for the nasty stuff, but he still harbors the hate, so he's more of a behind-the-scenes type of guy."

"If that's the case," Zack commented, "going to his apartment won't help. We might be better off right where we are, or in the stairwell. If he wasn't around when any of the people were murdered, Luis, Ebony and Lizette may have never seen his face. The only victims who would have seen him would have been the ones who lived here, and they would have seen him in common areas."

Jenny turned to Hailey. "Maybe that's why you keep getting visions here."

"That could be true," Hailey agreed.

"Well, then, the lobby it is," Jenny said. She headed over to the stairs, taking a seat on the bottom one. Resting her elbows on her knees and her chin in her hands, she waited in silence for something to happen.

Closing her eyes, she forced herself to forget about all of the things that constantly cluttered her mind, making herself available for a contact. After a few minutes, she saw it—a vision of Keegan, Cody and a tall, bearded stranger walking toward her.

She examined the stranger. With the beard covering much of his face, his features were difficult to discern. From what she could see, he was rather nondescript. Nothing jumped out at her as being particularly recognizable; he could have easily blended into a crowd.

Once the vision disappeared, she stood up and said, "I got a good look at his face. Now, I want to get back to the hotel and draw him before I forget it." She turned to the young girl. "Hailey, when I'm done, I'd like to show the picture to you and see if you agree with it."

"Okay," she replied with a nod.

The group thanked Andrei for letting them in, and they headed back to the hotel. The Newcombs said they would be visiting the pool for a while, which made Jenny happy. Hailey was a child, after all; she needed to have some fun. Jenny and Zack went back to their room, where she was able to recreate the image of Randy's face to the best of her ability. She marveled at how painfully average-looking he was, making him difficult to draw. When she was done, however, she stood back, taking a look at the completed image, feeling like it was an accurate depiction.

Shooting a quick text to Leslie, Jenny learned the Newcombs had returned from the pool and were now back in their hotel room. Walking barefoot through the hotel, Jenny found her way to their room, drawing in hand. She knocked and was let in, holding up her picture for Hailey. "Does this guy look familiar to you?" she asked.

Hailey's eyes grew wide when she saw the drawing. "That's him," she said. "That's definitely Randy."

Smiling from the affirmation, Jenny put the picture down on the bed, snapping a photo of it. "I'll just send this off to Detective Spicer," she announced, "and hopefully Randy will be off the streets, soon, too."

Chapter 29

Sunday

"So, what are your plans for the day?" Jenny asked the Newcombs over breakfast.

Hailey and her mother looked at each other. "Well, we plan to spend the morning at the pool, and then we are going to visit Luis's widow one more time and let her know about everything that happened," Leslie explained. "How about you guys?"

"Well," Jenny began, "we're—actually, I'm—going to pay Gordon Cox a visit in jail again so I can tell him that it's hopefully only a matter of time. I'm praying there's no snag or fluke that will prevent him from being released once the blood results come back. And then we've arrange to eat lunch with Ebony's mom so we can brag on her daughter."

"That will be nice," Leslie said.

"It will be, if I can keep myself from bawling like a baby," Jenny replied.

Jenny's mother spoke, patting Steve's hand in his high chair. "We're going to have some Grandma-grandson time. I was actually thinking of bringing him to the pool this morning, too. Hailey, would you be interested in swimming with him?"

Hailey smiled widely. "That sounds fun." It looked like she meant it.

"Amma, what about you?" Jenny asked.

Tucking food into her cheek, Amma replied, "You want me to swim?"

Jenny tried her best to keep from laughing. "No, I was asking what you are up to today."

"Following up with the phonies again. I'm having a little trouble with the guy's case...you know, the guy who works alone. Then I'm going on to the couple's case." She shook her head. "I don't feel right about leaving until they're all solved, or at least, on their way to being solved."

"That's admirable of you," Leslie noted.

Amma shrugged. "It's luck of the draw, you know? Some victims are having their cases pursued by real psychics, others by dingbats. It's not fair."

Zack snorted at her comment. "Dingbat," he repeated.

"Well, have you met them?" Amma asked.

"Only that first day," Zack admitted.

Jenny became instantly frightened. "Just how well do you know them, Amma? Have you been behaving yourself?"

"I'm always well-behaved," Amma replied.

This time, Zack let out a full-fledged laugh.

"I'm actually just talking about the wife in that husband-and-wife team," Amma continued. "She's not a psychic—doesn't claim to be. But she believes that her husband is, and that makes her a dingbat."

"What does that make the husband?" Zack asked with an amused smile.

"I won't say such a word in the presence of a child," Amma replied.

Jenny covered her forehead with her hand.

"Thank you for that," Leslie told Amma. "I've noticed that Susan is missing this morning. Where is she?"

Grateful for the subject change, Jenny replied, "She went home. She got her case solved, and her kids are home from college, so she wants to spend time with them while she can."

"Good for her," Leslie said. "I've honestly been wondering how long we can stay, ourselves. Unfortunately, I have to go back to work at some point."

"You can really leave any time you want," Jenny told her. "Since our cases turned out to be overlapping, I can take over if you need to go."

"I can stay a couple more days," Leslie replied. "While this work is intense, to say the least, I have to admit I'm enjoying the restaurant food and maid service."

"Amen to that," Isabelle said. "Even though it's just me in my little downstairs apartment at home, it's still nice to not have to cook or clean."

The waitress came by with the check; Jenny placed her credit card in the black folder and left it on the edge of the table.

"I wish you'd let us pay for our own meals," Leslie told her. "You're already paying for the room."

Jenny shook her head. "It's not my money—it's Elanor's, remember?" She thought for a moment and added, "You know, Elanor would be pleased with what we're accomplishing here. She and Steve absolutely hated prejudice. They were ahead of their time in that regard."

"Wait a minute," Leslie began, "did you say Steve?"

Realizing that the Newcomb's weren't aware that the baby's name had been a tribute, she added, "Yes...Elanor's boyfriend was named Steve, and he was apparently an amazing human being." She reached over and touched her baby's hand, looking at him lovingly. "This little guy has a lot to live up to if he's going to be worthy of the name." She watched him as he squinted, his face turning red. "Although, right now, I think he's pooping."

Jenny sat in the same chair as last time, waiting for Gordon Cox to appear. Nervous excitement buzzed in her stomach; she couldn't wait to see his reaction when she told him the man who had killed Lizette had been caught, along with one of his accomplices.

After a short wait, Gordon was escorted into the room; his wrists and ankles were shackled. She could hardly stand to look at him that way, but she knew in her heart it was only a matter of time before the sunlight hit his face and he could walk around without the burden of chains bringing him down.

He took a seat across from Jenny, his expression brimming with curiosity. "You again," he said, a half-smile appearing on his lips. "What brings you back to this place?"

"They caught them," Jenny replied, practically bursting at the seams. "They caught Keegan and Cody."

Gordon sat silently for a moment, a million thoughts clearly going through his head at once. "They've been arrested for Lizette's murder?"

"I don't know about that yet," Jenny replied, crossing one leg over the other. "I mean, they've been *arrested,* but for something different at this point. But it should be soon. I don't know how long it will take to process the blood evidence, but I can't imagine it will be long."

Shaking his head, Gordon asked, "What on earth did they get arrested for?"

"Church bombings," Jenny told him with disgust. "They were responsible for one in North Carolina that killed six people, and they were just about to do another one in South Carolina when they got caught."

He closed his eyes, trying to contain himself. He stayed quiet for a good, long time before he whispered through clenched teeth, "I worked with those people. I worked with those people every blessed day. Had I known what they were capable of, I would have torn them limb from limb." Opening his eyes and looking square at Jenny, he added, "I would have belonged here. After what I did to them, I would have spent the rest of my life here, and I would have deserved it."

"Well," Jenny replied, "they're in custody now, and I doubt they'll ever see the light of day again."

He wiped his hands down his face, the chain going with them, and finished with a scoff. "You told me last time that those two assholes were part of a white supremacist group. Is it safe for me to assume they targeted black churches?"

Jenny nodded solemnly. "It is."

He snorted, appearing as if he could actually laugh. "Oh, Lordy." The look of amusement never left his face when he added, "They'll never survive in here, you know. Two pretty little white supremacists in a prison? They'll be everybody's girlfriend before too long."

A huge smile splayed across Jenny's face. With a shrug, she replied, "Oh well. Perhaps they should have thought of that before they started killing innocent people."

With his eyes distant, Gordon said, "They'll end up dead. I guarantee it. And nobody will have seen a thing."

The door to the room opened, and five well-dressed men and a guard walked in with purpose. Jenny was surprised by their arrival; adrenaline surged through her as she wondered why they were there.

"Gordon Cox?" one of them proposed.

"Who's asking?" he replied.

One of the men stifled a laugh, saying, "Trust me. You're going to want to say yes to this one."

"Okay, then, I'm Gordon Cox."

"Well, Mr. Cox, I'm pleased to inform you that, in light of some new DNA evidence that has surfaced, a judge has thrown out your conviction, and you are now officially a free man."

Jenny felt her jaw drop. Gordon sat frozen, studying the man, who gestured to the guard. "Go ahead and remove the shackles."

The guard looked at another man in a suit, asking, "Warden?"

"You heard the man," the warden replied with a wide smile. "Take off the cuffs."

The guard stood still for a moment, looking over at Gordon with awe. "My pleasure," he eventually said. Putting the key in the lock, he added, "Apparently, this is long overdue. Happy this wrong got righted, my friend."

The wrist cuffs popped open, and Gordon wordlessly moved his arms around in a circle. The guard then released his feet.

After a moment, Gordon looked up at the men and said, "Please tell me this isn't some kind of cruel joke."

All the men laughed. "No, sir," the original man told him, patting him on the back. "This is not a joke. You are a free man. You can go back to your cell and get your things. Your sister is on her way here to pick you up."

Gordon didn't move, just scanning the faces of the five men over and over again as if he didn't believe it.

The men in the suits couldn't stop smiling. "Are you going to get up, or what?" one of them said playfully.

"I don't know," Gordon replied. "I'm afraid this is a dream and I don't want to get out of it."

This inspired a laugh among everyone in the room.

"I assure you, this isn't a dream. You are free to go."

Gordon wasn't the only one who hadn't been moving; Jenny was so still she had to remind herself to breathe.

"Do I have to go on trial again?" Gordon asked.

"No, sir. In light of the newest evidence, the charges against you have been dropped."

"Well," Gordon eventually said, once again moving his arms that weren't shackled. He slapped his lap, his blank look turning into a giant smile. "Well," he repeated, the truth apparently sinking in. He clapped his hands together, his face lighting up. "Well, well, well…"

"Well?" one of the men asked. "Are you ever going to get out of here?"

Gordon looked up at him, his face beaming. "Yes, sir. I do believe I will." He stood up, and the room erupted in applause.

"Let me be the first to shake your hand," one of the men said. The rest followed suit, giving Gordon emphatic handshakes and pats on the back.

"Hey, I want to be included in this," Jenny said, standing up and walking around the table to Gordon, who wrapped his arms around her in bear hug and lifted her off the floor. While she was certainly caught off guard by that, she reacted simply by laughing.

"Man," Gordon said after he'd put Jenny down, "this feels good."

"I guess I'll meet you out front?" Jenny asked.

"Out front," Gordon repeated. "I will meet you *out front.*" He shook his head and started to strut toward the door. Looking at one of the men, he raised his thumb toward Jenny and told him, "I'm going to meet her out front."

Jenny couldn't help but giggle as Gordon disappeared through that door for the last time.

"I'm glad you got to witness that," one of the men told Jenny after the door closed.

"I am, too," she replied sincerely. "That was awesome."

"Come on," the man said with a wave of his hand, "I'll see you out."

"So, this is the door he'll be coming out of?" Jenny asked the guard as she left the building.

"Yes, ma'am," he replied.

"Excellent, thanks."

The guard returned into the prison; Jenny stood by herself outside the door. She looked around, her shoulders low. An audience of one. If his sister didn't arrive soon, Gordon was going to walk out those doors after years of wrongful imprisonment, greeted by one clapping stranger. "No," Jenny said out loud. "Just, no."

She searched her phone for Dave O'Brien's number, letting Gordon's former boss know that he was about to be freed and that there was likely to be no fanfare. "Not as long as I can help it," Dave replied before quickly getting off the phone. Jenny thought for a moment about who else she could call, and absolutely no one came to mind. Sure, she could have called her family and the Newcombs, but those were strangers to Gordon as well. He deserved to be received by friends and family; unfortunately, Jenny didn't know who any of those people were.

So she waited, hoping the construction crew would pull up in droves at any moment.

The process was taking longer than she would have thought. She wondered if there was paperwork involved, or whether or not he would have had street clothes. A person's weight can change a lot in three years. Did they even keep the outfit the person was wearing when they arrived?

As Jenny's thoughts consumed her, a woman in scrubs approached, her likeness to Gordon undeniable. Her make-up was smeared from tears and she half-walked, half-jogged toward the door of the prison.

"Excuse me," Jenny called. "Are you Gordon's sister?"

The woman stopped, looking at Jenny with wide eyes. "Yes."

"He'll be coming out that door," she told her. "You can greet him out here with a big old hug."

"So, this is really happening?" the sister asked. Her voice cracked as she spoke, and tears filled her red eyes.

"Yes, ma'am, it's happening. They found out who really killed Lizette, and it wasn't your brother."

She held up a hand and closed her eyes, allowing her tears to fall. "Thank you, Jesus," she said passionately. "Thank. You. *Jesus.* I have prayed and prayed for this day. I never gave up hope that it would actually come."

Jenny smiled; the love this woman had for her brother was palpable. Even if no one else came to these doors, she carried enough love for an army.

Commotion caused Jenny to look in the direction of the prison. In an instant, Gordon's sister let out a shriek and rushed the doors as he came out. He was wearing street clothes, which hung on him, but he also wore a smile that would brighten up the dreariest of days. The siblings engaged in a huge bear hug, rocking back and forth, the sound of the sister's sobs filling the air.

Jenny looked down at her feet, in both an attempt to keep her composure and to give the two an uninterrupted moment. The sobbing continued, and Jenny found herself wiping tears from her own eyes. The effects of Keegan, Cody and Randy's actions reached so far beyond their victims. They destroyed countless lives with their hate.

She had to find Randy and make him pay for this.

Her phone rang from within her purse, breaking her out of her moment. Digging it out, she didn't recognize the number. "Hello?"

"Hi, yes, my name is Edward Williams; I'm a friend of Gordon Cox. Is he really getting out of jail?"

"Actually," Jenny replied, wiping her eyes, "he just came out."

She was met with a long period of silence. "Is that for real? You're not messing with me, are you?"

"No, sir, I wouldn't do that," she replied with a sniffle.

"Put him on the phone," Edward instructed.

"Well, he's having a moment with his sister right now. I don't want to interrupt them."

"I can wait," he replied. "I'll wait all day. It's already been years; I can handle a few more minutes." A long silence threatened to make the moment awkward. She was grateful when he continued to talk. "Do you know that it was a child who was responsible for this? I saw her with my own two eyes. She went to my river house, and she found blood in the crawlspace. The killer's blood. It was the damndest thing I'd ever seen. She knew right where to go, too. She said she was led there by spirits. *Spirits.* Have you ever heard of such a thing in your whole life?"

"I'm familiar with the notion."

"I never believed in that stuff before," Edward went on, "but I'm sure as hell a believer now. That was some crazy stuff right there."

"Wait a minute," Jenny said, interrupting him, "I might be able to give Gordon the phone now. He and his sister have stopped hugging."

"Put me on speaker," Edward instructed. "I want Cecelia to hear this, too."

Assuming Cecelia was the sister, Jenny pressed the speaker button and walked over to the siblings. "Gordon, I've got somebody on the phone who wants to talk to you." She held the phone out so everybody could hear.

"Who is it?" Gordon asked.

"It's Edward," he said through the phone.

With his arm still around Cecelia, Gordon said, "Edward! When are we fishing, man?"

"Today. Right now," he replied. "I'm going out to get some beer and steaks, and you can bring everyone you know out to the house to celebrate."

Cecelia wiped tears from her eyes, leaning her head on her brother's shoulder.

Shaking his head with disbelief, Gordon replied, "You crack open a beer for me and get a fishing pole ready. I'll be there as soon as I can."

"That's right. You get your ass over there," Edward said.

"You don't have to tell me twice, brother. I am *there*."

Jenny ended the call, noticing the time. She was supposed to be picking up Ebony's mother in four minutes.

Whoops.

With another giant bear hug, she told Gordon goodbye and sincerely wished him the best. The thought of him spending the next few hours fishing with a beer and eating steak warmed Jenny's heart. He should have been doing that all along, but at least now every moment will be much sweeter. He will inevitably savor every moment at that river for the rest of his life.

As soon as she got back in the car, she dialed Ebony's mother, Rhonda, and explained why she would be late.

"That's the best reason I've ever heard," Rhonda replied. "Go ahead and take your time. I'll be here."

With that, Jenny looked in the mirror at her red, puffy eyes and hoped they would go back to normal while she drove. She was certainly not looking like a woman about to go out to lunch; she appeared more like a woman who had just escaped from an asylum. Straightening her hair, she did her best to make her appearance more presentable, but it didn't help much. The only thing that would make her look better would be time.

She decided to drive slowly.

Chapter 30

Once they had been seated, Jenny and Rhonda looked over the menu while Jenny finished recounting the tale of Gordon's release. After placing their orders, Jenny smiled broadly and said, "I have another fabulous story to tell you, and this one involves you."

"I like fabulous," Rhonda replied.

"Then you will love this one. Your daughter, I will have you know, saved the lives of about two hundred people."

Rhonda's eyes grew wide. "How so?"

"She led me to the church she used to attend, and while she was there, she clued me in on the fact that there was a church bombing somewhere. Through Ebony's eyes, I was able to see the inside of the church that had been attacked, and I figured out it was the one from Falmouth, North Carolina a few Christmases ago. From there, we got led to South Carolina, where Ebony literally led me to the people responsible for that bombing." Jenny looked intently at Rhonda. "They were the same two people responsible for Ebony's death."

Rhonda sucked in a deep breath and held it for a long time. Managing to keep it together, she closed her eyes and said, "I'm a little bit confused, though. How did that save two hundred people?"

"They were about to do it again," Jenny told her, explaining the story behind Fifth Baptist Church. The story continued throughout the meal. She concluded by saying, "Based on the number of explosives they had made, I don't think any of those parishioners would have survived. Everyone would have died—including that baby."

Rhonda's face revealed a mixture of emotions, but pride trumped them all. "They say everything happens for a reason. I guess maybe my baby's purpose was to save all those people." She actually smiled, which was a surprise to Jenny.

At that moment, Jenny's phone rang. "Hang on. Sorry. I have to see what this is about," she said. "As a mom, I have to check my phone when my baby isn't around me."

"Absolutely," Rhonda replied.

Jenny fished around her purse for her phone, seeing it was Zack calling. A surge of fear ran through her as she wondered what horrible thing may have happened to inspire this phone call. "Hello?"

"Hey, Jenny," Zack said, "I just found out we're supposed to have a meeting with Detective Spicer at 2:30."

Unable to look at her phone since she was on it, she asked, "We are? What time is it now?"

"A little after two."

Jenny thought about it for a moment, stating, "I can get there by then. I may have to bring Rhonda with me, though. I won't have time to drop her off first. What is this meeting about?"

"Just to touch base, I guess," Zack told her. "I think we're supposed to update him with our progress."

"Susan's not here. Is that going to be a problem?"

"Does it matter?" Zack asked. "We can't do anything about that anyway."

"True." Pulling the phone down away from her mouth, Jenny asked, "Rhonda, would you like to come to a meeting about the progress that we're making? You can be there when I tell everyone about what a hero your daughter is."

"Am I allowed to go?" Rhonda asked.

"I don't think there are any rules about this. There haven't been enough psychic meetings for there to be official etiquette guidelines."

"Well, then, I'd love to," Rhonda told her.

"Alright, Zack," Jenny said into the phone, "Rhonda and I will be there at two thirty."

"Cool. Steve is sleeping, so your mom said she'd stay upstairs with him and I could go to the meeting, too."

"Okay, so I'll see you there?"

"Yup," he said. "You'll see me and your crazy grandmother."

Chapter 31

Jenny and Rhonda arrived at the hotel three minutes late. Everyone else had already assembled by the time they walked into the meeting room, taking the same seats as before. Jenny laughed to herself, noting what creatures of habit human beings are. Even when there aren't assigned seats, people often create them anyway.

"I guess we aren't late," Jenny informed Rhonda. "Detective Spicer isn't here yet." Remembering her old motto from college, she added, "You can't be late if you get there before the teacher."

"The teacher?" Rhonda asked.

At that moment, Jenny realized her comment may not have been a good one. "Just a joke," she said. "Come on, I'll introduce you to everyone. I have to warn you about my grandmother, though; she's a bit of a straight-shooter. That's putting it kindly."

"Oh, dear," Rhonda said with a giggle.

"Her intentions are good," Jenny replied. "She's just a little rough around the edges."

The pair approached the table, and Jenny introduced Rhonda to Amma, Leslie and Hailey. Zack also extended his hand to her, remarking, "It's good to see you again."

"You, too," Rhonda said.

"This is Ebony's mother," Jenny explained, "I thought she might like to be here when I tell everyone what a hero her daughter is."

"It's such an honor to meet you," Leslie told her, standing up and giving her a hug. "I can't imagine what you've been through, but you clearly raised an amazing daughter."

"Oh, thank you," Rhonda replied, rubbing Leslie's back. Jenny gathered this was the millionth hug Rhonda had received over the loss of her daughter.

"I'm glad we could actually make this meeting," Jenny commented. "We had just finished lunch, so the timing was perfect. But I'm surprised that Detective Spicer planned such a last-minute gathering. That's not like him."

"I'm wondering if they caught Randy, and that's why we're here," Leslie said as she walked back to her seat. "Hailey got this overwhelming feeling of joy earlier, and I thought maybe that was because the spirits knew he'd been arrested."

"Actually, I might know what that could be about," Jenny confessed. "Gordon Cox was released from jail earlier today. The charges against him have been dropped."

"What?" Leslie replied with awe.

Jenny nodded emphatically. "I was there when it happened. It was the most amazing thing. I was in the visiting area with him when the guards came in and told him he was free to go. The blood evidence must have come back, and they realized they had the wrong man."

Leslie and Hailey looked at each other. "What time did that happen?" Hailey asked.

"Around eleven, I guess?" Jenny replied with uncertainty.

"That sounds about right," Hailey noted. "That's around the time when I got that feeling."

"It was probably Lizette, then," Leslie added. "She must have been happy that her boyfriend finally got out of jail."

"Well, right about now, I suspect he's got a fishing pole in his hand and a steak on the grill waiting for him," Jenny said.

"As it should be," Amma announced. "Now, where is this detective? He called a last-minute meeting and now he is late for it?" She shook her head. "We probably have the wrong time. He must have meant tomorrow. I got the message through Dingbat; she must have gotten her dates confused."

Jenny put her hand on her forehead; at least she had warned Rhonda about Amma.

Before Jenny knew it, Amma was gesturing toward the fake psychic's wife. "Brianna, come here."

The woman, who was apparently named Brianna, dutifully came over, obviously unaware that Amma's nickname for her was *Dingbat*. "Hi, Mrs. Epperly," Brianna said cheerfully. "How are you today?"

"Are you sure the meeting is today?" Amma asked bluntly.

"That's what my husband told me," Brianna explained. "He's the one who got the message from Detective Spicer."

"And you trust him?" Amma asked. "There's your problem."

Jenny felt herself tense up.

"Why wouldn't I trust him? He's my husband."

"Your husband, the psychic, right?" Amma said sarcastically.

"Yes, my husband, the psychic." Brianna was being remarkably kind and pleasant under the circumstances. "What...you don't believe he's a psychic?"

"Amma," Jenny said, holding up her hand. She left it at that.

"I know psychics when I see them," Amma explained, "and he's no psychic."

Jenny closed her eyes. "Amma," she said again.

"Oh, believe me...he's a real psychic," Brianna began, without animosity in her voice. "He leads the police right to the clues they need in order to arrest people. I've seen him do it."

Jenny froze.

He leads the police right to the clues they need.

That would have been easy for him to do if he knew where the clues were. "Um...Brianna?" Jenny began slowly. "Was he, by any chance, involved in the Lizette Micheaux investigation?"

"Yes," Brianna said emphatically, shifting her gaze to Jenny. "He just knew right where to find the gun used to kill her." She turned her attention back to Amma. "See what I mean? I'm telling you, Randy is a real psychic."

Jenny looked up in time to see Randy close the doors to the meeting room.

Chapter 33

"Did you say Randy?" Zack asked.

Jenny closed her eyes, all of the pieces clicking into place.

"Well," Brianna replied jokingly, "that's his name."

"And he wouldn't have been invited here if he hadn't helped solve some crimes before," Jenny muttered, consumed with a feeling of stupidity. "We were all personally invited here by the Detective Spicer."

"Exactly," Brianna replied, the validation obvious in her voice.

"Jenny," Zack began quietly, "you have it with you?"

"No," Jenny told him softly, understanding that he was asking about the gun. "I was at the jail this morning, and then lunch. I left it in the hotel room."

A beardless Randy stood in front of the doors of the meeting room, his arms outstretched to the sides. When his sleeve inched up his arm, the edge of his Purify America tattoo became visible. "I'm glad you could all make it," he announced, his voice causing a surge of familiarity to run though Jenny's body. This was definitely their 'third man,' and he was guarding the only exit of the room.

Brianna left their group and walked over to her husband, standing by his side and smiling. She was unknowingly on the verge of discovering the truth about him, and it might have turned out to be the last thing she ever did.

"You've all done a good job," Randy went on. "I have to admit, I didn't think this would work. After all, who would believe in psychics? I sure wouldn't."

"Randy," Brianna said with confusion, "what are you talking about?"

He held up a hand to his wife, silently instructing her to remain quiet. "You figured it out," he continued, addressing the others, reaching into his pants and pulling out a gun with a silencer on the end.

"Randy!" Brianna shrieked.

"Quiet," he said to her. "I'm not going to hurt you."

The look on her face reflected utter dismay.

"But you all had to go out and put wanted posters out," Randy said to the crowd, "and now I have to go into hiding, thanks to you."

Jenny saw Amma walk over to the side, apparently trying to get close to Randy so she could tase him. Jenny purposely didn't cast her eyes in Amma's direction in an effort to not give her away.

Leslie took two steps to the right, positioning herself between Randy and Hailey. Jenny suddenly regretted having a child here.

"Nobody will recognize you," Zack told him. "You had a full beard in the picture. You look totally different now."

"I can't take that chance, now can I? Cody and Keegan are facing the death penalty. I will, too, I'm sure, if I get caught."

"The death…" Brianna couldn't even finish the thought. "What are you talking about? What did you do?"

"Everybody up against the wall," Randy instructed, ignoring his wife. Using his gun as a pointer, he added, "Even you," referring to Amma, who had worked her way even closer to him.

"But I don't feel well," she replied, demonstrating weakness that Jenny knew to be fake.

"And I don't care," Randy told her. "Get over there with the others."

The voice. Jenny could hardly stand to hear that voice. She felt the hatred of every one of his victims.

Amma walked helplessly over to the rest of the group, who had stood against the wall. Jenny's mind was racing at a million miles an hour, wondering how they were going to get out of this. It was an armed man versus the rest of them, protected only by a Taser that was tucked safely inside Amma's bag.

Randy walked a few steps toward them. "I'm going to make this quick," he announced. "Turn around."

In an instant, Brianna grabbed one of the chairs and hit Randy over the back of the head with it, causing him to fall forward onto his hands and knees. Zack and the other fake psychic ran over and tackled him the rest of the way to the ground, pinning his arms behind his back and holding him there. They pried the gun from his hand, casting it off to the side.

Leslie was already on the phone with the police. Jenny ran out the doors of the meeting room and told the people at the desk about what was happening. She returned with some of the hotel staff following her, finding Rhonda holding Randy's gun while he was still subdued by Zack and the other man.

Jenny wouldn't have blamed Rhonda if she shot him dead right then and there.

Glancing up, Jenny saw Brianna breathing heavily and trembling from head to toe. Leslie had gone over to comfort her, wrapping her arm around Brianna's shoulder. The 'Dingbat' may have been fooled by her husband for a long time, but she had inarguably just saved all of their lives.

Security came rushing in, taking over the duty of pinning Randy to the ground. They flex-cuffed him, standing him up, each of the large guards taking an arm.

Jenny took a good look at Randy's eyes, the only part of his face she could see when he had the long beard. They were indeed the same as the ones she had drawn in her sketch. She had to look away, disgusted by the hate hiding behind those eyes.

Hopefully, those eyes would only see the inside of a jail cell from this day forward.

That is, if Rhonda didn't put a bullet between them first. Jenny glanced at Rhonda, who held the gun by the barrel, giving no indication that she planned to use it.

Jenny wasn't sure she would have been quite so strong when faced with the man who helped kill her child.

Instead, Rhonda sat the gun down on an empty table and approached Randy, who was still being detained by the large guards. He was motionless, although his face reflected anger. He looked up at Rhonda when she came up to him, smiling defiantly at her as if to taunt her. He almost seemed proud of what he'd done.

Even though she apparently didn't plan to shoot him, Jenny hoped she gave him a good, swift kick to the jewels.

That didn't seem to be her plan, either. She held her head high and asked Randy, "Do you know who I am?"

"I know *what* you are," he replied.

Jenny closed her eyes, fighting the urge to go kick him in the jewels herself.

"You killed my daughter," Rhonda said calmly.

With those words, Brianna dropped to her knees. Leslie was still there to calm her.

"I would ask why, but I know why," Rhonda continued. "I've thought a lot about what I would say to you if I ever got the chance, especially over the last few days." She drew in a breath and looked down at her feet, gathering strength for a moment before adding, "My first instinct is to hate you." She looked back up at him. "But that only hurts me. I'm the one who feels the pain when I hate. So, I've looked into it a little deeper. I've tried to figure out why you think the way you think and act the way you act. I realize you must have been taught this behavior. Nobody is born harboring this much hate. Somebody, somewhere along the line, brainwashed you into believing that the white race is the superior race—that people of color must be...evil somehow." She shook her head. "I'd like to think that most people don't believe that. Most people have learned to look at the individual. But not you.

"If you had looked at the individual when you saw my daughter, you would have seen an intelligent, caring, sweet young lady who only wanted to help people. But that's not what you saw. You only saw the color of her skin, and that was enough for you to cast judgement.

"But look at you now," Rhonda continued. "Just like my daughter, you are a man who had the potential to do great things. You could have become anything you wanted to be, but somebody taught you to hate instead. And for that, you will likely spend the rest of your life in jail. It's a shame, really. You are a victim of this, too. And for that reason, I forgive you."

"I don't." Amma's voice was followed by an immediate zapping sound, and Randy fell to the floor.

"She tased him," Zack said with dismay. Looking up at Amma, he repeated, "You tased him."

"He deserved worse," Amma declared flatly.

Jenny looked down at this motionless man on the floor. "Is he dead?"

"He'll be fine," Amma said.

"Amma," Jenny began, "he was *detained.* You could get into trouble for this."

"I had to," Amma replied. "He was starting to get unruly. Didn't you see him? It was in the interest of safety."

A long pause was followed by Zack saying, "I saw it. He was getting pretty agitated."

"He came within inches of kicking Rhonda," Leslie added.

"Mom!" Hailey said with dismay. Leslie only shrugged in response.

The larger of the two security guards let out a laugh as they picked Randy back up and stood him on his unsteady feet. "So that's our story? Self-defense? I'll buy that."

"Good," Amma said. "We're all in agreement, then." After a moment she added, "So, can I tase him again?"

Once the chaos had subsided and Randy had been taken away, the group sat with Detective Spicer at one of the tables in the meeting room. The hotel staff had supplied them with snacks and drinks and had given Brianna a blanket to wrap in. Jenny knew first-hand how comforting that could be.

"I never dreamed..." Brianna said, shaking her head and looking distant.

"We're both victims of the same man," Rhonda told her as she took her hand. "Don't be so hard on yourself. Remember, you saved all of our lives today."

"It's the least I could do," Brianna replied. "He killed your..." Tears prevented her from saying the rest.

"Were there any other cases that he 'solved?'" Leslie asked while making finger quotes.

Brianna nodded, stating, "There were two others."

"And were the victims minorities?" Leslie asked.

Turning her head to the side, Brianna nodded again. She was unable to speak due to the crying.

All eyes turned to Detective Spicer. "We'll get on that," he said flatly. "Those cases will be reopened immediately."

"Something just happened," Hailey announced.

Everyone looked at her, waiting for her to elaborate.

"It was like a...swirl," she explained, "and now I feel empty." She squinted as she spoke, as if she was unsure how to explain what she'd experienced.

Jenny, however, knew the feeling well. "One of the spirits has left you," Jenny told her. "Someone is satisfied and has crossed over, as it should be."

"I wonder who it was," Hailey remarked.

"I'm not sure there's a way you can tell," Jenny said, "but it's definitely a good thing."

"Well," Leslie began, clasping her hands, "can we declare that these cold cases are officially solved now?"

"I think we can," Detective Spicer said with a smile.

"I guess that means we can head home?" Leslie asked.

"I see no reason why not," the detective replied.

"Although, Hailey..." The tone of Leslie's voice indicated she was up to something. "We do have a stop to make before we go back home."

Hailey looked at her mother. "We do? Where?"

"South Carolina. We have a dog to pick up."

After a brief look of dismay, Hailey asked, "We're picking up a dog?"

"I've arranged for us to take Keegan and Cody's dog. After all, the dog didn't do anything wrong, and now he's homeless."

Hailey's face lit up. "Really?"

"Sweet," Zack said with a smile.

Jenny was grateful for this, too, in part because it meant Zack wouldn't be asking to take the dog home. A baby, one overactive dog and a juvenile husband kept Jenny busy enough; she didn't need another dog shaking things up.

"His name is Rascal, and he's a mixed breed," Leslie explained. "They're keeping him at the shelter until we can get him."

"Can we go now?" Hailey asked eagerly.

"I think so," Leslie said. Looking around the table, she asked, "Are we all done?"

Detective Spicer nodded. "We're fine for now. If we need anything else, we'll call you."

"Come say goodbye before you leave," Jenny instructed as the Newcombs got up to pack.

"We will." Hailey practically ran to the doors of the meeting room.

"I guess I should go and start looking into those two other cases," Detective Spicer said. "Brianna, are you able to come with me to the station to give me details."

With a sniffle, she nodded and stood up.

"Hey," Amma said to Brianna. "You'll be fine. You're a tough one—you just proved that."

Brianna smiled and nodded again. "Thanks."

"She means it," Jenny said with a point in Amma's direction. "She only says things she means."

With that, Brianna left the lobby with Detective Spicer's arm around her.

"You," Amma said, pointing to the fake psychic who remained at the table. "Are you willing to admit you're a fraud and let me officially take over your case?"

Jenny wasn't even unnerved at this point; she was far too numb to feel anything.

"I don't know about a *fraud*," the man said.

"Shake my hand," Amma insisted. The man obliged, and she said, "Did you feel that?"

"Feel what?" the man asked.

"Exactly," Amma replied. "If you were a real psychic, you'd have felt something."

After a brief moment of silence, the man said, "Let's just say I have good instincts."

"Good instincts. Okay. You have good instincts. Do you want to work as a team to get this done?"

The man thought for a moment before ultimately replying. "Deal."

"And then, after that, we work on Randy's case," Amma told the man, who really had no choice in the matter.

Jenny turned to Rhonda, who hadn't said much in a while. "Sorry to risk your life like this," she said flippantly. "Seriously, how do I even begin to apologize for bringing you here and putting you in jeopardy like this?"

"Please don't," Rhonda replied. "I got to speak my peace to the man who conspired to kill my daughter. I think I will sleep more soundly tonight than I have in years."

"You should go down to Fifth Baptist Church in South Carolina—the one that was spared by Ebony. The parishioners are praying for her, and I'm sure they'd love to meet you," Jenny told her.

"I will definitely make the trip. Thank you."

A wave hit Jenny, and she spoke the words before she even contemplated them. "Later, Sunshine."

Rhonda looked at her with awe. "What did you just say?"

Jenny felt the joy of Ebony leaving her body and crossing over into the beautiful world after this one. "I think Ebony is saying goodbye."

Rhonda closed her eyes. "I used to say that to her every morning before she left for school." Raising her face up to the ceiling, she added, "I will see you again, my baby."

"You will see her again," Jenny said softly, "and, in the meantime, you can be assured that she is in an amazing place. She is just fine, right where she is."

"I hope so," Rhonda replied.

"I know so," Jenny told her. "I know so."

To be continued in Cursed...

Made in the USA
Middletown, DE
09 July 2017